Weekend Arrangement

Sophie Penhaligon

Published by Sophie Penhaligon, 2021.

WEEKEND ARRANGEMENT

First edition. August 1, 2021.

Copyright © 2021 Sophie Penhaligon.

ISBN: 979-8532278592

Written by Sophie Penhaligon.

Also by Sophie Penhaligon

Weekend Arrangement
Safety in Numbers

Watch for more at https://www.sophiepenhaligon.com.

Olivia Jefferson could hear the sound of running water bouncing off the shower curtain, accompanied by cheerful whistling. The overwhelming scent of cheap body wash was billowing under the bathroom door, making her feel slightly nauseous. Twirling her hair around her finger, she thought back to the first time she saw Mark Hazelton.

At the time, she had been flattered by his attention, a beautiful bad boy with messy blonde hair and an equally bad attitude. It had been on one of those crazy Saturday nights when she was out with Lottie. She knew who he was, of course. He always hung out with the loud-mouthed jocks from the college soccer team, and on that particular evening, they were raucously flicking peanuts at each other, while everyone else in the bar was trying to avoid their poor aim.

Mark and Olivia had both been in their final year of their journalism degrees. They had shared some classes, but they had never really struck up a conversation, and he wasn't someone Olivia had considered dating material; too sporty and definitely too full of himself.

It had shocked her when he approached her at the bar, just as she was chugging down her third rum and coke of the evening. Wiping her mouth with the back of her hand, she was suddenly aware of his presence, flicking his hair away from his eyes.

"Hi. It's Olivia, isn't it? You're in my Media Ethics class."

Surprised by the fact he even knew her name, Olivia swung around to face him, trying not to breathe Bacardi fumes in his face. He had shocked both Olivia and her friends by spending the rest of the evening with her and then asking her out for coffee the next day. She had always thought he went out with her because he had lost a bet in the bar that night, and she had been the forfeit as the slightly crazed and fiery untouchable. She never got him to admit to that, but she remained convinced this was the truth of the situation.

That was six months ago, and since then, they had been a fixture. Moving in together when they finished their degrees was more of a practical move than a romantic one. The word "love" had never come into the equation. They had an easy-going relationship, with neither expecting too much from the other, and Olivia often wondered why they were still together. The first flush of excitement that you get from a new relationship had passed and had been replaced by an amicable and relaxed arrangement. Sex was occasional and a little underwhelming, but it was there, and Olivia wasn't complaining.

Olivia flopped onto the sofa while she waited for Mark to emerge, burying her head in a copy of *Mrs. Dalloway*. As a veritable bookworm, she consumed novels with a passion, losing herself in the intricacies of lives so far removed from her own. She looked at the mess of books on the coffee table, punctuated by Mark's copies of Sports Illustrated. *Chalk and cheese*; that's what her dad called them, and he wasn't far wrong.

Mark had fallen into a job straight out of college, working as a sportswriter for a local rag. Olivia was still freelancing but had dreams of one day becoming a famous author and travelling the world. Freelancing didn't exactly pay the bills, and she was grateful that she shared a place with Mark so she could make ends meet. She had kept her part-time job at the local library, working in the children's section. She only worked there two days a week and although the money helped, she really kept doing it because she loved it.

She looked up from her spot on the sofa to see Mark emerge from the bathroom, looking shiny and fresh and smelling like a Lynx commercial.

"God Mark, have you been marinating in that stuff?" Olivia wrinkled her nose at the overpowering aroma, wafting her hand in front of her face.

"Why don't you come with me, babes?" he said.

Olivia rolled her eyes. "You know I hate these soccer club things. I've been with you before and I just don't feel very comfortable. All the other girlfriends have legs up to here, boob implants, and veneers. I can't compete with that." She stared at her feet sadly. "Not only that, I have nothing in common with those girls. I was trying to talk to Megan about Jane Austen, and she asked me if she was an Instagram influencer. For fuck's sake, Mark. How can you not know who Jane Austen was? She must be a complete Smurf."

Mark grinned at her from under his floppy bangs. "I guess she just has different priorities in life, Olly."

Olivia did not really like being called Olly; it made her feel like an owl, or someone's pet Schnauzer, but she put up with it because it was Mark. "Well, what time do you think you'll be back?" Mark grabbed his keys as he was heading out the door.

"Dunno. Probably late. Don't stay up, babes. I'll try not to wake you." He gave her a quick peck on the cheek and then he was gone. She could hear him whistling in the hallway as he approached the elevator.

Olivia stomped off into the living room and slumped onto the sofa, throwing *Mrs. Dalloway* onto the coffee table. She started flicking through the channels and eventually settled on watching a couple of re-runs of *Friends*. Feeling the familiar pang of hunger, she loped off to the fridge and stared into the cavernous space. There were slim pickings, as neither of them were particularly good at remembering to pick up groceries. Grabbing a jar of dill pickles, she headed back to the couch.

Mark had been gone for about an hour and she felt bored and resentful. She should have gone with him, she told herself. At least there would have been plenty of alcohol, and some of Mark's friends were always fun to flirt with. She looked at the clock and decided she still had time to make it to the bar. He would be pleased she had come, and they could play pool. She went into the bedroom to change. *Now, what am I going to wear that will compete with the Barbie girls?* she thought. If she were being truthful, she would have admitted that she always felt slightly inferior to these beautiful, if somewhat superficial, girls. She'd always sensed that these were the type of women that Mark was really interested in. Perhaps he wasn't really invested in their relationship because it always felt like he was just passing through.

Examining the contents of her rather eclectic wardrobe, she pulled out a short sundress, a sweater and a pair of white sneakers. In the bathroom, she applied a thick layer of foundation to cover the freckles she disliked so much. Adding a slick of pink lip gloss, she stared at her reflection before heading out the door, smiling to herself that Mark would be surprised to see her.

The bar was only a couple of blocks away and it was a nice evening, so she decided to walk. She breathed in the warm air, singing to herself as she made her way down 11th Avenue. Pretty soon, she came to the sports bar where Mark's team always congregated. It was a bit rough, and it wouldn't have been Olivia's choice, but she figured a night out was a night out and she headed through the door. She saw Chas, one of Mark's teammates, and waved. Chas waved back, but he didn't smile, and something about the way he looked at her was off. She made her way into the bar and had the strange feeling everyone was staring at her. It was awfully quiet. And then she saw them. Sitting in the corner of the bar was Mark. He looked a little worse for wear, and there was a table full of empty beer bottles in front of him. Sitting astride him, on his lap, was a tanned, blonde girl with very white teeth and large breasts. Mark clearly appreciated her breasts because Olivia noticed his hands were inside the girl's t-shirt, massaging them with an inebriated smile on his face.

He hadn't noticed Olivia, so she strode up to the table. As soon as he saw her, he quickly retrieved his hands, a shocked look on his face. "Hi, babes. This is Kimberley."

Feeling totally humiliated and incandescent with rage, Olivia grabbed the remains of the bottle of Budweiser that Mark had been drinking and emptied it over his head. She turned and smiled sweetly at Mark's companion. "It's very nice to meet you, Kimberly. I'm Mark's girlfriend. At least, I thought I was, I now see I was mistaken. I can see that you two were having a very intellectual conversation, so I don't want to disturb you. I just had a message for Mark."

Mark stared at her, open-mouthed, wet through from his beer shampoo. He looked slightly terrified.

"Sorry Mark, I'm going to have to shout over the music," she continued, although the music wasn't that loud in that part of the room. "I just wanted to let you know a package came for you today while you were out. I think it's that penis pump you ordered. I really hope it works–jeez, that thing is tiny."

Kimberley shot a quick look at Mark's crotch and then retreated to the other end of the bench seat. Happy her work there was done, Olivia strode out of the bar with a smile on her face and her head held high.

She reached the sidewalk and took deep breaths, unable to comprehend what she had just seen. Her stomach was in knots, and she was so angry she thought she was going to throw up, but she kept walking at a fast pace, feeling the need to expend some pent-up emotion. A few moments later, she heard someone running up behind her; it was Mark.

"It's not what you think, babes," he spluttered. "We were just having a bit of fun. You know, letting off steam." Olivia turned to face him. Her green eyes were flickering with rage.

"I am so happy you were able to come out and have *fun* tonight. Don't rush home. You'll find all your stuff conveniently located on the sidewalk when you get there. I'll try not to break your vinyl collection as I throw them out the window."

Mark followed her for a few more steps, with a doleful expression. "Does this mean we're over?"

She turned on her heel again. "Yes, Mark. We are most definitely over. We should have been over a long time ago."

Unexpectedly, Mark angrily grabbed her arm, and she could feel his fingers pressing uncomfortably into her skin. Suddenly, she was glad there were other people in the vicinity. "What do you mean?" he said through gritted teeth.

Taking a deep breath, she shook herself free, rubbing her sore arm and said, "Let's face it. We both want different things. I hate sports; I get tired running for a bus. And besides that, you wouldn't recognize romance if it bit you on the ass."

He looked offended. "That's not true. I bought you flowers on your birthday."

"No, Mark. Your mom bought me flowers on my birthday. You just gave them to me. Now go back to the bar. I think Kimberley's tits are getting cold."

When she got back to the apartment, she slammed the door and leaned against it, breathing hard. After a few minutes, the realization of what had just happened hit her and she wasn't sure whether she wanted to laugh or cry. The whole scenario with Mark and Kimberly was like something from a sit-com, but this was her life being played out in front of her. It surprised her that she didn't feel sad, but she did feel humiliated and angry. She couldn't believe she hadn't seen this coming; it really should have been obvious. In reality, they'd allowed this relationship to continue because it had been the easy option for both of them. They probably should have parted ways amicably at the end of university, but neither of them seemed able to make the break. It had just been too comfortable and had become a habit, as these things often do.

She went into the bedroom and pulled Mark's clothes out of the closet. She found a large Rubbermaid and packed everything inside, and then hauled it out into the hallway, followed by his record collection, his crappy old manual typewriter that he was so fond of, and some other odds and sods. She was going to put it out on the sidewalk, but she didn't have the energy, so she decided to just leave it outside the door. The apartment looked strange and lonely without many of his familiar things, and she felt exhausted by the weight of her emotions. She was heading to bed, but first, she secured the deadbolt so Mark wouldn't be able to get in. She wrote a note and left it in an envelope on top of Mark's stuff, asking him to leave his key with the night security guard.

Climbing into bed, she wrapped the duvet around herself like a fat burrito. It was hard to sleep with her feelings all churned up, and she heard Mark outside the apartment door around midnight. He was calling through the door with slurred speech.

"Olly, please let me in. We need to talk. I've got nowhere to go."

Olivia ignored him and put the pillow over her head. He tried a few more times, a little louder, until someone from a neighbouring apartment told him to *"shut the fuck up,"* and then she heard him pick up his things and leave. She breathed a sigh of relief. This felt strange. This relationship had been like a comfy sweater or a familiar blanket. She was filled with mixed feelings of hope and terror.

2

Olivia woke the next morning to the sound of her phone buzzing on the kitchen counter. Dashing out of bed, she got her feet tangled in the abandoned clothes she'd thrown off the night before and landed with a resounding thud. Rubbing her knees, she headed into the kitchen, unable to reach her phone before her caller hung up.

She perused the pile of mail she hadn't been able to face opening, knowing full well that none of it would contain good news. Padding over to the coffeemaker, she threw away yesterday's grounds and made a fresh pot. At least she would have a strong coffee in her hands before facing the inevitable. Her stomach grumbled, so she grabbed a pack of Frosties and went to sit at the kitchen island.

Three brown envelopes sat in front of her, and she fingered them nervously. She looked at the official logos printed on the front and didn't need to open them to know what they contained. She knew one would be from the bank, to discuss her overdraft, one would be from Student Loans, and the final one was her utility bill. To top it all, her rent was due at the end of the week.

Mark's departure, whilst welcome in some ways, presented her with a whole new set of problems. At least he had a regular income and helped with the bills. Now she would have to face all this on her own, and she had no idea how she was going to do that. She knew she couldn't move back home. She hadn't lived at home since she left for college, and the thought of moving back with her volatile mother filled her with dread. She couldn't even find a roommate as this was only a 1-bedroom apartment. She loved living here, and it had great security, but she didn't see how she was going to be able to stay with only her paltry and infrequent freelancing money and her library job to support her.

Pouring Frosties into a bowl, she looked in the fridge for milk, but then remembered neither of them had bought any. *Oh well, dry Frosties are better than no Frosties,* she thought grimly. She considered her options. She could give up freelancing and find herself a regular job in an office somewhere. Although she had a journalism degree, the thought of going into that profession filled her with dread. It was too cut and thrust, and she really didn't enjoy that kind of writing. She considered taking on some extra hours at the library if there were any available. She realized she would have to ditch her ideas of being a full-time author and either face reality or face poverty.

She grabbed her phone to see who had been calling her. *Probably Mark trying to wheedle his way back in,* she thought. Seeing there was a message, she entered her code and listened. The voice announced herself as Lumi Rogers from Lane & Associates Publishing. Olivia immediately felt excited. It was the first call back she had received from any of the twenty plus publishing houses she had contacted, and out of all of them, Lane's was the most prestigious. She really hadn't considered that they would contact her, as they were renowned for supporting well established non-fiction authors. Getting your work accepted by Lane & Associates was like finding the golden ticket in a bar of Willy Wonka's chocolate.

Lumi told her that their lead editor, Ms. Dresden, would like to see her tomorrow at 11:30 and that she should call to confirm. Olivia punched the air in celebration and did a short victory lap of her tiny living space, knocking over a side table in the process. This was it; her luck was going to turn around. She just had to get herself out of the financial hole she currently found herself in. As she was considering her options, her phone rang.

"Hi Livvy, it's Dad. How's it going, sweetheart? We haven't heard from you for a while."

"Oh, you know. It's going, I guess. I wasn't expecting to hear from you this early. Is something up?"

Her father sounded immediately sheepish. "Well, Mark called me this morning. I guess you two have had a bit of a falling out?"

"Falling out! Falling out!" she yelled. "Is that how he described it?" *Devious bastard*, she thought, *trying to get on Dad's good side.* Her dad was a bit of a softie, and he had probably fallen for Mark's sob story.

"All righty calm down, love. Just tell me what happened."

Olivia proceeded to tell her father about the incident in the bar the previous evening. She'd always had a relaxed relationship with her dad, and she felt she could share things with him.

Her dad listened intently and then he said, "Livvy, are you sure you didn't just read the situation wrong and jump in with both feet? You know you can be a bit of a hothead at times, just like your mother. Sometimes it's best to take a breath and consider things. He sounded pretty upset, love."

Olivia was indignant. "*Dad*! He had his hands on her breasts. Under her t-shirt, no less. How do you think Mom would react if she caught you doing something like that?"

Greg Jefferson thought for a moment. "I think she would cut my balls off and feed them to the dog, sweetheart."

Olivia exploded with laughter. "Good one, Dad. Why didn't I think of that?"

Greg continued. "To be honest Olivia, you don't sound very upset. You two have been together for a few months now. It must be a bit of a wrench."

Her dad was right, of course. Now that the deed had been done, she felt more of a sense of relief. "We were really different people, Dad. I don't think he was right for me. I just didn't want to admit it. I think he was more of a convenience than anything else."

Her dad was quiet for a while and then he said, "Well, I never liked him anyway. He took too long in the bathroom doing his hair." Olivia knew her dad was trying to cheer her up. Greg and Mark had actually gotten on quite well and they enjoyed talking sports together. "Any luck on the job front?" he added, hopefully.

"Well, funny you should say that. I got a call back from a publishing house. They're interested in my travel series. I'm going to see them tomorrow to pitch my ideas. Out of all the companies I applied to, this was the one I thought I'd never hear from. They're the most prominent publishing house in the city."

Greg offered encouragement. "That's great, sweetheart. I'm sure they'll love you. You've put a lot of work into those guides; you deserve to do well." She heard him cough nervously before he said, "Wear something suitable, okay?"

Olivia grimaced. "What exactly do you mean by *suitable,* Dad?" She remembered the look on his face when he'd picked her up from the station at Christmas. Maybe the sequin boob tube had been a mistake in December, but all the same, he was her dad, and he should understand her creative side. And besides, it was definitely festive.

Greg drew a breath. He could tell she was on the defensive. "Just try to wear something businesslike. You need to look professional if they're going to publish your books. You want them to take you seriously after all."

Olivia backed down. He was only trying to be helpful, and she needed to let him play the dad role sometimes. "Okay, I promise, no sequins. I have to go now. I love you, Dad."

"Love you too, Livvy. Knock 'em dead tomorrow, sweetheart! I'll tell your mom. She'll be thrilled."

Olivia wasn't sure if her mom would be thrilled or not. Nothing she did ever seemed to please her, and she had long since given up trying to gain her approval.

Olivia was up early the next morning, giving herself plenty of time for her appointment. She showered and rummaged through her closet. It was really just a mishmash of things she had put together during her college years. She had never been one to spend money on clothes, mostly because she didn't have that kind of money to spend. Her style was a little eclectic, verging on quirky, and she tended to just pick up individual pieces she liked from a whole manner of places, including the local thrift stores. She also regularly acquired some rather stylish hand-me-downs from her elegant mother, who quickly became bored with things.

She fingered the lilac feather boa and dismissed it. *Definitely not,* she thought, *although it might be fun.* She thought about the kind of impression she wanted to make and remembered what her dad had said about something businesslike. She looked through her wardrobe and wailed. There was nothing that fitted that description. It was no good; she was going to have to call Lottie.

Carlotta Partington was one of Olivia's best friends from college. Lottie was everything that Olivia was not. She shopped in all the designer stores, courtesy of Daddy, and she was always beautifully turned out with matching accessories. Lottie was a beautiful, intelligent girl, and she'd pulled off a double first with a combined degree in English and History whilst still being the perennial party girl, but she had no intention of getting a job as her parents were ridiculously wealthy.

Olivia dialled her number. "Lottie, I'm having a full-scale fucking emergency here! I don't know what to wear."

Lottie listened to what the occasion was and asked Olivia what was in her closet. "No, Olivia. Not the green leather pants. That won't do at all. Okay, listen. I'm going to put together an outfit and I'll put it in a cab. It will be with you in twenty minutes." Olivia thanked her friend profusely and then talked about their plans for the weekend. She told Lottie about her breakup with Mark, and her friend breathed a sigh of relief.

"Well, thank fuck for that. He was dragging you down. You just didn't see it." It surprised her to hear her friend say that. She always thought she liked Mark.

"Let's face it. Mark is like one of those disappointing bags of Doritos. You know the ones I mean. You go to the store and you pick up the fullest, shiniest bag, and then when you get home and open them you find there's only two inside. He's vacuous, Livvy. Full of air. Throw him back and forget about it." Olivia giggled at her friend's Doritos analogy. "Well, we definitely need to celebrate, girl. You got rid of Dorito Boy, and you are going to get this publishing deal. I can just feel it," Lottie continued.

As promised, the cab drew up at the front of Olivia's apartment block in twenty minutes and the driver collected the clothes contained within. Olivia noticed a classy-looking dress bag on the back seat. Lottie had already paid him in advance, so she thanked him and ran in to take the elevator.

When she unzipped the expensive looking dress bag, she was suitably impressed. Lottie had come through, as always. A sleek navy sheath dress topped off with a matching jacket lay on her bed. Lottie had also sent a beautiful silk scarf and a pair of expensive-looking leather pumps. Olivia wasn't sure if they had the same sized feet, so she tried them on. They pinched a bit, but she decided she could put up with the pain for a couple of hours. Lottie had placed a handwritten note with the clothes.

"Wear decent underwear, put on some makeup, and put your hair up for fuck's sake! Good Luck. L xx

Decent underwear! Olivia wasn't sure what she meant, so she went to her underwear drawer and threw the contents out onto the bed. She selected something she deemed to be conservative and got dressed. Lottie was decidedly less well endowed than Olivia in certain areas, so the sheath dress was a little more fitted than she would have liked, particularly across her boobs and her backside. Smoothing the dress over her curves, she hoped it didn't look too indecent. The look she was trying to achieve was business-like, not Ms. Naughty Secretary.

Heading to the bathroom, she tipped out the contents of her makeup drawer. She went for an understated look and carefully applied a neutral coloured eye shadow, mascara, and a pink lipstick, not forgetting to cover those freckles. "Freckles do not exude sophistication and charm," she muttered to herself.

She then had to decide what to do with her hair. Olivia's hair was the envy of her friends; long, honey-coloured, and super thick with heavy bangs that were always too long, but it wasn't always the easiest thing to put into an updo because of its weight. She searched through her drawers for something to put it up, but she couldn't find anything. Her eyes caught on a brand-new orange pencil; perfect! She had watched a YouTube video on how to put your hair up with a pencil, and she thought it was a neat idea. She also thought it was a great finishing touch in her role as a writer. She pulled her hair into a high knot, inserted the pencil and voila!

Lottie would be proud of me, she thought. As she left the apartment, she realized she'd left it in a bit of a mess. "Oh, well" she thought. "As I am the only one living here now, it hardly matters." and with that thought of newfound freedom and independence, she headed towards the elevator.

3

Olivia took a cab to the publishing house. Although she knew she couldn't really afford it, she didn't want to wrestle with public transit in Lottie's nice clothes and risk getting all sweaty before she arrived. As she approached the building, she sighed in appreciation. It was located in an older part of the city, in an area of heritage buildings. Lane & Associates Publishing House was arranged over three floors, and Olivia nervously approached the heavy glass doors with the brass handles.

Entering the building, she walked over to the imposing reception desk and the beautiful, impeccably dressed Asian woman who sat behind it. Her name plate read "Lumi Rogers", and Olivia recognized the name of the person who had called her yesterday. Lumi smiled stiffly at Olivia as she approached.

"Hello," Olivia said nervously "My name is Olivia Jefferson, and I'm here to meet Evangeline Dresden."

Lumi nodded and looked Olivia up and down with an expression of mild distaste. "I will check that Ms. Dresden is ready for you."

Olivia nodded and watched Lumi as she spoke on the phone. Her clothes looked expensive, and Olivia pondered that her make up must take her an inordinate amount of time in the morning. Although she was beautiful, there was something about Lumi that made her feel distinctly uncomfortable. Eventually Lumi put down the phone and pointed to the elevator.

"Ms. Dresden's office is on the third floor. Take the elevator and she will meet you at the top."

Olivia stepped into the elevator. It was old and creaky, and Olivia felt a little nervous as it took off with a jolt. When she reached the third floor, the doors slowly slid open and waiting in the hallway was a tall woman with grey hair and blue eyes. The elegant lady extended her hand and greeted Olivia warmly. Her hair was styled in

a chic bob, and she wore beautifully tailored clothes. Olivia silently thanked Lottie for the loan of the outfit she was wearing and decided the feather boa would not have gone down well. Olivia looked
around at the stunning office space. The building was beautifully
preserved, and the various items of technology scattered around on
desks seemed out of place.

"Come down to my office and please, call me Eva," the woman
said as they passed several cubicles separated by old panelling. Eva's
office was tastefully furnished with a large pedestal desk and a selection of leather chairs. Olivia wrinkled her nose happily at the smell
of aged leather. It looked like the kind of place she would have liked
to work if she hadn't decided to go freelance. *Maybe I could get a job
here if my travel books don't work out,* she thought to herself.

Eva sat behind her desk and indicated to Olivia that she should
sit down. Olivia was nervous, but keen to give it her best shot. *Remember not to talk too much,* she thought to herself, *and don't open
your mouth unless you know exactly what you're going to say.* When
she was nervous, she had a tendency to ramble on in a disconnected
manner.

She liked Eva, and soon felt comfortable telling her all about her
ideas for the travel guides she was writing. She had brought along
some examples of her work, and Eva looked suitably impressed.

"It's a great idea, and very on point. I really like it!" Olivia smiled
in relief and with that, someone entered the office. Olivia didn't see
who it was at first because she had her back to them, but Eva quickly
introduced him.

"Olivia, this is Daniel Lane, our CEO. I'm sure he would be extremely interested in your work."

Olivia spun around in her chair to face the new person in the
room. She held her breath as her eyes ran over the man who had just
arrived. He was immaculately dressed in an expensive tailored suit
and a white shirt. He wore a vest, but no tie, and the top of his shirt

was unbuttoned. She unconsciously held her breath as she took in his thick dark hair and magnetic blue eyes. She noticed they weren't an insipid blue but more of an unusual deep indigo, like a pair of deep dyed jeans. He had to be the hottest guy she had ever seen. She wanted to just sit there, soaking him in, but as he extended his hand out to her, she desperately tried to re-engage her frazzled brain.

Clutching her hand, he shot her a panty-dropping smile. "I'm very pleased to meet you, Olivia. I always enjoy meeting new, young talent."

She opened her mouth and closed it again, desperately trying not to blush, but failed miserably. Whenever she tried not to blush, it just made things ten times worse. Eva seemed not to notice her predicament and rushed on enthusiastically.

"Olivia is working on a great new project for a set of travel guidebooks for single women. I think it's something that would fit our new mandate and help to get us into the young adult market."

He stared at Olivia intensely for a moment and then suddenly said, "Are you hungry, Olivia? I want to hear about your ideas, but I need to eat. Maybe we could chat over lunch?"

Olivia looked back at the beautiful man, a little terrified. *Oh, God,* she thought, *I can't go to lunch with this guy. I'm bound to make a fool of myself.* She didn't voice her concerns, but instead just smiled brightly. "Oh, I'm always hungry, Mr. Lane."

He laughed. "I'm very glad to hear that. Come on, we can take my car. It's not too far."

Olivia felt very self-conscious in the elevator, staring at her feet from beneath her dark lashes. Standing across from her, Daniel Lane did not make conversation as he leaned casually against the handrail, but she could feel his eyes on her, and it was as if his stare were burning into the top of her head. It felt as if the brief journey down took forever, and she was relieved when the elevator halted with a thud.

As he passed Lumi, he said, "I'm taking Ms. Jefferson to a lunch meeting. I'll be about an hour."

"Right you are, Mr. Lane." Lumi replied sharply, looking at Olivia as if she were something she'd just scraped off her shoe. Heading out the back entrance into the parking lot, Olivia noticed that Daniel Lane's car was a classic red M.G. sports car imported from the U.K.. She looked nervously at the small sports car and wondered how she was going to get in elegantly whilst wearing a rather tight sheath dress and heels. *God, I hope I don't split Lottie's dress*, she thought.

She looked across at him with an anxious expression. "Oh dear. It's awfully low, isn't it?"

He smiled back at her in an amused way. "Don't worry, I'll give you a hand." He crossed to Olivia's side of the car and swung open the door. Then he grabbed her hand and clasped it as she got in. She was dreading the inevitable sound of tearing fabric as the seams gave way around her ample backside, but thankfully everything seemed to stay put.

Thank God for expensive clothes, she thought, *they must reinforce the seams for people with fat asses like me.* She concealed a small laugh behind her hand.

"I'm afraid I have a passion for old cars," he said as she buckled herself in. "They are not always very practical."

Olivia looked at the wonderful leather steering wheel and the walnut dashboard. "But it is lovely." she whispered.

"Thank you," he smiled "I think so too. Beautiful things are one of my weaknesses."

He drove across town at breakneck speed, and soon, they were pulling up to an elegant Italian restaurant in a tree-lined street. He hurried around to Olivia's side of the car to help her out, and Olivia marvelled at his long legs. Looking up, she realized he was almost a foot taller than her, even in Lottie's heels.

The owner fawned over Daniel like an old friend as they entered the restaurant and they were soon seated in a corner booth, away from many of the other diners. Lottie's shoes were pinching her feet, so she quickly kicked them off under the table. She looked at the menu and thought about what to eat. *Nothing too messy*, she thought to herself, *so that rules out spaghetti*. She ended up choosing a seafood salad and stuck to water. This was a business lunch, after all. She made a mental note not to pig out.

As they waited for the food to arrive, Daniel asked Olivia to tell him about her ideas. *Okay Olivia, watch your mouth*, she thought grimly. Trying to take a professional stance, she flew straight into her rehearsed pitch. He immediately put his hand up to stop her.

"No, Olivia. I don't want you to pitch it to me. Just tell me about it in your own words. And please, call me Daniel."

Olivia took a breath and started again. She told him about her idea for a series of guidebooks for single women who wanted to travel to Europe alone. Her guidebooks would be different in that they would emphasize safe travelling practices geared towards single women. There would even be a section on basic self defence and important things like where to obtain the morning-after pill in different countries. Daniel looked interested.

"How many do you have ready so far?" he asked.

Olivia felt comfortable talking about her work. "I have one already completed about Paris and two more semi completed for Rome and London. I could have them finished in a month or so."

The food arrived, and she watched Daniel Lane elegantly use his fork to twirl his fettuccini, looking totally at ease. *He obviously doesn't have to worry about being a messy eater*, she thought enviously. He took a sip of water and looked across at her. Olivia was lost in the moment as she contemplated his long, dark eyelashes. *You fly too close to this one, Olivia, you're going to burn*, she thought grimly.

He was staring at her expectantly, and she realized she must have missed his question. She flushed and took a sip of water. "I'm sorry, would you mind repeating that?"

Daniel smiled at her, his dark blue eyes twinkling. "You looked like you were away with the fairies for a moment there."

She looked down at the table, mortified. "That's one of my *many* faults. I'm always away with the fairies. I have the attention span of a goldfish."

Daniel looked at her seriously. "I didn't intend it as a criticism. You are very creative. Your mind probably just wanders a bit. It's nothing to be ashamed of."

Olivia looked up. *Unfortunately, my mind is wandering on you right now*, she thought knowingly. She immediately felt guilty. Two nights ago, she had been throwing Mark's stuff out of the apartment, and here she was lusting after a publishing god.

"I was interested to know how you went about researching your books. Did you travel to these places on your own?"

Olivia was pleased to be back on topic again. "Yes," she said, smiling. "I did three extended trips spaced out over three summer breaks, but I also spent a lot of time in Italy when I was growing up. I'm really looking forward to getting back to Florence when finances allow."

"So, you had no significant other to go with you then?" he asked.

She thought for a moment. "No, not really. I had a boyfriend for a while, but he went on a soccer tour this summer, and I really wasn't interested in that, so I did my thing, and he did his."

Daniel looked a little surprised. "And he didn't mind you travelling on your own?"

Olivia thought about Mark. The only thing he was really interested in was sports. Playing sports, sports on television, talking about sports. "I don't think he minded at all. And besides, I couldn't really write a travel guide for single women if I hadn't travelled as one. It wouldn't seem right. The perspective would be all wrong."

Daniel nodded. "I can see you've gone into this seriously. What other research have you done?"

"Well, I've contacted women's advocacy groups in all three places, to get advice on what's available for women if something happens. I told them about my guides, and they were all really impressed and wanted to help as much as they could. I want to mention them in my books and let people know how to get hold of them if they need to."

Daniel looked impressed. "This seems like a project that's close to your heart. What made you want to write these in the first place."

Olivia took a deep breath, wrapping her napkin around her finger. Talking about her friend Georgie's experience always put her on edge, and she wasn't sure she wanted to talk about it now. Georgie's violent rape at the hands of a group of men in Rome had devastated her friends and left Georgie like a different person. "Let's just say I know someone who had a terrible experience in Europe. I wouldn't want anyone else to go through what she did." Olivia was shredding her paper napkin into pieces, and she knew Daniel was watching her intently.

"Are you okay?" he asked quietly. "Or has that poor napkin done something to offend you?"

Olivia turned her head to the side because she thought she was going to cry. She could feel the tears welling up, threatening her carefully applied mascara. Thinking of beautiful, proud Georgie, just a shell of her former self, always affected her like that. Taking a deep breath, she tried to compose herself. *For God's sake, pull yourself together. You're making a fool of yourself,* she thought.

Olivia blinked a few times. "Yes, I'm fine." She turned back to face him, her face more composed, although her green eyes were still sparkling with tears. "I want all the guides to be dedicated to my friend Georgie and to women like her, who have been afraid to do things on their own. And I would like to call my guides *Single and Safe: A Girl's Guide to Solo Travel.*"

He nodded and smiled his approval. "So, have you got plans for more single trips to research more cities, or will the boyfriend be going this time?"

She smiled ruefully at him. "Well, I have lots of plans, but I want to sell these first or I won't be able to afford to go anywhere else. And," she added, "the boyfriend is no more, so he definitely won't be going with me." He studied her carefully.

"I'm sorry to hear that. Is that recent?"

She laughed. "You could say that. Two days ago, actually."

He looked surprised. "Very recent then." She nodded. He leaned forward and studied her face. She wanted to move back away from his intense gaze, but she felt rooted to the spot. Finally he said, "You don't seem heartbroken. Are you heartbroken, Olivia?"

She tried to conceal a smile. "No, it was on the cards. Just took a while for me to see it. There's only so much soccer a girl can take." She looked across at him. "Do you like soccer, Mr. Lane?"

He looked like he was trying not to smile. "Once again, my name is Daniel, and no, soccer is not one of my sports. I enjoy *other* physical activities." The way he said "other" seemed strange. Like he was really emphasising it. Olivia wondered what he meant. It seemed like the meal was coming to an end and Daniel indicated to the server that he wanted to pay. "So, you're a newly single woman. What are you going to do with your newfound freedom?"

"I'm planning to go out on a girls' only celebration night to get totally smashed. No guys allowed. Although, I guess I could fondle someone at the bar. That seems popular these days."

Daniel choked on his water, trying to suppress a laugh. Olivia blushed when she realized what she'd done. "Oh, I'm so sorry Mr. Lane. I have a habit of thinking out loud. I have no social filter."

She looked across at his face, but she couldn't read his expression. "I think I've shocked you. That's not a good impression to make."

He looked into her eyes. "I wouldn't say it shocked me. More intrigued. The fondling part definitely sounds interesting." His mouth was neutral, but Olivia could see the amusement register in his eyes.

"I'm a bit of a disaster, really." There was a long pause, then she added, "but then I shouldn't be saying that to you either, should I, when you've just agreed to promote my books?"

Daniel looked down at the table and bit his lip, trying not to laugh. Finally, he looked up with a hint of a smile and said, "I don't think you're a disaster. I think you are quite unique. And I also think you should make every effort to stay that way."

He was looking at her intently and she felt his gaze burning into her skin, so she dove under the table to grab Lottie's shoes. In horror, she realized that she had inadvertently kicked them over to Daniel's side of the table and they were now out of reach.

She looked up at him and said weakly, "I'm sorry, I think I'm going to have to ask you to retrieve my shoes. I kicked them off under the table because they were hurting and now I can't reach them. You see, they aren't my shoes. They belong to a friend. As does the rest of this outfit. None of it is mine. I rarely wear clothes like this. None of my clothes seemed suitable. My father said I should wear something *business-like*, whatever that means." Olivia drew a breath to continue with her rambling, but Daniel reached over and gently placed a finger over her lips.

"But am I right in guessing that the pencil is yours?" Olivia suddenly remembered her updo secured with a pencil.

"Yes" she whispered, smiling, as if she were revealing a big secret. "The pencil is, in fact, mine. I got the idea from YouTube. Look!" She pulled the pencil free and shook her head. Her thick, honey hair fell around her shoulders in soft tendrils, and she looked up at him with a wide smile.

Daniel's mouth dropped open. "I think I prefer it without the pencil," he mumbled with a strange look in his eyes that Olivia couldn't figure out.

After a few seconds, Daniel composed himself and stood up to go. "Well, I think you are just the kind of author we want at Lane & Associates." I will get my assistant to contact you, and perhaps we can get together again to firm up the contract and discuss details.

"Wow," exclaimed Olivia. "I thought I'd blown it because I'm such an idiot."

Daniel looked at her seriously. "You're certainly not that. You're a very smart young woman with great ideas. Now, I must go, but we will be in touch. I'm assuming Evangeline has all your details. Address, phone number etc." Olivia nodded her head numb with excitement. Daniel extracted a beautiful pen from his pocket as he signed the bill. "Do you need a ride back?" he asked.

"No, I'm fine from here," she said. She didn't want to risk trying to get in the sports car again. She would probably fall on her ass.

"One more thing, Olivia." She looked at him eagerly. "Next time I see you, come as yourself. You don't need to try to be something you're obviously not." He shook her hand warmly, looking into her eyes for a moment too long, and then headed out of the restaurant.

She wondered what he meant by that last statement. Did he mean she wasn't sophisticated and businesslike? She wondered about the type of women Daniel Lane dated. *Not my type, that's for sure.* She thought about his elegant suit and his long dark lashes and felt regretful that she couldn't imagine herself on his arm. Cheering up, she remembered the upcoming girls' night out, and rushed home to call Lottie and tell her the good news.

As soon as Olivia got in the door, she was on the phone with Lottie. Lottie screamed in excitement when Olivia told her the news "And," Olivia continued, "the guy who owns the publishing house is seriously hot. I thought I was going to spontaneously combust during lunch."

Lottie laughed. "What's his name?"

"Daniel Lane," Olivia replied.

"Daniel Lane? You mean *the* Daniel Lane from Lane & Associates?"

Olivia sighed. Lottie knew everyone. "Yes, that's the one," she said, a little annoyed that her friend knew him. She could see that Lottie would definitely be his type. Tall and willowy with beautiful auburn hair, her designer clothes were always impeccably cut, and she looked like a million dollars, even when she got out of bed in the morning.

"Oh, my God. He is like *the* most eligible bachelor around. He's rich and philanthropic and he is, as you say, seriously hot. Women flock around him like bees around a honey pot. He goes through girlfriends like you go through a bottle of tequila."

Olivia thought Lottie sounded unusually giddy. "Well, how come I've never heard of him?" she grumbled. She didn't need Lottie to answer that question; she already knew. She didn't move in the kind of circles Lottie did, with her charity balls and polo matches. She realized she had absolutely nothing in common with Daniel Lane. Maybe that was just as well if he was really the type of man that Lottie was describing.

"Okay, well, moving on." Olivia wanted to change the subject. "Where are we going on Friday? I want to drink tequila and dance on the tables."

Lottie laughed. "Olivia! You remember what happened last time you did that? You fell off, and we ended up in the ER for four hours because you had a concussion."

Olivia winced at the memory of it. "I know. I never learn, do I? Maybe as my best friend, you could keep me off the tables."

"I'll do my best Olivia Jefferson," Lottie promised, "but you've always been a bit of a wild child!"

4 - Daniel

Maneuvering his sports car back into its original spot in the executive parking lot, Daniel smiled to himself. It wasn't his habit to mix business with pleasure, and when he did, it invariably came back to bite him on the ass. Eva had already warned him off schmoozing the female authors since the Vanessa Lambert escapade; God, that woman was persistent.

It wasn't as if he'd even slept with her, but he never should have taken her to that charity ball two months ago. At the time, he thought she would have made a suitable date for the evening and the chance at some extra-curricular pursuits afterwards wouldn't have gone unappreciated. Beautiful with flawless style, she certainly looked great on his arm as they ran the gauntlet of the inevitable press photographers on their way in. It wasn't until halfway through dinner, after Vanessa had polished off two-thirds of a bottle of vodka, that he realized he was in serious trouble. Having her climb into his lap before dessert and proposing marriage was one of the most embarrassing things he'd ever had to live through, especially when she launched into a rather raunchy rendition of *It's Raining Men*. He thanked his lucky stars that she had passed out shortly afterwards and he could get her into a cab before too many people clued in to what was going on.

He could only imagine what his father would have said about the situation. There probably would have been words of advice about never dipping your nib in the office ink. It didn't help that the press viewed him as a perennial playboy. He wouldn't deny that he had enjoyed an active and creative sex life, but all the women he slept with were well aware of his "no-strings attached" expectations. He told himself that it was only fair. He'd worked damn hard to turn the business around, and he expected to play hard as well, and he certainly wasn't ready to get tied down.

Sitting in his car, he ran his hands over the leather steering wheel and thought about his lunch with Olivia. She was so different from the women he usually dated, but he felt himself inexplicably drawn to her. Unlike most of his past girlfriends, whom he could read like a book, Olivia was a complete enigma. Nervous and yet feisty, naïve and yet worldly; a complete innocent wrapped up in an unintentional cloak of overt sexuality.

Thinking back to how mortified she was when he caught her staring at him, he chuckled to himself. She had been caught ogling him and she had no idea how to hide it; she really was quite adorable. When she had taken that pencil out of her hair and looked across at him, her smile seemed full of allure and promise, and yet he knew full well that she was completely unaware of her effect on him. He looked down at the bulge tenting the front of his dress pants. "You need to go down before I can go back into the office," he growled.

Ten minutes later he swept into the building and Lumi shot him a seductive smile. *You can forget about that*, he thought grimly. *You definitely fall under the category of office ink.* He knew he had to stay in her good books, as she was great at heading off the string of women who came looking for him, and she was always cooperative about fielding his calls.

He didn't like the fact that his private life sometimes invaded his business domain, but he didn't really know how to prevent it. Limiting himself to women who were very clear on his inability to provide anything other than a warm bed for the night was the only way forward. He successfully compartmentalized his life into business and pleasure. Blurring the lines had only gotten him into trouble.

Breezing into his office, he flopped down into his leather chair and closed his eyes. It couldn't have been many minutes before he heard Eva's heels click down the hallway and stop outside his door. "Do you have a minute, Daniel?"

Oh no, here we go, he thought.

"How was your lunch with Olivia Jefferson? She's a bright little thing, isn't she?"

The question sounded casual enough, but Daniel could see she wasn't particularly impressed. Her lips were tightly pursed as she waited for a response.

"It was good. We talked about her books. She's very enthusiastic." He prattled away in brief spurts.

"She's also very young. I do hope we won't have a repeat performance of the Vanessa issue. You almost had to take out a restraining order against one of our own authors."

He frowned and shook his head. "She's nothing like Vanessa, and besides, I just wanted to give her some encouragement."

"Daniel, I saw the way you looked at her when you walked into my office. She doesn't need *that* kind of encouragement. I know you're my boss, but you're also my friend. Think about how bad this would look. She's only twenty-four, the same age as my Lily."

He rubbed his face with his hands and sighed. "You make me sound terrible. Like I'm some kind of serial womanizer. I'm always very clear with the woman I date I can't be seen as a long-term prospect. I can't help it. My interest always ebbs too quickly."

He looked across at her and saw that although her head was down, her shoulders were shaking lightly with laughter. "Have you ever considered that maybe you're dating the wrong types of women?"

He looked incredulous. "Eva, you've seen some of my dates. They're all beautiful and sophisticated. What more could I possibly want?"

She smiled at him fondly. "I think you should ask yourself that question, not me. Anyway, lecture over. I have a pile of work I need to get through this afternoon. I know it's none of my business, but just think about what I've said, please. Leave her be. For your sake and for hers."

He watched as she walked from his office and quietly closed the door. He knew she was right. He was seven years older than this girl and besides, he certainly couldn't imagine attending a stuffy charity function with her; she would be completely out of her depth. Her deliciously unfiltered mouth would raise an eyebrow or two; it might be amusing though.

He chuckled to himself as he tried to imagine Olivia on his arm at one of those fancy events, a borrowed gown and her hair tied up with an HB pencil. Her shoes would be off and her hair down before they'd made it through the first course. A few drinks inside her and who knows what might happen. It might just be the most fun he'd had in years.

He immediately felt guilty for thinking of her in this way. *God, when did I become such a fucking snob*, he thought grimly to himself. Running the most prominent publishing house in the city came with its pitfalls. Since he had taken over from his father, he discovered that as a public figure with obligations to many local charities, his private life had become a matter for public consumption. On a slow news day he would often see a picture of himself on the front page of the local rag, attending something with someone. Some of the more creative journalists loved to hint about long-term relationships or even wedding bells, but Daniel made sure he lay those nasty rumours to rest by trying to never attend two events with the same woman. This of course contributed to the playboy executive label he had earned over the past few years.

He'd had a bit of an epiphany a couple of weeks ago when he found himself in bed with a beautiful woman, only to discover that he had completely forgotten her name. He knew it began with an "F" but whether it was Fiona or Felicity or something else completely escaped him. He realized he was sleeping with women who no longer held any interest for him. They were cookie cutter women, like the cookie cutter life he'd carved out for himself.

Looking down at his desk, he noticed that Eva had inadvertently left a manilla file. Picking it up, he could see it was Olivia's information. Under the notes that Eva had taken, there was a copy of her resume and he studied it carefully. At the top of her resume was a small headshot photograph. Her head was cocked to the side and her hair fell loosely around her shoulders. Her mouth was open in the same inviting smile she had given him in the restaurant, and he caught his breath. Even in this tiny image, she was captivating, and he unconsciously ran his finger around the outline of her face. Reading down through the information, he noticed she had a part-time job at the Evergreen Public Library. Without thinking, he picked up his phone and entered the number.

"Evergreen Library, how may I help you?" a chirpy young female voice at the end of the line greeted him.

"Oh, hi. Could you tell me if Olivia Jefferson is working today?" He knew what the response would be, given that it hadn't been that long since he'd seen her at the restaurant.

"No, she doesn't work today. She will be in tomorrow at 9. Would you like me to give her a message?"

He hesitated for a moment. "No, there's no message, thank you. I'll catch up with her later."

Putting down the phone, he looked down at the small photograph. He knew what he should do, of course. He should return the file to Eva's office and forget all about his growing fascination with Olivia Jefferson. The best thing for Olivia would be for him to leave well alone, but somehow he knew that wasn't going to happen. For some strange reason, she had managed to get under his skin in a way that confused him. He couldn't remember the last time he felt this way about a woman, if ever. He was the king of playing it cool. Don't chase, don't encourage, let them come to you.

He realized he had long since tired of the constantly revolving door of beautiful socialites he had at his beck and call. There was nothing fresh or new in his life, and Olivia seemed to him to possess all the freedom he lacked. He had been tied to the business since his father was forced to step down and although he didn't hate it, this was his future, here in this office. She had travelled extensively, was street savvy enough to stay safe in a foreign country and was advocating for other women to do the same. What did it matter if she couldn't hold her own at one of those superficial events he had to attend?

He reflected on the last time he'd really had fun and was troubled to realize he couldn't remember. Harvard had been fun, despite being bone achingly hard work. He considered his sex life. Surely, if anything, that aspect of his life should be fun? Giving it some serious thought, he contemplated that even that sometimes felt like it was on autopilot. He suddenly felt rather depressed. What the fuck was wrong with him today, and why was he letting this unusual woman get to him?

The next day was one of Olivia's regular work days at the library. She had loved libraries since she had been a young child and had found solace in her hometown library when she was a confused and sometimes angry teen. She enjoyed working in the children's section, and the head librarian gave her a free rein with the school programs that she handled. Olivia loved to find imaginative ways to get kids excited about books and reading, and she threw her creative side into her job.

Evergreen Library had been lucky to receive a grant a couple of years ago to revitalize the children's section, and it had been done beautifully. Olivia had provided some input on providing a magical space for the kids, and she was really proud of how they had transformed the space. A local architect had been called in to help with the design, and she had watched in wonder as he'd transformed the rather dull and utilitarian space into something amazing. He had actually won awards for it, which Olivia thought were well-deserved.

Set at the back of the library, the youngest library members entered through a beautiful wooden archway made to look like the entrance to a tree house, complete with a carved wise owl. At the back of the room there was a gorgeous stained-glass window of a castle and a beanstalk that created colourful rainbows of light around the room. The desk where Olivia sat also looked like the front of a tree and her favourite area was the story telling section, where small tree stumps were located for the children to sit on. The storyteller got to sit on a rather opulent throne, much to the envy of all the tree stump residents. The throne was strictly out of bounds for all but the storyteller, and it was roped off when not in use.

Olivia never thought she would enjoy reading stories to children, but it had become one of the most favourite parts of her job, and she got to know all the school groups as they trooped through on a weekly basis. Today she was expecting a kindergarten class followed by a rather lively grade three class, and she got her reading material and props ready for their arrival. For the grade threes she was going to carry on reading a chapter book she had started a few weeks ago, but the kindergarten class was going to be treated to one of her special performances.

Olivia loved to dress up for her kindergarten friends and today would be no exception. She trolled through the local thrift stores looking for costumes and props and had amassed quite the collection.

She entered through the staff door and immediately saw Harry Jacobsen at the coffee machine. Harry was the head librarian and was probably no more than thirty-five, but he looked more like someone in his fifties. He lived with his elderly mother and their collection of Maine Coon cats, and consequently, his knitted vests were always a little on the furry side. With his big round face, he reminded Olivia of the man in the moon. He was the sweetest person she had ever met, and she had adored him ever since she first met him four years ago, when he interviewed her for her part-time job.

This morning he quickly filled her in on his mother's arthritis and the birthday celebration they had held over the weekend for Rufus, one of their more senior cats. Harry had already made Olivia's coffee for her the way she liked it and he handed it to her, smiling. "Harry, you are such a sweetheart. You know that don't you?" she teased him. He blushed, as he always did when Olivia said this to him. They had an uncomplicated relationship, and he was always excited to see what props she had brought in for kindergarten story time.

"The theme this week is dragons," she revealed with a grin. "Just wait till you see what I have. I really scored!" Harry looked quite breathless as she dove into the large tote she had brought with her. Out of her bag she pulled a green, luminescent cape, complete with dragon spikes running down the back. It was silky and embellished with shimmering dragon scales that caught the light as she moved. "And now for the pièce de résistance. Ta-da!" she announced, and out of her bag she pulled a beautiful blue and green dragon mask intended for a masquerade ball.

Harry gasped, "Olivia, that must have cost you a fortune. Put it on. I can't wait to see it!" He was clapping his hands together like an excited child. Olivia grinned at him, remembering why she liked him so much. He was child-like and innocent, and she knew he would always be that way. He was so comfortable in his own skin and knew exactly who he was. Olivia sometimes wished she could be more like him, instead of constantly being concerned what other people thought of her.

She threw the cape over her shoulders, wrapping it around herself, and then she put on the mask and pulled up the hood to cover her hair. There was nothing comical about this costume; it was actually quite theatrical and mysterious. The mask itself was a piece of work, and Olivia had been thrilled when she had spotted it. "You look amazing!" Harry shrieked. "The pipsqueaks are going to lose their minds!"

Harry slapped his forehead like he had suddenly remembered something. "I almost forgot. Someone called for you yesterday afternoon. Maisie took the call; I think she told them you would be in today."

"Do you know who it was?" Harry shrugged his shoulders. Olivia wondered who would call her at the library, rather than using her own phone, but she didn't have time to give it much thought. "Okay, Harry. It's almost time. Let's get this show on the road."

Beaming a huge grin, Harry went to open the library doors whilst Olivia positioned herself at the archway to the children's section, sitting rather dramatically on one of the tree stumps. She knew the class wouldn't be arriving for another ten minutes, so she spent the time skimming through the books she was going to read and thinking about the voices she was going to use and how to embellish them.

Glancing up, she caught sight of a tall, dark-haired man in a suit entering through the main doors, headed towards the adult fiction section. Something about him looked familiar, and it piqued her curiosity. Gathering her cape around herself, she jumped off her tree stump and headed toward the adult section. As she rounded the large bookcase, she suddenly walked smack bang into Daniel Lane. Shocked, she jumped back, clutching her hand to her chest. "Oh my God. Mr. Lane. You scared me!"

He looked her up and down with a look of utter bewilderment until his face broke into a wide smile of recognition. "Why Olivia, what a pleasant surprise. And you appear to be dressed as... a dragon?" She was extremely glad to be wearing her mask as she felt the colour rush to her face.

"Yes, you're quite right. Today, I am a dragon," she said dryly.

"Quite a sexy dragon, I must say." His eyes shone playfully. "I'm almost afraid to ask, but I just can't resist. Why?"

She didn't have time to respond before twenty-two five-year-olds came barrelling through the library door, their enthusiasm almost deafening. "Ms. Olivia! Ms. Olivia! Where are you?"

"I have to go," she blurted out hurriedly, and she sprinted over to the children's section to greet them at the treehouse entrance. Trying to ignore the strange effect Daniel Lane had on her, she got straight into character as soon as she saw the children. "Good morning, children. Ms. Olivia is not here today. I am her friend, Ember, and I will be reading to you today. Come with me, please." She was using a voice that she considered to be dragon-like, which was coming out as low and sexy, and maybe not wholly appropriate for five-year-olds.

The children were completely spellbound and followed her as if she were the Pied Piper, sitting on their little tree stumps like angels.

The class teacher, seeing that Olivia had them entirely under control, took the opportunity to browse the books and enjoy her coffee.

Looking up to confirm she had their attention, Olivia noticed it was not only the children who had followed her to the reading corner, as she observed Daniel Lane trying to fold himself small enough to sit on one of the tree stumps. He looked so funny that she had to turn her head to suppress a laugh and pretended she was coughing. "Sorry, children. I've been breathing a bit too much fire today, and it's given me a tickle in my throat."

The children were mesmerized during Olivia's session, and she read all three books without so much as a murmur. When she put down the last book, her young charges groaned. "That is all the time I have with you today, children. I would like you to choose your books now. I will tell Ms. Olivia that you were all very well behaved, and I didn't have to eat anyone."

The kindergarten teacher gave her a brief wave and escorted her class off to choose their books for the week. Olivia sat behind her desk and checked them all out, giving each child a dragon sticker before they left.

"Goodbye, Ember. We love you." The little voices trailed behind them until the teacher had shepherded them all out of the door, and the library was left in silence except for the sound of applause from a solitary pair of hands.

Daniel approached her as she shed the mask, rubbing her face where it had dug into her nose. Grabbing the barrette from the back of her hair, she let her hair down and shook her head, massaging her scalp where it hurt a little.

Looking up at him from her desk, she saw he was smiling down at her in wonder. "That was the most amazing performance I've ever seen. You had them eating out of your hand. How often do you do that?"

She wasn't sure if he was teasing her, but she didn't want to be rude. He had, after all, agreed to produce her travel guides. She distractedly braided her hair into a long side braid before realizing she had nothing to secure it with. With a frown, she rummaged around in her desk until she found a yellow rubber band, only to find she had creatively knotted it together with about fifty others when she had been bored one day last week. Pulling out the long chain of rainbow coloured bands that seemed to go on forever, she knew that Daniel was watching her with apparent fascination. *He obviously thinks I'm a nut job*, she thought, trying not to laugh.

"I only dress up for the little ones on Wednesday mornings," she said a little bluntly. "I'm not a dragon every week, you know. It just depends on what I'm reading." She rambled on, speaking rapidly. "At Easter, I'm always a bunny, and then on Halloween, I'm usually a witch, and at Christmas, I'm an elf. In between times, I have been known to be all manner of things. Last week, I was Ms. Frizzle." She noticed Harry crossing the floor, looking excited and, relieved at the distraction, she shot him a lovely smile.

"Oh my goodness. That was amazing. You were an absolute hit!" He quickly nodded at Daniel in acknowledgement, and then he threw his arms around her rather inappropriately, pulling her in for a bear hug. Releasing her, he brushed a few stray cat hairs off her cape and smiled down at her affectionately. "I'm going out for Starbucks, sweetie. Mochaccino okay for you?"

"That would be lovely Harry, but it's my turn, remember?" He shook his head determinedly and headed for the door, humming happily to himself. She couldn't remember the last time he'd allowed her to pay for coffee.

They both watched Harry depart and then he turned back to her. "What do I need to do to get a hug like that?"

She looked at him incredulously. "You need to be a middle-aged bachelor who lives with his elderly mother and has a family of extremely hairy cats.

Daniel winced. "I don't think that's going to work for me. I don't really like cats that much."

Olivia rolled her eyes, "God, neither do I. They make me feel uncomfortable. I always think they're secretly plotting to overthrow the planet–smug little bastards. I went to Harry's place for dinner one night and all seven of them crawled all over me. I think they were trying to break down my resistance and pull me over to their side. It didn't work; I was practically hyperventilating by the time I left. That constant meowing haunted my dreams for months. Don't tell Harry though, he'd be devastated. I dressed up as a black cat for Halloween one year, and I think he thought he'd died and gone to heaven."

"Your secret it safe with me." He smiled. "You're hilarious, Olivia. You know that don't you?"

She sighed heavily. "Oh yes. People tell me that all the time. Particularly men who I was hoping for a second date with, and then I never see them again. Most guys find me too... now, which adjective shall we use?" She considered thoughtfully. "There have been so many. I've been called unusual, weird, quirky, short, too curvy, rude, scary; one bastard even told me I was too aggressive. Can you believe that?" She wasn't really talking to him at this point rather than ranting to the universe. Shaking her head in disbelief, she looked back at Daniel, who seemed rooted to the spot. "I have to get ready for my grade three class now, Mr. Lane. You must excuse me." She whipped off her cape and put it into her tote after folding it carefully.

"Is there going to be a different costume?" he asked hopefully.

"No, not today," she smiled. "The grade threes are a much tougher audience. No costumes, and strict Ms. Jefferson will probably have to put in an appearance."

He suddenly grabbed her hand and circled her wrist with his thumb, causing a strange warmth to travel up her arm. "That sounds even more interesting than the dragon costume. If I didn't have a meeting, I would stay and watch. Strict Ms. Jefferson sounds like my kind of girl." Olivia pulled her hand away sharply and narrowed her eyes at him.

"Was there something in particular you came in for today that I can help you find, or was this just a detour to make fun of me? Being a struggling author doesn't exactly pay the bills, you know. I've been working here since college to make ends meet, rather unsuccessfully unfortunately. I do love the kids and working here with Harry."

He looked apologetic. "I found exactly what I was looking for, thank you. I certainly didn't intend to make fun of you. As I told you yesterday, I think you are quite unique, and that is intended as a compliment before you ask. I hope you don't mind if I come and visit you again." Without waiting for her to respond, he pivoted and headed out the door, leaving Olivia with her mouth slightly agape, wondering what the hell just happened.

At lunch time, she shot a quick text off to Lottie:

Are you free tonight? I need to decompress after a weird day.

Always free for you darling. How about margaritas at my place at 7?

Olivia confirmed with a thumbs-up emoji and looked at the rather interesting sandwich she had packed for lunch. She realized she would have to do some grocery shopping before she went over to Lottie's and swore to herself she would only buy cheap and healthy food and not several pints of Ben & Jerry's like she normally did.

....

Sitting on one of Lottie's white leather couches, Olivia took a large swig of her drink and pulled a face like she was sucking on a lemon. "Good God, Lottie. How much tequila did you put in this exactly? I have to work again tomorrow. You know that don't you?"

Lottie laughed in her deep, sexy tone. "What's the point of a virgin margarita, sweetie? Anyway, spill the beans. Something brought you over here to indulge in my booze mid-week."

Olivia gave her a full rundown of her day and her strange encounter with Daniel Lane whilst dressed as a dragon. She was always a great storyteller and tended to embellish things, much to the amusement of her friends. Lottie sat on the couch with her legs crossed and her eyes sparkling, gasping at the part where he grabbed Olivia's hand.

"Well, he obviously came in just to see you. Your library is nowhere near his office."

Olivia flushed. "It certainly seemed that way. But why, for fuck's sake? Do you think he wanted to make fun of me? Although I have to say he seemed quite taken with the dragon costume."

Lottie's eyes grew wide. "I'll bet he has a costume fetish. All these bored rich guys have some kind of fetish and I bet his is getting women to dress up. He'd be ideal for you. You have a ton of amazing costumes."

Olivia looked incredulous. "That's ridiculous, Lottie. Who the hell has a costume fetish? I've never heard of it."

"Willard Beasley for one." Lottie replied darkly.

Olivia frowned as her mind went back to one of Lottie's past boyfriends. Willard's family owned a chain of upmarket bookstores and like many of Lottie's suitors, he was rolling in money. "What do you mean? I always liked Willard. He was sweet, in a daft, rich guy kind of way."

"Well, do you remember that time I borrowed your unicorn costume to go to that party with him in the Hamptons?"

Olivia smiled and nodded. It was one of her favourite costumes and much loved by the children, even though it was a little hot to wear. It had a white, star-covered body suit with a hood and a rather magnificent silver horn with a long pink wig to represent the mane. Like many of Olivia's costumes, it verged on the sexy side.

"Well, Willard was more than a little excited by that costume. He insisted on fucking me while I was wearing it, and he wanted me to make unicorn noises."

Olivia exploded, spraying margarita out of her nose as she doubled over. "What noises do unicorns make?" she spluttered as tears ran down her face.

Lottie was struggling to keep it together. "I'm not sure. I improvised with horse whinnies. It really turned him on!" she shrieked.

"Wait a minute," Olivia said seriously. "Are you telling me you had sex in that costume and then you gave it back to me? Lottie, I read to 5-year-olds in that costume. That's really not appropriate!"

"I had it cleaned Olivia. I'm sure it's perfectly hygienic. Anyway, what I'm saying is maybe Daniel Lane is like old Willard."

Olivia thought about Willard. He'd seemed like such a sweet guy, if a little gormless. Who knew what hidden depths people had? "Didn't Willard end up marrying Felicity Venables? You know that girl with the large teeth who looks like a... *horse*," they both said in unison, laughing so much their sides were aching. "Do you think he gives her a good rubdown after he's taken her for a ride?"

"Stop or I'm going to throw up!" Lottie begged.

Olivia found it hard to believe that Daniel had a costume fetish. He just didn't seem the type, but maybe Lottie was right. She shook her head to remove that rather troubling thought from her mind and downed another one of Lottie's extremely addictive margaritas.

"Or maybe," Lottie speculated, "he's into a bit of S&M. Obviously the possibility of strict Ms. Jefferson had him hot under the collar. Perhaps you should invest in a Ms. Whiplash costume."

Olivia rolled her eyes. "You know how I feel l about that kind of thing. I have no time for kinky perverts."

Lottie smiled knowingly. "Don't limit yourself, darling. There are a lot more flavours than just plain old vanilla you know."

"I know that, and my particular favourite is Chunky Monkey, but I am not about to get involved with any kind of sex that involves bananas or any other fruit for that matter."

"Well, fetish or not, he definitely has the hots for you. He clearly made a special trip to seek you out. He likes you, Olivia. Give him a chance. Don't blow him off like you do everyone else who's interested in you."

Olivia made a face. "Don't be ridiculous. He's so far out of my league he's in a different universe. Have you actually seen him up close? Men like that don't date girls like me. You've seen me first thing in the morning. I look like a deranged Troll with decent boobs."

Lottie sniggered at the rather disturbing imagery, even though she couldn't disagree more. She'd always envied Olivia's petite but curvaceous figure and her hair was to die for, even if it did have a mind of its own. Despite Olivia's insistence to the contrary, men often found her irresistible, but she was usually blissfully unaware of the fact, passing off their attempts to gain her attention as inebriation or temporary loss of mental faculties. Her unfiltered mouth gave the impression she was brushing them off and eventually they gave up, convinced she wasn't interested.

Lottie looked affectionately at her friend, watching her lick the salt off the edge of her margarita glass with the tip of her tongue. "I think you have it backwards, Liv. You're way out of Daniel Lane's league. He'd never find another woman like you."

Olivia stopped mid lick with her tongue stuck to the glass and gave her a tipsy smile. That last margarita was definitely one too many. "I always thought you were slightly insane, Lottie, but that last statement just proves it. Anyway, it's a moot point. Mr. Lane and I will never be an item. Never, never, ever," she slurred emphatically. "Holy crap. My lips appear to have gone numb."

Sensing it was time to call it a night before one of them did something they would regret in the morning, Lottie called Olivia a cab, hugging her friend warmly as she watched her take a rather convoluted route to the elevator.

6 - Daniel

D aniel arrived for work inordinately early the next day, even by his standards. He was normally in his office before anyone else arrived, but lack of sleep meant he was behind his desk by 6:30. It was still dark outside, and he looked out at a city waking up from its short-lived slumber. Last night sleep had eluded him, and his dreams were haunted with visions of shimmering masks and questioning green eyes.

He tried to rationalize what was happening to him. He decided it was the forbidden fruit card coming into play. Eva had warned him off; Olivia was too young, and it was inappropriate for him to hook up with one of their authors. That had to be the reason he was feeling the way he was. There was nothing worse than being told you couldn't have something—or someone. But, even as he justified it to himself, there was a lingering doubt deep within his chest. He was breaking all his own rules with this girl, and yesterday he had gone out of his way to see her at work. For the first time in his life, he was openly pursuing a woman, a very unusual one at that.

He closed his eyes and leant back in his chair, recalling the moment she came flying around the bookcase and ran slap bang into him like an iridescent freight train. Although her appearance had surprised him momentarily, it also made perfect sense.

Looking down at his impeccable suit, he sighed. This was his work uniform; it didn't come with many variations. Different shades of grey or sometimes black, but nevertheless, he was the archetypal executive. He imagined himself 20 years from now, still wearing the same suits and sitting in the same office overlooking an identical cityscape.

In contrast, Olivia felt perfectly comfortable going to work dressed as a dragon. Watching her enthusiasm as she read to the little guys yesterday was nothing short of enchanting. Perhaps that was part of the attraction. He felt bored and trapped by his life, and he was witnessing someone living out their life in a way that suited them. Not that he wanted to walk into the office dressed as a dragon, of course, but having those kinds of choices in life had to be liberating.

He considered that he had always been destined for this life. If he had taken up law, as he had originally intended, he would have spent his days in the same uniform, with a similar office. When he bought the house on the coast, he thought it would afford him some of the peace he was looking for in life. At least there, no-one really knew who he was, and he wasn't followed by the press. He got to relax a little, but still, it was a bit of a lonely existence. His decision not to take any of his female flings to the cottage had been very deliberate. He didn't want them there, but it meant he spent his weekends without company, rattling around in his self-imposed ivory tower.

After fixing himself a second cup of coffee, he sighed and stared gloomily at his schedule for the day. He had an early meeting at 8:30 which would probably last for two hours with a break until one, and then more meetings. *A usual run-of-the-mill day,* he thought. He looked at the block of time he had after his morning meeting and before his 1 o'clock and thought about how he would fill it.

He should go through the quarterly forecasts that the Head of Finance had left on his desk yesterday, but another idea was forming in his head. He grabbed the manilla folder containing Olivia's information, which he had hidden in his desk. He had copied her resume and returned the original file to Eva, who would be none the wiser, but he had no intention of losing this small link to her, and besides, he enjoyed looking at her picture.

He realized it was still quite early, but he had to phone her before he got trapped in his 8:30 meeting. Picking up his phone, he nervously punched in her number, but it went directly to voice mail. He smiled as he listened to her quirky message, and then he spoke.

"Good morning, Olivia. It's Daniel Lane. I'm wondering if you could meet me for coffee this morning around 11. I will be at the Mean Bean on 32nd Street, probably at a table on the mezzanine towards the back. I hope to see you then."

After hanging up, he took a breath. What the hell was he doing? This was exactly what Eva had asked him not to do, but it was just coffee. What harm ever came from meeting someone for coffee? It could even be construed as a business meeting, and they could continue talking about her books. "Who the hell are you kidding, dick brain?" he mumbled to himself.

Just before 11, Daniel found himself settled at a table at the back of the mezzanine of the Mean Bean. He liked this particular coffee shop, as it was easy to hide yourself away on the upper floor without being recognized or bothered by anyone. It was also far enough away from the office to ensure that he was unlikely to run into anyone from work.

Looking at his watch, he wondered if she had received his message or if she would even show up. She hadn't seemed that impressed to see him at the library yesterday. In fact, at times, she verged on hostility. He sipped his espresso and decided that he would wait until 11:30 and then if she didn't arrive, he would head back to work.

After a couple of minutes, he saw her heading towards him with an enormous cup of coffee perched in one hand and a sandwich in the other. He took in her appearance and held his breath. Dressed in a pair of faded, ripped jeans and a snug black t-shirt that showed off a section of midriff, she completed her ensemble with a pair of black Doc Martens and a long, flowy black cardigan. An oversized pair of sunglasses were perched on top of her head and her still-damp blonde hair hung around her shoulders. She shot him an uncertain smile as she approached. She looked young and stylish, and he thought she could easily pass as an art student from the local campus. He rose, like the true gentleman he tried to be, and pulled out a chair for her. "Thank you for coming, Olivia. It's lovely to see you again."

"Sorry I'm five minutes late. I just got up actually."

He looked at her questioningly. "You just got up?"

"Uh-huh. I went to see my friend, Lottie, last night, and she plied me with a few of her outrageous margaritas. By the time I got home, my entire face had gone numb." She rubbed her face as if she were still afflicted. "Do you ever get so drunk your face goes numb?" she asked, looking at him directly with that questioning look in her eyes.

He watched her with amused wonder. "It hasn't happened for a long time. I'm glad you got home safely." He paused for a moment and looked her up and down. She looked so different from when she had visited the publishing house—younger and definitely more comfortable. "You look..." He paused, lost for what to say.

She giggled. "Ah, I can see you're struggling to find the right adjective. I'll give you five and you can choose the one that fits the best. I'm great at this game; are you ready?" He nodded dumbly. "Okay, so you said, 'you look' and the adjectives are: edgy, scruffy, bewildered, grungy, or disillusioned. Which one are you choosing?"

Frowning, he considered his choices. "Do I have to choose one of those? I was thinking of something quite different. I was going to say, 'you look amazing.'"

She wrinkled her nose adorably. "Hmm. I wouldn't have thought of that, but I guess it fits. Thanks. Well, I took your advice. You told me to come as me the next time I saw you, and I guess this is me on some days, when I'm not gainfully employed as a dragon that is."

Flopping into the leather chair, she looked across at him with her head on one side. "You look great too. Business suits really do something for you. You've got that whole smoldering executive hottie look going on." She immediately clapped her hand over her mouth with a look of horror. "Shit, I'm so sorry. It's early and the filter's off. I really should put duct tape over my mouth until I know all my brain cells are firing."

"Executive hottie?" He grinned. "So, you like what you see?"

She looked at him skeptically. "Are you seriously asking me that question and expecting an honest answer? Besides, according to Lottie, half the state's rich and sophisticated female population are constantly prostrating themselves at your feet, so it's a bit of a moot point really. Anyway, going back to last night. It's your fault I found myself shitfaced mid-week."

He looked confused. "My fault?"

She nodded seriously. "You completely threw me a curve ball turning up at the library like that. I had to go over to Lottie's to debrief and one drink led to another, so to speak." She paused and sipped her coffee. "So, why were you there exactly? It's nowhere near your office, and you don't seem like the kind of guy who needs to use the library at 9 a.m. You own a publishing house. Lots of books there I would imagine," she added shrewdly.

Daniel winced. He wasn't expecting to explain his actions so early into the conversation. In fact, he wasn't really sure he could, as he didn't understand it himself. He couldn't think of anything clever to say, so he simply said. "I came to see *you*."

"Why?"

"Because I like you and I wanted an excuse to see you again."

"Oh. Okay."

And with that, she seemed to have accepted his explanation, and she turned her attention to her sandwich. He watched her as she started to carefully tear off the crust before she ate it. She looked like she was keen to take the crust off in one piece and stuck her tongue out as she focused on the task at hand.

"Don't you like the crust?"

"Oh yes, I love the crust, but I eat that last. Not with the sandwich. I know it's weird, but it's just the way I roll. Sandwich first, crust last." Satisfied that she had done a good job, she tucked into her sandwich, humming happily to herself.

"What if it's a baguette?"

"What?" she mumbled with her mouth half-full of food.

"What if you're eating a baguette? Do you tear the crust off that as well?"

She looked at him as if he were quite mad. "No! You can't tear the crust off a baguette! There would be nothing left. What's the point in that?" In her passionate diatribe about leaving the crusts on baguettes, she almost sounded aggressive, with her hands waving wildly to emphasize her point. He could see why some guys would be put off by that, but it just seemed to intrigue him all the more.

He tried to conceal his laugh behind his hand, and she narrowed her eyes at him. "You think I'm crazy, don't you? I saw you watching me when I was pulling out those rubber bands from my desk drawer yesterday. You had that look, I've seen it before. It's that '*let's humour the insane person*' look. I see it a lot."

Daniel grinned. She was being wickedly unfiltered today, and he loved it. It lifted his spirits in a way that he couldn't even comprehend. No-one ever spoke to him like this. There were far too many kiss-asses in his life. The press would have a field day if they caught him tucked away in the back of this coffee shop with Olivia dressed like this.

Looking more closely, he noticed her earrings didn't match. One was a turquoise feather and the other a trailing silver moon and star. "I don't think you're the least bit crazy. You do however fascinate me beyond words. Your earrings are really interesting."

She looked up at him and smiled as she chewed on her sandwich. "I've lost so many earrings in the past, I don't even bother trying to match them up anymore. I just rummage around in my jewellery box with my eyes closed and wear the first two that I grab. I've made a rule that I have to wear them even if the combination is really wacky.

I find it makes for intriguing conversation. I've met some really nice people because of my earrings." She looked thoughtful for a minute. "On the other hand I've met some really weird ones as well, but who am I to judge?"

He leaned closer to her with his elbows on the table. "Is it just your ears you have pierced, or do you have other piercings?" It was out of his mouth before he could stop himself. *God, talk about inappropriate,* he admonished himself silently.

She looked across at him with a smirk and raised her eyebrows. "I'm not sure I want to answer that question. It's a little personal, don't you think?"

He rubbed his face with his hands. "I'm sorry, Olivia, you're absolutely right. That was totally...."

She interrupted him before he had a chance to finish. "I don't have any other piercings. Having my ears pierced freaked me out so much I had to do it in two sessions. I passed out cold the first time, and they carted me off to the ER. I'm on first-name terms with those people for one reason or another. God, imagine having your nipples pierced. Holy crap!" She pulled a pained expression as if she were sucking on a lemon and paused thoughtfully before continuing. "I do, however, have a very discreet and tasteful tattoo." She raised her eyebrows at him suggestively.

He could see she was in a much more playful mood today. God, he loved playful Olivia. She made him feel like he could put away all his stress just for a short while and bask in her naughtiness. "Am I allowed to ask where it is?"

She sipped her coffee and looked over her cup at him with dancing eyes. He could tell she was flirting, even if she wasn't aware of it herself. "I'm not sure I know you well enough to tell you the location of my tattoo. I will however tell you what it says. *L'amore vince sempre,*" she said with a dramatic flourish. He looked at her quizzically. "*Love Conquers All.* Well, actually the literal translation is *Love Al-*

ways Wins. It sounds so much better in Italian, don't you think? I had it done in Rome last summer."

He nodded his head thoughtfully. "Do you think it does? Does love conquer all?"

She shrugged her shoulders. "I'm probably not the best person to ask, as I have never been in love as far as I can remember anyway, and I think I would remember. It's a nice thought though, isn't it? Loving someone so much that nothing else matters? My dad loves my mom like that, which is amazing because she can be vile at times. It's crazy what people put up with when they're in love." She stared off into space thoughtfully before shaking her head as if she were trying to bring herself back down to earth.

"I'm so sorry, I've been totally inappropriate today. I think my blood sugar is low. It really affects my social filter when I haven't eaten; I feel better now. God, I can't believe I called you an executive hottie. How rude! I rarely objectify people like that. At least not to their face."

The change in her was quite astonishing, as if she suddenly realized her behaviour might not be quite right. She looked across at him with a puzzled look. "Was there a reason that we're meeting here today, or am I just providing you with a distraction?"

He tried to think fast on his feet. Obviously she was expecting this to be an extension of their business lunch, and he had been led into an entirely different direction by her apparent hypoglycemia. "Oh, I just wanted to talk about your next project. You touched briefly on it on Tuesday. It's good to know what direction you're headed in, so we know what to expect."

She smiled and launched into telling him about her future plans with enthusiasm. He watched as she gesticulated with her hands and told him all about her planned trip to Florence and Tuscany and her desire to live in Italy on an extended basis. Her excitement was infectious, and he found himself wishing he could accompany her. It had been so long since he had been anywhere exciting, and she would certainly make an interesting travel companion. He dismissed the idea as a pipe dream. She had made it obvious that her goal was for solo travel, and why would she go with him anyway?

At noon he indicated that he had to get back to work, and she told him she was due to be working at the library at one. "Dressed like that?" he asked, a little bemused.

"Yes, absolutely dressed like this." She laughed. "I'm going to be building Lego castles all afternoon, so I needed to wear something I can crawl around the floor in." He looked at her quizzically, so she continued. "Today I'm working with the *Stepping Stones to Literacy* project. We work with a small group of kids from disadvantaged backgrounds and try to get them into reading in creative ways. You don't turn up in a business suit to work with kids like that. They'd never relate to me at all."

He watched her in amazement as she explained the project and how it worked. She clearly loved working with this particular group, and her enthusiasm for the project was palpable.

She rose from her seat, and they left the coffee shop together. She pulled her sunglasses back down over her eyes and put out her hand to him to shake. Taking her hand in his, he shook it briefly, wishing he could pull her in for a kiss but decided against it. "Can I see you again?" he blurted out without thinking.

"Oh, I have the distinct impression we'll run into each other again." She laughed. Then without another word she turned, plugged in her earbuds, and headed off down the street. He watched her depart, her head bouncing to the music, and her hips swaying gently. He felt himself release an enormous sigh. *You're in deep shit, Daniel,* he said to himself.

7

The next day, Olivia was aimlessly wandering around her small living space, trying to drum up inspiration to sit down and write for the day. Her phone rang from the depths of her messenger bag, and she emptied the contents onto the floor in her efforts to find it. Seeing Daniel Lane's name flash on her display, her hand hovered over the phone momentarily before she decided to answer.

"Good morning, Mr. Lane. This is becoming a bit of a habit, don't you think? Didn't we see each other only yesterday? Are you stalking me by any chance?"

He didn't answer her directly but launched into something unrelated, speaking as though it was she who had called him. "Hello, Olivia. I'm going to the park at lunchtime to feed the ducks, and I thought that might be the kind of activity you would enjoy. Do you want to come along?"

"You think I'm into ducks?" she said incredulously.

"Hey, I'm just throwing stuff at the wall here and seeing what sticks. I'm completely out of my depth with you. I think I just need another Olivia fix."

She pondered this for a moment. "I'm not a class A drug, you know. I really wanted to get on with my writing today, and besides, I Googled you last night. I'm not sure I like you anymore."

She heard him heave a sigh. "I really don't want to get into this on the phone. Look, you need a break away from your computer for an hour. Just meet me at noon and we can chat. What do you think?"

After a little gentle persuasion, she agreed and hung up. Olivia was actually a total sucker for ducks, but she didn't let him know that. She really didn't know where this thing was going with Daniel Lane. It was all very odd. It wasn't the type of dating she was familiar with at college, not that she'd dated much then anyway. She wasn't even sure that this *was* dating. He seemed interested in her, but it all seemed so weird.

What was even stranger was that since the incident in the library, she had chosen not to tell Lottie about these outings with Daniel. She wasn't really sure why this was because she was sure Lottie would approve. God, she was practically panting over him. For some inexplicable reason, she felt she needed to keep this to herself. Anyway, it was hardly as if they were compatible in any shape or form. She definitely wasn't expecting this situation to go anywhere. He was just using her as a little comic relief. Well, if that's what he wanted, she was happy to oblige.

She forced herself to forget about Daniel for a couple of hours and got on with some work, not stopping to look at the clock until 11:30. Realizing she was still wearing a pair of fuzzy Hello Kitty jammies, she thought she probably should change.

She was really tempted to wear something totally outrageous, just for the shock value, but looking through her closet she noticed one of her mom's castoffs, a pretty blue linen jumpsuit with a tropical print. It was one of those things her mom had ordered online and then never wore when she realized how impractical it was. It was the colour that appealed to Olivia. She loved all shades of blue, but this particular blue reminded her of the sky in Provence. Not wanting to look too conventional, she pulled on a pair of leopard print sneakers and grabbed a denim jacket before heading out the door.

As she approached the pond in the middle of the park, she couldn't see him at first, but then looking across the water she realized he was on the far side, where few people ventured. *Hiding away in the shadows again*, she thought.

She could tell he was watching her as she walked around the pond to reach him, but she kept her head down, not acknowledging him. He stood as she got closer and for a moment, he looked like he was going to step forward and kiss her in greeting, but she side-stepped him and moved around the back of the bench. He smiled and shook his head as if he'd just been out-maneuvered.

"You came. I wasn't sure you would."

She looked at him with her lips pursed. "I wasn't sure I would either. I guess curiosity got the better of me."

"You need to be careful with that. You know what curiosity did to the cat."

"And *you* know I totally hate cats, so the thought of one dying from a case of nosiness does not scare me. One less to take over the planet as far as I'm concerned."

He opened a large paper grocery bag he had brought with him and pulled out baguettes and coffee for them both, setting them down between them on the bench. "I had to guess at what you might like. I have brie and cranberry or ham and Swiss. I bought baguettes so you wouldn't have to go through the trouble of tearing off the crusts."

She gave him a dry smile. "How thoughtful." She chose one and then tore the end off it, throwing it into the water and encouraging an entire flock of ducks to come rushing toward them, skating across the water excitedly.

"I like your dress. You look lovely."

She looked down at herself, slightly surprised at his comment. "Oh, it's not a dress, it's a jumpsuit. Look." She stood up and showed him that the legs were actually wide pants. "My mom bought it before she realized it's impossible to pee in these things without taking it all off, so she gave it to me. Don't you think designers would have considered that before they initiated a resurgence in women's jumpsuits? What's wrong with them? Do they not need to pee?"

His eyes creased up at the corners in amusement. "And I guess you're not bothered by those kinds of things."

"Well, I would be if I had to pee behind a bush, that would be impossible, but I know there are restrooms here so it shouldn't be a problem. Men are so lucky they have magical plumbing. It must be so much more convenient that you can just whip it out at a moment's notice."

"I'm not sure how magical it is," he said, laughing.

She raised her eyebrows. "From what I've been reading on Google, yours must be pretty magical." She looked thoughtful for a moment before she murmured, "Daniel's magic dick. Hey, that would be a great title for a book, don't you think?"

He shot her a serious glance. "Olivia, don't even think about it."

She shook her head. "But you're not seeing the marketing potential in this. It could be one of those books that looks like a kid's book, but it's actually written for adults. Someone requested one at the library; it's called *Go the Fuck to Sleep*. Have you heard of it? Apparently, it's for sleep deprived parents."

He stared at her, looking slightly bewildered.

"Anyway, going back to the magic dick idea, there could be a whole series of them like *Daniel's Magic Dick goes to the Grocery Store*, or *Daniel's Magic Dick has a Bad Day*. I think we could be onto a winner here. God, I'd love to be the illustrator on this series." She chewed her baguette thoughtfully, as if she were pondering the idea.

"Olivia, I forbid you to write a book about my dick, magic or not, and we certainly won't be publishing it."

She glanced at him slyly. "You'll be sorry when Penguin Random House picks it up. Don't say I didn't give you a chance."

"You are joking, aren't you?"

She laughed. "Not completely, actually. I'm always on the lookout for a good idea. The next Harry Potter is always just around the corner, and this could be it."

He pondered this for a moment. "Well, how would you like it if someone wrote a book about your magical vagina?"

She gasped in admiration. "Oh, my God, you said the V word. I can't believe it; you're sitting there in your suit, and you said the V word. Out loud. There's hope for you yet. I guess it could have been worse. You could have said magical pussy, but then we'd be back to those damn cats again." She sniggered as if she were enjoying a private joke before he drew her back to his question.

"You haven't told me what you would think."

"Okay, first, I think I would take it as a compliment. No-one's ever described it like that, but I think it could work. We could truly be onto something here. *Livvy and her Magic Vag*." She suddenly collapsed into peals of laughter, burying her face in her hands. "Oh my God, I just had an amazing thought, but I'm absolutely not sharing it with you."

He looked a little offended. "Why on earth not? You don't normally seem to have problems sharing things that would be seen as completely inappropriate in most conversations."

She grinned across at him. "Yes, but this is worse than inappropriate. Even I know my limits."

"But you'd share it with your girlfriends, I guess?"

She nodded slyly. "Oh, yes. This is just the kind of thing they would really appreciate. I could get some real mileage out of this idea."

"Well, is that not what we are? Are we not friends?"

Olivia thought about this for a moment. She really had no idea what they were doing; it seemed completely surreal. At times he came across as a somewhat formal executive who was a little stiff and reserved, but at other times, she could see the possibilities in him. He definitely had a sense of humour hiding in there somewhere. "Okay, I'll tell you, but you mustn't think badly of me. Remember, you pressed me on this one." She made a dramatic flourish with her hands. "It's like the story of Aladdin: Livvy and her Magic Vag; rub it, and it will grant you three wishes." She looked across at him with an enormous smile of satisfaction as he choked on his baguette.

Mission accomplished, she thought wickedly. *Maximum shock value achieved.*

After he composed himself, he turned to her with a seductive smile. "Sweetheart, if you let me rub it, you'd grant all my wishes."

She felt herself blush and put her hands on her hot cheeks before turning to him with tight lips. "You see what you did there? You completely stepped out of the friend zone, and you made me blush, and I really hate that. It's so fucking gauche. This is exactly why men and women can't be friends, unless you were gay, of course, and then it would totally work."

He held his hands up in surrender. "You can't blame me for that, Olivia. You led me right into it. I couldn't resist."

"Okay, I'll give you that, but it proves one thing. You do have a sense of humour concealed under that suit. I think you could be a lot of fun if you allowed yourself to be."

He smiled a little sadly. "I guess it's been well hidden for a while. I don't know when I became this boring person. It's amazing what a big dose of responsibility does to you. There are... expectations." His voice trailed off, and he shook his head as if he were bringing himself back to reality. "Anyway, how the hell did we get onto this topic in the first place? I'm completely confused. You seem to have the ability to wreck any conversation."

Olivia tore off another large piece of her baguette and flung it into the pond, hitting one duck on the head and causing her feathered friends to embark on a watery skirmish. "I'm good at confusing people. No-one ever knows whether I'm serious. It's great. Keeps people on their toes and weeds out the riffraff."

He looked puzzled. "What do you mean?"

She grinned mischievously. "Well, when someone seems interested in me, I think it's only fair that they see me at my most unfiltered, so they know what they're getting into. If they can't deal with it, they soon give their excuses and leave." She paused for a moment. "But, strangely enough, you're still here. You're the last person I would have thought would be interested in someone like me."

He shook his head and smiled. "Yes, odd, isn't it? It's like being sucked into another dimension."

She looked a little offended. "You are free to leave at any time."

His voice took on a wistful quality. "That's just it. You kind of scare me, but I can't seem to get enough of you. You're like no one I've ever encountered before."

They both sat in silence for several minutes, digesting his words and the remains of their baguettes. She riffled through the paper bag, looking for cream and sugar for her coffee, humming happily when she found a cache of it at the bottom of the bag.

Taking a sip of his coffee, he continued. "So, why don't you tell me about your Google search? It sounds like you've been a busy girl."

She rubbed her hands gleefully as if she were going to impart some secret information. "So, this is what I've discovered about you. You appear to be a serial dater. You're never pictured with the same woman twice and the press love to make inferences about your dating habits." She launched into a dramatic voice. "*In society news, love 'em and leave 'em publisher Daniel Lane hits the town with yet another beautiful woman this week.* I've no idea how many of these women end up in your bed but looking at you, I figure your batting average is pretty good."

He sat quietly for a while. "What you describe is mainly accurate, although I think my batting average is much lower than whatever crazy number you have in mind. Mostly, these women are just accompanying me to social events that require an escort. For the past few years, I've avoided committed relationships. I haven't felt I've had anything to offer apart from something casual, and I'm always brutally honest about that. What I really need to know is how *you* feel about all this."

She leaned her head back and stared at the sky. "Well, you're obviously some kind of playboy, player, whatever they call them these days. What I can't figure out is why you're sitting on a park bench feeding ducks with a slightly deranged and impoverished writer. It hardly fits your game plan, does it?"

He looked down at his hands sadly. "I never really had a game plan as such, but I can see where you're going with this."

Looking across at his dejected face, she actually felt a little sorry for him and sighed. "Listen, I try not to be judgmental about people. Look at me. I'm a well-known crazed loon, and I hate it when people claim to know who I really am because, generally, they don't. But I don't subscribe to this hump 'em and dump 'em mentality, so if you're just looking for another fling, that's not who I am. Casual sex messes with my head. I just can't do it. I like to think I have more self respect than that."

"I don't like who I am, Olivia. I don't like who I've become. It was never intentional, it just kind of evolved and became a habit. There's something missing in my life, and I have no idea of how to go about fixing that. Part of my attraction to you is that I envy you. I envy your freedom and your lack of inhibition. I don't have choices in my life in the way that you do. Never believe someone if they tell you that success buys freedom, it doesn't. It's far better to be anonymous."

He looked down at his watch and started to pack up the debris of their lunch. The ducks had long since lost interest and had hurried off to harass another unsuspecting diner. He stood up and looked down at her with a sad smile. "I guess I should get back to the office. Thank you for meeting me for lunch."

She stood up with him and without thinking threw her arms around him. She couldn't bear that he felt so bad about himself. She'd been in this position herself so many times. God knows, she wasn't without faults. At least he wasn't trying to hide anything. He froze for a moment as if he were confused, but then he returned her embrace, wrapping his arms around her tightly and burying his face in her hair. Eventually he pulled back and regarded her thoughtfully. "Was that a pity hug?"

She screwed her nose up at him and smiled, shrugging her shoulders. "Who knows? Maybe I just like you." And with that, she turned and headed off down the path.

8

Girls' night arrived at last, and Lottie and Olivia decided they would go to The Red Room, a rather classy wine bar with great music and dancing. They were also going to invite Emily and Jordan, a couple of friends from their college days. They arranged to meet up at 7 p.m. and Olivia headed off to her closet to do her worst.

Zipping speedily through the contents, she suddenly spied a pair of black, ruffled dance pants with a low-cut waistline she had bought for kizomba lessons. The pants had a row of loose pearl buttons on the back waistline that moved when she shook her hips, like an exotic belly dancer.

Olivia was a natural dancer, and she was always ready to try something new. The sensual moves of kizomba had really appealed to her and when she had dragged Mark along for lessons, he had been less than enthusiastic about it, even though she loved it. Pretty soon, he was making excuses not to go, so Olivia had gone alone.

This was her first Mark-free night out and she wanted to let off steam and be a little outrageous, so she paired the pants with a black, sequined, cropped camisole top that left her stomach and back exposed. She put it on and was thrilled with the result. She completed her outfit with some strappy sandals and took more care than normal over her makeup. Pulling her hair into a messy updo, she applied some dramatic eye makeup and flame red lipstick and smiled at herself in the mirror. "You are one hot babe," she laughed at her reflection.

She took a cab downtown and pretty soon she was entering *The Red Room*. It was an upmarket place, as Lottie only went to places her parents would be happy for her to be seen in. As usual, Olivia was a little late, and she saw her friends as soon as she entered. They screamed a greeting as she headed over. The friends embraced, casting appreciative eyes at Olivia's outfit.

"I guess this is your revenge outfit," Emily said. "I've never seen you look so amazing! There are going to be some stiff dicks on the dancefloor tonight! Look at your toned abs, you lucky bitch. No-one who eats the amount of ice-cream you do should look like that."

Olivia laughed. "That's because it all goes to my ass. I currently have 15 litres of Ben & Jerry's stored in there. I guess that's 7 ½ litres per cheek." She slapped her backside for added effect.

After they were settled at the table, she regaled her friends with her story of going to the bar and finding Mark "in flagrante delicto," so to speak. Her friends roared with laughter at the story as Olivia gesticulated wildly to show how Mark was rubbing Kimberley's boobs.

"What a douche bag," Jordan drawled. "Kimberley probably has the IQ of a fart." And with that, their table exploded with laughter again. It was going to be a rowdy night.

The girls got another round of tequila in, and Olivia wanted to dance. The Red Room was one of a few bars that hosted regular kizomba nights, so she was hoping there would be someone to dance with. Suddenly, she recognized one of the instructors from her class, and she gave him a wave.

Paulo had olive-coloured Mediterranean skin and short dark hair. He had the body of a dancer, slight and muscular, with sharp angular cheekbones. He was wearing loose linen pants and a distressed looking t-shirt, giving him a casual, artistic look. Olivia loved it. He came over to her immediately and air kissed her loudly on both cheeks.

"Olivia! I've not seen you for the longest time, darling. Where have you been?"

She looked at him apologetically, having stopped her classes when Mark complained. He looked at her outfit appreciatively. "Well, I can see you've come prepared to have fun tonight. You look amazing! Dance with me, please, darling," he said, extending his hand.

There were several couples already entwined in close embraces, swaying to the heady beat of the music. She considered dancing to be one of her only talents. She refused to play a musical instrument, so her mother had insisted she take dance lessons from a young age, and being unable to stick with anything for long, Olivia had experienced every dance genre known to man from ballet to bachata.

She had a natural rhythm, and her friends were always envious that she could dance with anyone and always look good. Paulo led Olivia to the small dance floor and held her against his chest, their hips swaying together while they found the beat of the music. Lottie always said that kizomba was the closest you could get to fucking on the dance floor, and she wasn't far wrong.

Paolo's leg was firmly lodged between Olivia's thighs as she leant into him with one hand around his neck, and their faces pressed together. Paolo was an amazing partner. He was light on his feet and gentle, and she was really enjoying his expertise. He was extremely fit, and she could feel the outline of his muscles through this thin t-shirt.

Olivia had danced with a lot of inexperienced partners who thought kizomba was all about grinding their sweaty groin into their partner, so it was great to be with someone who knew what he was doing and treated her with respect. When the song ended, he kissed her hand sweetly and headed off to join the group he had arrived with.

Olivia headed back to Lottie, who had been watching from the edge of the floor. "Wow, he is so hot. Why did he disappear like that?"

Olivia nodded her head toward Paulo's all male party. "Gay," she whispered, "but a wonderful dancer." Lottie gave her a conciliatory look and smiled.

Deciding she would get another round of tequila in before more dancing, Olivia spun around and found herself staring into the eyes of Daniel Lane, who was watching her from the other side of the dance floor. He smiled slowly at her and she almost fell to her knees, dizzy from the booze, but also from the heat of his stare.

She grabbed Lottie's arm a little too tightly, inadvertently digging in her nails. "Oh, holy crap, Lottie," she whispered out of the corner of her mouth, "Daniel Lane is here, and he just saw me make a complete exhibition of myself with Paulo. He probably thinks I'm a complete slut, and what's worse is he looks fucking amazing."

This was an altogether more casual version of Daniel, dressed in black jeans and an untucked white linen shirt. His hair was gleaming like he'd just gotten out of the shower and his mouth was drawn up in a relaxed half smile. He was the very definition of sex on a stick. Lottie glanced over to where Olivia's eyes were fixated and gave a little gasp. "Good God, Olivia," she gulped. "That's not a man. That's an orgasm on legs."

The two-legged orgasm provider made his way over to where the girls were standing. The music had started up again and Jordan and Emily had started to dance with each other, gyrating their hips dramatically. Olivia stood riveted to the spot as he approached them.

"Good evening, Olivia. I didn't expect to find *you* here. That was quite the performance."

She stared at him silently. She opened her mouth to speak, but nothing came out. Lottie could see Olivia was struggling, so she pushed herself forward in an effort to save her friend and extended her hand.

"Hello, Mr. Lane. I'm Carlotta Partington, Olivia's best friend."

He smiled briefly at Lottie, but quickly turned back to Olivia, ignoring the fact that she hadn't spoken. "You really are quite accomplished. Have you taken lessons?" Olivia nodded silently at him, and Lottie chimed in again.

"Livvy's a natural, Mr. Lane. She can dance to anything. Men are always clamouring to dance with her." Daniel smiled gratefully at Lottie, making her blush.

"Well, in that case I hope you won't mind if I steal her away from you for a few minutes."

Without asking, he grabbed her hand and pulled her onto the dance floor. Olivia's favourite dance track was playing and before she knew it, he had her in a close embrace. She mentally prepared herself. *Okay, Olivia,* she said silently to herself, *show him what you're made of.* The music started to thrum, and she gently gyrated her hips, feeling the rhythm.

"Ready?" he asked her, brushing his hand against her back. She nodded, and they started to dance. He led her expertly around the dance floor. She felt his hand on her bare back and at the same time, he was fingering the pearl buttons at the top of her waistband. He was obviously as skilled as Paulo, and Olivia wondered how the hell he had come to be so good. He was obviously a closet kizomba expert as well as being a publishing god.

She had her head turned away from him as they danced, pressing into his shoulder, and he pulled her other hand up to wrap around the back of his neck, to pull her closer, placing both his hands on the small of her back. Wherever his hands touched her bare skin, she felt like an electrical charge was running through her body, awakening something deep inside. It was incredibly erotic, and she suddenly felt extremely exposed, contemplating that the cut off sequined top might not have been such a good idea.

They were starting to draw the attention of others in the bar who obviously recognized some serious talent on the floor. He was dancing with her with an air of possession, in a much more sensual way than Paulo did. She could feel the heat of his body through his shirt and her mind started to wander in a direction she hadn't planned on going. The song came to a slow, sultry close, with Daniel dipping Olivia down low to finish, causing everyone to applaud.

Pulling her back up, he didn't release her, instead keeping her in a close hold. Olivia thought he was just going to lead her into the next song, so she continued to gently gyrate her hips in time to the music. Instead, he pulled her in closer and whispered in her ear.

"You look amazing tonight. The dragon costume was sexy, as were the ripped jeans, but this is in another league altogether. Am I correct in thinking *this* is who you really are?"

She turned her head to look at him and said reflectively, "To be honest, most of the time, I don't know who I am." Her face was flushed from too much tequila, and her hair was falling out of the messy updo cascading in damp wisps around her shoulders. She felt like she needed to respond, so she started, "You look..." but found herself unable to come up with anything that adequately described him.

He laughed softly. "Ah, I think we need to play the adjective game again. Now, I think I remember how this goes. I have to give you 5 adjectives and you need to choose one. Okay, here we go: devastating, dreamy, delectable, delicious, or dangerous. Wow, they all start with 'd'. I think I should get extra points for that. Well, come on, Olivia. Don't keep me in suspense. Which one are you choosing?"

She looked directly at him and swallowed hard. "Dangerous. You look dangerous, Mr. Lane."

He stared into her eyes with a searing gaze that almost knocked her off her feet. "I wish you would call me Daniel, particularly in view of our closeness right now." He paused. "Although I have to say, it is unspeakably hot when you call me Mr. Lane."

Olivia turned her face away from him in confusion. The tequila was doing a great job of giving her total brain fog, and her body felt hot and heavy. She was concerned she might collapse to the floor like a rag doll. It was a good thing he was holding her so closely.

He brushed her dishevelled hair behind her ear and continued. "We seem to have some kind of magnetic attraction. Maybe it's time to explore our relationship in a little more depth. Would you come home with me tonight?"

She turned to face him, mesmerized by the deep blue of his eyes. They were eyes you could lose yourself in if you weren't careful, like deep blue pools full of seduction and promise. She was in grave danger of falling down the rabbit hole. He smelled so good; not cologne, something better. She could feel the heat of his body up close, and it was making her feel dizzy. She was trying to think of a smart response, but it was hard when he was so near; the tequila was numbing her thought process. "Why would I go home with you?" she asked, finding her words at last.

"Because every time I see you, all I can think about is getting you beneath me." She felt like her head was spinning as he pulled her closer into his arms and murmured in her ear. "You are the most beautiful and unique woman I have met in a very long time. I find you intoxicating."

Olivia swallowed hard. "That would be the tequila," she croaked, barely able to speak.

"But I haven't had anything to drink," he replied. "Will you come with me?" His lips were practically on her ear now and she could feel both her resolve and her knees weakening. "Come on Olivia. It will be fun. You like fun, don't you? I can tell."

Shaking herself out of the spell he had put her under, she suddenly pushed away from him with both hands, green eyes flashing with anger. She came out of her corner fighting, as if someone had suddenly poured ice cold water on her.

"I don't know what impression you have of me, but I am not some easy fuck you can just come in and pick up. I thought I'd made myself clear on that. I will not become just another notch on your bedpost. I came here with my friends to have fun, and I am going to leave with my friends. Thank you for the dance. I hope you have a good evening."

Olivia spun on her heels a little unsteadily and headed back to the table to reunite with her friends, flopping down heavily into her seat, her face flaming hot. Daniel Lane stared at her departing form for a moment before quietly slipping out the door.

Nobody spoke for a moment, and then Lottie broke the silence.

"Christ Olivia, what just happened? You look like you swallowed a frog."

She looked around at her friends with a shocked expression and said. "He wanted to take me home and fuck me."

The girls were silent for a moment, and then they all exploded in laughter, gripping their stomachs and hitting the table.

Lottie looked horrified. "Olivia! I can't believe you just turned down Daniel Lane. I already told you he is one of the most eligible bachelors in the state."

Olivia looked disgusted. "Lottie, he just wanted a quick fuck. The guy's a complete player. I don't suppose for one moment he's looking for a long-term relationship, particularly not with me."

Lottie reached over and stroked Olivia's hair. "Don't be stupid, Livvy, you're beautiful. It's only you who can't see that."

They all decided the best course of action was to get another round of drinks, and Olivia got in a couple more dances with Paulo. She was the only person Lottie knew whose dancing actually improved with copious amounts of alcohol. Thankfully, they all persuaded Olivia not to dance on the table. The girls left the bar at around one and shared a cab, singing all the way home.

9–Daniel

D aniel walked into his penthouse apartment and poured himself a large glass of whiskey. Looking down at his hands, he realized they were shaking, and he laughed. That was *not* how he had
expected his evening would play out. How the hell had going out to
buy a bottle of wine turned into that fiasco?

When he had left his apartment a little over an hour ago, he'd
had no intention of running into Olivia Jefferson. He was going to
celebrate his first quiet night in weeks with a good bottle of Malbec
and an evening of vegging out in front of the TV. The sight of her ex-
iting the cab and walking towards The Red Room had been enough
to drive all sane thoughts from his head.

Of course, he knew immediately it was her. She was unmistak-
able. He'd watched as she bent in to pay the driver before straighten-
ing up and walking into the wine bar. He could see she was dressed to
have fun, the kind of fun that had been eluding him for so long. She'd
indicated the type of evening she was expecting when he had taken
her for lunch, and her comment about fondling someone at the bar
had urged him into action. If she was going to be doing any fondling,
he wanted to make damn sure he was on the receiving end. He wasn't
about to let some anonymous Joe sweep her out from under his nose.

Slipping into the bar through a side door, he found a small table
set well back in a dark corner, knowing that she was unlikely to spot
him. From his vantage point, he watched the girls embrace before
Olivia launched into her animated display. He could tell by the way
her friends were watching that she was holding the conversation in
the palm of her hand. They were falling around and laughing the way
girls often do when they are on a fun night out, and he watched the
first two rounds of tequila go down without touching the sides.

Even from a distance, he could see she wasn't just pretty, she was
fucking gorgeous, and he noticed he wasn't the only man in the bar

who was staring. Admittedly, she was dressed a little unconventionally, but that only added to the attraction. The sequin bra top hugged her full breasts and the dance pants showed off her curves perfectly. He had already decided that he would just sit in his corner and enjoy watching her. It wouldn't be fair to interrupt her evening when she was having such a good time with her friends.

Of course, his plan went to hell when that guy approached her to dance. She obviously knew him by the way he greeted her, and he wondered if she had arranged to meet him there. She was, after all, newly single, and perhaps this guy was the replacement. Well, that was not going to happen—not on his watch. But, before he could get up and intervene, she was on the dance floor with him.

He'd stood up from his seat to get a better view and was immediately mesmerized by what was going on. She had her face pressed into the guy's neck and they flowed around the dance floor like quicksilver. They were so connected that Daniel wondered if they had been dancing together for years. He watched her hips flutter to the beat as she pulled herself closer to her partner and his gut lurched in envy.

He was well aware of the lure of kizomba. He had taken lessons with Serena several years ago, but recently, there had been no-one he knew who could dance in that way. It was not the kind of dance that featured greatly at the charity functions he attended; it was a bit too racy. He watched as the music ended and her partner chastely kissed her hand before disappearing into the crowd. Perhaps he had gone to buy her another drink. He knew this was his only opportunity. If he was going to act, he had to act fast before that asshole returned and took her away.

Recalling the moment, he realized that this was the point all logical thought had flown out the window. As he reached the edge of the dancefloor, she turned to face him and the look on her face almost floored him. Her mouth was open, but she didn't smile. A look of confusion crossed her face; but there was something else that he hoped to God he wasn't imagining. Her hair was messy, and her cheeks were pink from the exertion of the dance, but what he saw on her face was unadulterated desire. He'd seen this look on women's faces before, but it was never this visceral. Was it directed at him? He wondered if she was even aware of it, or if it was something that was happening subconsciously.

He expected her to recover when he reached her and waited for her unfiltered mouth to kick in, but there was nothing. For the first time since he'd met her, she seemed dumbstruck. It was a good job pushy Ms. Partington was there to guide the conversation, otherwise he might not have even gotten her to the dancefloor.

But then she was in his arms, pressed up against him, and his body immediately reacted. He had held more women in his arms than he cared to remember, but nothing felt like this. Something radiated out of this girl that felt like a punch to the solar plexus. She was glowing with warmth, and she smelled amazing, not one of those expensive cloying perfumes, but something much more subtle.

Added to that, he could feel the shape of her curves pressed up against him, and he thought he would lose his mind. There was nothing bony about her; she was full of womanly softness. During the dance she gave him everything. It was as if she were surrendering herself to him through the heady rhythm of the music. Her hips instinctively pulsated against him, and he'd felt himself instantly harden.

The music came to an end, but there was no way he was going to let her go. He was too intoxicated by her presence. The right words never came to him, and he heard himself using a string of trite pick up lines that were completely wrong for the situation. He couldn't help himself. All the years of practice at picking up women and he had nothing. It was embarrassingly pathetic!

Then she had turned and faced him, and he watched the fire return to her eyes. No doubt about it, she was mad! She had seen him for who he really was, a shallow player, a rich boy with nothing better to do on a Friday night than come out and pick up young women. The worst of it was that she thought he'd wanted to pick her up like a cheap hooker. She was offended, and so she should be. He'd been a complete asshole.

He knew there was no way he could explain that he had become lost in the moment, that her very presence was doing things to him he wasn't familiar with, so he let her go and came home feeling frustrated and confused. He had to get this girl out of his system one way or another. He couldn't go on living like this. This week had been a complete disaster for him from a business perspective, as he found himself unable to focus on anything for more than a few minutes before the thought of her popped into his head. This was a serious obsession he needed to deal with it before it wrecked him.

He needed to rationalize this in the way that he had always done with past relationships. He was pretty sure she would not go for the "no-strings" crap he fed most of his partners. She was younger than most of the women he hooked up with and he didn't want to hurt her, but there was something else clawing away in the back of his mind. Why had she become so important to him in such a short span of time?

A thought came to him that might just work out really well. He needed to take her somewhere where there would be no risk of the prying press taking photos, somewhere where he could be assured she wouldn't be able to blow him off again. As he crawled into bed, the plan solidified in his mind. He would need to make an early start in the morning if he were going to pull it off, but it would all be worth it. As he slid into a deep sleep, his face settled into a satisfied smile. Olivia Jefferson would soon be his.

10

Olivia woke up with a hefty hangover the next day. "Eww, my mouth tastes like a sewer. God, that's it. Tequila and I are definitely taking a break," she muttered to herself as she rolled out of bed. It was around 10 a.m. and she headed unsteadily into the kitchen to make herself some strong coffee and find the Tylenol. As the caffeine rushed through her bloodstream, she thought about the events of the previous evening, and she remembered Daniel Lane's proposition.

It all seemed so bizarre. She was wondering if it had actually happened, or whether it had been the tequila playing tricks on her brain. It wouldn't be the first time she had suffered alcoholic hallucinations while she was out with the girls, although on that occasion they had all indulged in too much Absinthe for purely experimental reasons, to find out if the rumours about it were true.

Her phone rang, and she looked at the call display. It was Lottie. "Good morning, you wicked woman," Lottie greeted her. "What have you got planned for the day? You gonna slay another publishing mogul?"

"So, it did actually happen then? I was beginning to think I had imagined it all."

Lottie laughed. "Oh no, it definitely happened. Your face was priceless; I wish I'd taken a photo. I bet he was really pissed, Olivia. I can't imagine many women turning down Daniel Lane."

Olivia snorted. "Well, I'm not many women. I'm me!"

Lottie giggled. "You can say that again."

"Well, I think I can safely say I won't be hearing from him again." She said a little sadly. "I only hope he won't change his mind about my travel guides."

"I don't think that's going to happen, hon. He was being the creep, not you." Lottie quickly changed the subject. "Well, it's Saturday, sweetie. What do you have planned?"

Olivia thought for a moment. "I thought I would binge watch *White Collar* with Ben & Jerry," Olivia said.

"Yummy; can't beat a bit of Matt Bomer to pass the time," Lottie agreed. "Come to think of it, Daniel Lane looks a bit like Matt Bomer. Do you think you're secretly lusting after him?"

Olivia sighed a little regretfully. "Well, he is incredibly hot. God, I lost the power of speech when I saw him smoldering at me like that. I can't help wondering if I made a mistake last night. But fuck it, Lottie. What nerve! Did he think I was just going to fall into his arms and let him drag me off to his cave?"

Lottie laughed her low, sensual laugh. "Well, he can drag me off to his cave any day. Be careful your principles don't get in the way of you having fun, Olivia. I bet he's fantastic between the sheets. You could probably learn a lot from that man."

Olivia snorted, "I'm not sure that's the kind of education I'm looking for. This conversation is over, Ms. Partington. I'm off to find Ben & Jerry. They are always great company at a time like this." And with that, she hung up.

Olivia was still rummaging through the freezer when her phone rang again. Thinking it was Lottie calling back, she reached up to grab her phone from the counter and answered it without looking at the display. "Good morning, Olivia. How are you feeling today? Not too much of a hangover I hope." The honeyed voice flowed through her body, causing her temperature to rise by several degrees.

Oh, holy crap. It was him. She took a deep breath and sat back down on the floor shakily, hugging her knees. She considered hanging up, but she knew that this man held her dreams in his hands, so she just said bluntly, "I'm fine, thank you. How are you?" She heard him take a breath and sigh.

"I'm just a bit disappointed to be waking up without my favourite little dragon for company this morning, but apart from that, I'm fine." There was a brief pause. "You don't mind me calling you, do you?"

Olivia bit her lip and looked at the contents of the half-eaten tub of Chunky Monkey she'd retrieved from the back of the freezer. "Actually, I do mind. I mind very much. I want you to stop playing games with me and leave me alone."

"Whatever do you mean?"

She sighed impatiently. "The other day in the park, do you know I actually felt sorry for you? Poor misunderstood playboy, trying to mend his errant ways. Well, I think last night proved that a leopard can't change its spots."

He obviously chose to ignore this last comment. "What do you have planned for today?" he continued.

"I'm about to get stuck into a tub of ice cream and then I'm going to watch TV," she said. "Why?"

"Well, I behaved badly last night, and I feel I owe you an apology. I wondered if you would come out and have a picnic with me. I could pick you up in about an hour if you like?"

Olivia hesitated. "You don't owe me anything, and I'm not going anywhere with you today or any other day. I think it's best if we just keep this professional."

She heard him take a breath. "Olivia, please don't be like this. At least let me make it up to you."

Listening to his soft, husky voice, she could feel herself caving. She tried a compromise. "Look, why don't we meet for coffee again. That was nice."

His voice took on a pleading quality. "But I have something special planned. Please, Olivia. It'll be fun, I promise."

She stared down at the sad tub of ice cream and the unappetizing crunchy frost crystals that had accumulated from being in the freezer too long. Suddenly neither Ben nor Jerry seemed to hold any interest for her. "Okay, I'll go with you under one condition."

"Name your terms."

Olivia took a breath and tried to sound assertive. "I want to go somewhere where there will be other people around." She heard him cough like he was suppressing a laugh.

"I would never do anything you weren't comfortable with. It's hardly in my best interest, is it?"

She wasn't sure what he meant by that, so she simply said, "Single and Safe, Mr. Lane. Single and Safe."

There was a pause, and he quickly said, "I'll see you in an hour," then he hung up without giving her the opportunity to voice any more concerns.

As soon as he'd hung up, she was in a blind panic. Her mind filled with questions: *Should I have said no? What shall I wear? Should I take condoms? - God where did that last question come from?* She thought.

She jumped into the shower and quickly washed away the remains of her tequila-filled night. She shampooed her hair and dried it in record-breaking time. I've only got an hour, she panicked. She flew to her closet and looked in. Her black dancewear was still laying sadly on the floor where it had been abandoned the night before, so she picked it up and put it on a hanger.

She considered what the occasion called for. Not wanting to wear anything too pretty or girly, she searched for something that would show him how kick ass she really was. She grabbed a pair of black, tight-fitting jeans which showed off her curves to perfection, before looking for the perfect top to go with her outfit.

Laughing, she pulled a white t-shirt from her drawer that Lottie had given her as a joke birthday gift. It was emblazoned with the slogan, *If my mouth doesn't say it, my face definitely will.* To top it all off, she pulled out her favourite item of clothing, a beautiful, buttery-soft black leather moto jacket. It had been a Christmas gift from her brother, Luca, although in reality, she knew that his fiancée, Molly, had bought it. There was no way Luca could have been that inspired. The jacket looked hideously expensive, and something she could never afford normally.

Okay, now I need some awesome footwear, she thought to herself. Sneakers would make the most sense, as they might go somewhere where she needed to walk, but that would be too sedate. She shoved a pair of Converse in her bag and instead chose a pair of lilac suede ankle boots that she had bought for half price because of their colour.

Rushing off to apply makeup, she overdid the smoky eyes and applied a hefty slick of Ruby Woo lipstick before bending at the waist and back combing her hair a little to give it a wild look. She was examining the results of her efforts with a satisfied smirk when her phone rang. "I'm in the parking lot behind your building. Are you ready?"

She confirmed that she was and headed to the elevator, wondering why he hadn't parked out front. As she exited the back door, she saw him immediately leaning against a large black SUV, arms folded with a huge grin on his face. Shielding her eyes with her sunglasses, she walked towards him, trying to keep her gaze impassive and not register the apprehension that she felt inside. She watched as he took in her appearance, seemingly amused, and as she approached, he gave her a slow clap.

"Holy crap, Olivia. You really have pulled out all the stops today, haven't you? Is this for my benefit? Very sexy! Definitely love the boots."

She looked at him seriously. "I like to think the way I dress conveys a message. I'm not sure sexy was what I was going for. I've obviously failed."

"And what message are you trying to express today?" He asked with a smirk.

"This is my *fuck you* outfit, but it's obviously not hitting the right buttons. Perhaps I should go back and change." Turning away from him, she eyed his car suspiciously. "Is this another one of your cars?"

"It is," he said, opening the passenger door for her. "I thought you might find it more comfortable than the M.G. Not so low." He winked at her playfully.

"Ah, but I'm wearing kick ass jeans today, so it wouldn't have mattered if you'd turned up in a tractor."

He climbed in and looked across at her. "Okay, let's get one thing out of the way. Are you still mad at me?"

"I am, but I feel I shouldn't be. You were, after all, just doing what all men do, thinking with your dick. Although I think we've already established it is a magic dick, so I guess I should give you some leeway there."

"Olivia," he sighed, "I walked into The Red Room last night and I saw you looking utterly beautiful, dancing very provocatively. I don't know anyone who can dance like that. I do have blood running through my veins, you know. You were hot in ways I didn't even know existed. Now, can we please call a truce?"

Realizing she couldn't stay mad at him when he was being so charming, she nodded.

He looked relieved. "Great, I'm glad that's settled. Now, can we please go and eat? I'm sure you haven't had any breakfast and you must be starving. The last time you didn't eat breakfast after a heavy night, you were trying to get into my pants."

Olivia gasped and stared at him with her mouth open. "I most certainly was not!"

He was grinning widely. "What was it you called me? Smoldering executive hottie if I recall correctly. If that's not a come on, I don't know what is."

"Just because I was admiring your physical attributes and saying how nice you look in a suit does not mean I was trying to get into your pants! You see what happens when a woman finds a man attractive? She gets accused of being a jezebel!"

He shot her a wicked smile. "So, you do find me attractive then."

"If you weren't driving, I would hit you!"

"Are you feeling a little more relaxed now?" he asked.

"What do you mean?"

"You seemed a little uptight when you got in the car. You're looking a lot better now."

She looked at him in astonishment. Did he just spar with her to try to make her feel more relaxed? Whatever he had done, it had worked. She laughed and shook her head. Clever bastard.

As they headed out of the city, Olivia asked him where they were going, but he just gave her a secretive smile and put a finger to his lips. He really was the most beautiful man. She took time during the journey to study him. He had movie-star looks for sure. Her mother would have said that a man who looked like that must be up to no good. She wondered if that was the case, and if so, just what the 'no good' might entail.

It was warm in the car, and she quickly shed her jacket and took off her boots, revealing her multicoloured toenails, which seemed to amuse him. As the journey progressed, things got a little easier between them and they chatted.

He told her that his father had run the publishing business for thirty years, but that he had a heart attack while Daniel was at Harvard studying law. He finished his law degree, but he never got to practice law as his father asked him to return home and take over the business. "I had to learn everything from the bottom up," he explained. "It was quite a learning curve for someone who thought he was going to be a barrister." Once his dad had finally bowed out, he wanted to rejuvenate the company and bring in some more progressive ideas. He brought Evangeline on board, and with her help, they attracted work that appealed to a new, younger audience. "Hence, our interest in you," he added.

"Can I ask you something?" She interrupted. "Do you have a costume fetish or any other unusual preferences? I think I should be aware of things like that."

He put his head back and laughed, and for a moment Olivia felt like the car had suddenly been filled with instant sunshine. It was the first time she'd seen him really laugh. It took him several minutes before he could compose himself enough to answer her question. "God, you make me laugh." He said, wiping at the sides of his eyes with the back of his hand. "I don't have a costume fetish. You're quite safe. I'm not going to ask you to dress up unless you want to, of course. I am, however, concerned that I might have an Olivia fetish." He smiled teasingly at her, and she turned her head to look out the window, trying to ignore the fact that her stomach was doing back flips. Being confined in the car with him felt very different from meeting him in the coffee shop or in the park. She was very aware that she was in uncharted territory and her typical jocular bravado was failing her.

Pretty soon then pulled up at a small seaside town that Olivia remembered visiting regularly when she was a child. There were narrow streets of pretty whitewashed cottages with wood shingled roofs. Daniel pulled into the driveway of a bigger cottage that overlooked the ocean. There were metal gates that opened when he hit a button above his head. The gates closed slowly behind them as they pulled through. "We're here," he smiled across at her.

Olivia climbed out, breathing in the sea air and looked at the beautiful house. It was traditionally styled with painted shakes on the outside and a big welcoming porch. "Where are we?" she said, "I thought we were going to have a picnic."

He started towards the house, carrying a picnic basket and reaching into his pocket for keys. "This is my place, and we *are* going to have a picnic. Come on in."

11

Olivia hopped out of the car barefoot, carrying her boots, and walked cautiously into the house, catching her breath. It was the kind of place she always admired in the expensive home magazines when she was at the dentist's office. The interior was painted white, and it was simply but tastefully furnished. "Don't you live in the city?" she asked.

"I do during the week, but I try to get down here as much as possible. I love it here."

Olivia looked around. It was just the sort of place she would love to live in. There was a large, white farmhouse kitchen with an expansive blue island, which opened out into the dining area and living room. As she walked through the house, she gasped when she saw the deck overlooking the ocean. Without thinking, she unlocked the French doors and stepped outside, allowing the sea breeze to blow through her hair. Leaning on the railing, she watched a family playing on the beach, building sandcastles, and her mind was taken back to when she used to visit with her family. Of course, they never stayed anywhere as stunning as this.

Daniel was watching her thoughtfully from the kitchen. "Do you approve?"

She turned back to him excitedly. "It's beautiful–I love it. I want to go down to the beach. Can we go now?"

He grinned, obviously pleased. "Let's eat first, then we can go for a walk."

He took the picnic basket into the kitchen and started to take things out. Olivia watched him intently as he unloaded a couple of bottles of wine into the fridge, followed by strawberries, some large shrimp with tails on, and crusty bread. This didn't look like an impromptu picnic to her. *You certainly wouldn't find stuff like this in my fridge*, Olivia thought, remembering the solitary jar of dill pickles and some rather dubious cheese. "Mr. Lane, I thought we were going to have a picnic?"

He looked at her, amused that she insisted on using his formal title. "We are, Ms. Jefferson. We are going to have a civilized picnic on the deck. Is that okay?" She narrowed her eyes and looked at him suspiciously. "You will be perfectly safe. I remember what you said about being around people. Look, there are several families down on the beach. If you scream, they will hear you."

"And why exactly would I need to scream?"

He stared at her with a dark look in his eyes. "Oh, I don't think you'll be screaming from the deck. There might be other rooms in the house where I could make you scream though."

Olivia tried not to smile. This new, playful Daniel was different from the man she had been encountering all week. She wondered what had brought about the change in him. He seemed lighter and younger, definitely more carefree. In addition, he was looking seriously hot, and she was aware of the arousal building inside her that she hadn't felt for a long time. Its warmth extended into the pit of her stomach and between her thighs. *Probably just hungry,* she told herself.

Daniel busied himself getting out plates and laying things out. "Can I help?" she asked.

"Well, it's all just about ready, but you can help me carry some things out to the deck if you'd like." The food was beautifully arranged on white plates with crisp white napkins. He got some ice from the chiller and put it in a silver bucket, placing the wine inside. Then he grabbed two elegant wine glasses from one of the upper cabinets. Olivia thought about her own kitchen and reflected on the fact that when her friends came round, they normally drank wine from coffee mugs. "Okay. I want you to go and sit down. There are just a couple of quick things I need to do."

Olivia sat at the aged teak table and breathed in the sea air. It was absolutely heavenly. As she sat there, beautiful and familiar music filled the air. She closed her eyes listening to the dulcet tones of *O Mio Babbino Caro* and memories of her childhood came flooding back to her. She sang along softly to the piece, mesmerized by the intense feelings that consumed her body. She sensed Daniel come through and place something on the table. He stood staring at her for a while as she sang.

"That's beautiful. I didn't know you were a singer."

She shook her head. "I don't sing very well. It was never my strength, and besides, I'm more of a contralto than a soprano, but I love Puccini. My mom used to sing this song to me when I was a little girl. Do you know what the song means?" He shook his head, silently. "The woman is telling her father about a man she is desperately in love with. She wants to go and buy a ring, but if he rejects her, she's going to jump off the bridge and throw herself in the river."

Daniel frowned. "That's a bit overdramatic. I don't think women do that kind of thing these days."

She laughed. "It's opera! It's supposed to be overdramatic! My mother was an opera singer before she had my brother and me. She always filled our house with this kind of music."

He looked suitably impressed "I didn't know that."

Olivia nodded. "She's Italian and deeply passionate, and quite the hothead. We used to go to the opera on a regular basis when we were growing up."

Olivia's mind was taken back to the beautiful opera house with the plush velvet seats and ornate balconies. Opera nights always meant a special new dress for her and her mother, and she loved how she could lose herself in the emotion of the music. She found the whole experience captivating, and one of the few passions she could share with her rather formidable mother.

He regarded her thoughtfully. "I think you might be a bit of a hothead yourself, am I right?" She narrowed her eyes at him, but he continued. "I thought you were going to give me a black eye last night." He laughed.

Olivia tightly pursed her lips, remembering the events of the previous evening. "What did you expect? You were being an animal. I'm not used to such predatory behaviour. I had to defend my honour."

"Well, that is a noble cause indeed," he teased. "I can't blame you for that." He seemed keen to change the subject and move on. "You obviously speak Italian."

Olivia nodded. "Both my brother and I are bilingual. My mother insisted on it. We spent a lot of time in Italy over the years, visiting family. It's a beautiful country. They live so differently there. Life is just less complicated, I guess. There's no subterfuge. When something upsets you, you yell and gesticulate. Everyone knows where they stand. I can't abide the mind games that people play here. Most of the time I don't understand them."

He smiled. "So, you like straight talking then?" He piled food onto a plate for her and poured two glasses of crisp white wine. "Tell me about your family."

She took a gulp of her wine. "My mom is the typical Italian matriarch. We didn't get on too well when I was growing up. I never felt I was the daughter she really wanted. Too short, too blonde, too curvy, and a smart mouth to boot. I think I embarrassed her—a lot. You've probably noticed I have a knack for saying what I think, and it's not always wholly appropriate." He laughed, shaking his head, as if he were recalling some of the things she had said to him. "My brother, Luca, is four years older than me and he made my life hell. I guess as all big brothers do. And then there's my dad; he just tries to go with the flow and put out all the fires we create."

Daniel laughed. "Sounds like a lively household."

She looked at him grimly. "It was hell for a while. I used to take refuge in the local library. At one stage I thought about taking my sleeping bag and living there." She stared off at the ocean, deep in thought, before she continued. "There's an awesome kids' book I read to the kindergartners called *Library Mouse* about a mouse who lives in the library, and every night after everyone has gone home, he comes out and reads amazing books. My favourite line is *'his imagination brimmed over with wonder and fantasy.'* Well, that's me. I'm library mouse. Sometimes my imagination gets the better of me."

Looking across at him, she noticed he seemed miles away. Maybe she was boring him. She had a tendency to monopolize the conversation a bit. He blinked a few times as if he were processing what she had just said, and she thought he looked a little emotional, but she must have been mistaken. Eventually he looked up at her. "That's a lovely story. I can see I'm going to have to come back to visit you in the library and borrow that one."

She laughed. "Well, you could just wait until I read it to the kids again and you will have the added bonus of seeing me dressed as a mouse."

"Oh, I think that is definitely worth waiting for," he laughed. "Now come on, let's eat. You look half starved."

He was right of course, Olivia was starving. The shrimp were fresh and delicious, and the crusty bread tasted divine. The awkwardness between them had gone, and they chatted easily, sharing their love of opera, and Olivia told him about performances she had seen on her travels to Europe. He also wanted to hear all about her solo travel trips, so, through mouthfuls of food, she regaled him with stories of the temporary jobs she'd had during her extended visits.

In Paris, she had connived her way into a short term serving job at a café close to Montparnasse. He asked if her French was as good as her Italian and she giggled, shaking her head. "It's good enough to get by. I definitely perfected the Gallic shrug, which works for a whole multitude of situations." She mimed it out for him as a response to a slew of different questions and was happy to see him laughing along with her. Thinking she was being over the top as usual, she tried to dial it back a little. She knew all too well that most people could only take this side of her in small doses.

"Okay, tell me about your favourite memory from that trip."

She had to think long and hard about that. There was so much from her travels that stood out to her. Working there and immersing herself in the country's culture meant that she experienced things that other travellers might not see. Ultimately, something came to the front of her mind. "It's a little touristy, but here goes. After Paris, I travelled down to Provence on the train for a couple of weeks. I remember standing in a lavender field in Provence in July. It felt like it stretched on forever, and it was an absolute assault on your senses. The colour of the lavender, the fragrance as it rose up from the warm earth, and the humming of the bees all around. The heat is so arid at that time of the year, it seems to intensify the scent. It was one of those experiences that sears itself into your brain forever. I have some photos on my phone, but it really doesn't do it justice. You have to be there and feel it for yourself."

She trotted off to find her bag and retrieved her phone, quickly zipping through the contents of her gallery until she got to the photos she was looking for. Showing them to him, she registered her disappointment. "These tiny images don't suffice. You have to go. You need to get away from that stuffy office for a few weeks in the summer and go stand in the lavender fields."

"If only it were that easy."

She looked puzzled. "It is that easy; just do it. Life's too short, you don't get another shot at it, you know. If I could make it happen as a struggling student, I'm pretty sure you could if you really wanted to."

He didn't look convinced. "What about holiday romances? You must have had a few of those."

She shot him a playful look. "Hmm. Now we're moving into completely unfamiliar territory. How did we get from lavender fields to the horizontal mambo? And you say I destroy conversations!"

He looked apologetic. "You don't have to tell me if you don't want to."

She shook her head. "Nothing to tell really. I have a strict no sex rule when I'm travelling solo. It's the safest way. I'm not very good at casual sex, and I didn't want to return from my travels with a broken heart or worse, so abstinence seemed like the best course of action."

They were both drinking quite a lot of wine and she was too caught up enjoying the afternoon to even notice. They had already finished one bottle and were well on their way with a second. "Tell me about your family, Daniel. What are they like?"

He looked thoughtful for a moment. "My mom and dad are great. Dad was thrilled I agreed to take over the business. He knew how much I wanted to practice law, but at the end of the day, I really just wanted to make them happy. They'd been through enough already." Olivia looked across at him. He was shifting in his seat restlessly, folding and unfolding his napkin. Eventually he looked up.

"I had a brother who was two years younger than me, but he died in a motorcycle accident when he was 19. That was ten years ago now."

Olivia automatically clasped his hand. "Oh my God, Daniel. I'm so sorry."

He squeezed her fingers. "It's been really tough. I sometimes wonder if that's what brought on my dad's heart attack. Family gatherings are always difficult. It's as if everyone is waiting for Simon to walk back through the door and take a place at the table." Olivia felt tears welling up in her eyes, but she didn't want him to see, so she turned her head away.

Daniel shook himself. "Okay, that's enough of this depressing conversation. I'm here with a gorgeous girl and I'm making her cry. Have another glass of wine and let's talk about something else. Tell me about college."

Olivia could see he was trying to pull himself out of a dark place, so she started chatting unreservedly, telling him funny stories about evenings out with Lottie and Georgie. "When I arrived at college, I was totally unprepared," she laughed. "My mother hadn't let me date, and I would never take a boy home while Luca was in the house, so I had no clue about men." She watched the smile return to his beautiful face. "I was a typical bookworm with no social life, and then I met Lottie and Georgie."

Daniel nodded. "The irrepressible Ms. Partington. She's scary."

Olivia hooted with laughter. "She's not scary. She's just protective. She and Georgie took me under their wings and taught me a great deal about what I had been missing."

Daniel cocked his head to one side. "That sounds interesting. Tell me more."

She pulled a face. "Not that kind of interesting. I discovered a taste for alcohol, and realized I had a wild side. Most of the time we were just having fun. I have danced on a few tables. In fact, I'm famous for it."

He laughed. "Well, I can clear this one if you're feeling in the mood." She smiled, running her finger around the edge of her wineglass, making it ring.

There was a break in the conversation, and she looked up from under her bangs and caught him staring at her. "Have I got food between my teeth?" she asked, giggling.

"No, I'm just enjoying the view. It's breathtaking."

Olivia was stunned at his candour and didn't know what to say, so she jumped up out of her seat awkwardly. "Let me help you clear this away."

He grabbed her wrist, pulling her back down. "There's no rush. We don't have to go anywhere. Just relax and enjoy being here. Okay? This place is all about relaxation. That's why I bought it. I needed a place where I could unwind. The business can be pretty stressful at times. I'm very aware it's Dad's legacy and I don't want to screw it up. This is my bolthole. It's the only place I feel I can really be myself. Whatever that means," he muttered.

She looked across at him, not wanting to ask the question on her lips. "Do you bring people here often?" She tried to make it sound light, but there was a weight to it she couldn't avoid.

"I've never brought anyone here. Only you." He stared at her for a moment longer, and then he stirred. "Okay, would you like to go for a walk on the beach? Let's clear this away first and then we'll head down."

They took all the dishes into the kitchen and stowed away the uneaten food. Daniel washed the dishes in the sink and Olivia stood beside him and dried. She enjoyed the familiarity of doing something domestic with him. Somehow, it made him feel less intimidating. Pretty soon they had everything looking shipshape again.

He looked at what she was wearing. "Hmm. I don't want you to get cold. It's usually windy on the beach, and you probably don't want to take your leather jacket. I'll grab one of my sweaters for you." She heard his heavy footsteps on the stairs, and then he was back at her side with a navy cashmere sweater.

"Thank you," she whispered, feeling the softness of the sweater against her skin.

They took the steps off the deck and followed the winding path down to the beach. The wind was brisk, and Olivia pulled Daniel's sweater on over her head, noticing that it smelled like him in a way that was slightly intoxicating. It looked great with her jeans, and she wondered if she could sneakily steal it. He probably had hundreds, she reasoned with herself.

She'd rolled up the bottom of her jeans and changed into her sneakers, but when she reached the beach, she sat on a rock and took them off. Walking barefoot on the sand, she curled up her toes in delight. It felt magical, just as it had when she was a child, and she danced along in front of him, doing ballet twirls with her arms out wide. Eventually Daniel held out his hand to her, and she took it without hesitation, feeling its warmth and strength. The wine she had consumed over lunch had loosened her tongue and she could feel herself talking too much.

"I used to come here when I was a child," she told him.

"Really?" He looked amazed. "We came here when we were kids as well. That's one of the reasons I bought this place. How often did you come?"

"Oh, usually every summer. We would cram into the car and stay here for a week. I haven't been for the longest time, but I have such happy memories of being here. It's one of the few places we never seemed to argue. I guess the sea air was good for my mom's foul temper."

They walked for about an hour and then headed back to the cottage. The warmth had gone out of the day and the sun was starting its journey down toward the horizon. When they walked into the cottage, she could taste the salty air on her skin and her hair felt tangled from the wind. He didn't let go of her hand as he gently led her into the house. "I guess we'll need to head back soon," she said a little sadly.

He spun around to face her. "Oh, we're not going back. We'll have to stay here tonight. I've had far too much wine to drive, and besides, I always stay for the weekend."

Olivia looked stunned. "But I haven't brought anything with me. No change of clothes. Nothing."

He smiled over at her. "Think of it like camping. I'm sure we'll figure something out."

You sneaky bastard, she thought. She felt anger rising in her and turned to face him, her hands on her hips, green eyes flashing with fury. "You planned this, didn't you? You had no intention of going back, but you failed to inform me." He smiled at her stance. It clearly amused him.

"It was a slight oversight, I agree, but if I'd told you, would you have agreed to come?"

"Absolutely not!" she hissed. She was aware that her breathing had quickened, and she took some deep breaths to calm herself. "I feel like Red Riding Hood after she's wandered too far into the forest," she muttered.

He raised his eyebrows archly. "That's a little melodramatic, Olivia. What does that make me? The wolf?"

She looked over at him gravely. "Well, I think you're playing that role now, don't you?"

Daniel sighed and ran his fingers through his hair. "Have you had a good time today?" he asked.

She looked thoughtful. "I've had an amazing time. It's been wonderful."

He looked pleased. "Then let's not argue over a tiny detail." He paused and then said, "Olivia, there are plenty of bedrooms upstairs; I'm not expecting you to share a bed with me. I'm not in the habit of forcing women to sleep with me."

Olivia could see how that was true. He was absolutely gorgeous. *I'm sure they must be lining up for you*, she thought to herself. She felt foolish for reacting the way she had. He probably thought she was an immature idiot.

After a while, he spoke. "I'm sorry if you think I deceived you. I just wanted to spend some time with you. Is that such a bad thing?" She shook her head and smiled warily at him. "Now, come on into the living room. I want to see if I can beat you at Snakes and Ladders." Daniel opened a large wooden trunk which contained a selection of old board games. "We used to have them at home," he explained. "My mom wanted them gone, so I brought them down here."

They had a couple of rather raucous rounds of Snakes and Ladders. There were obviously both competitive and there was a fair amount of cheating going on.

"I don't think you're playing fair, Ms. Jefferson," he growled.

"Good grief," she replied. "I played with my brother for years. There is no fair play with Luca. He takes no prisoners."

He grinned. "I guess we better not play Monopoly then. You'll probably take all my money."

12

The light disappeared from the day, and Daniel lit some side lamps. A gentle glow filled the cottage, and he pulled the drapes across. He fetched an armful of logs from outside and lit a fire in the grate. Olivia sighed with contentment. It didn't get any better than this–a log fire, a cozy cottage, and a red-hot man who seemed keen for her company.

He smiled at her. "Happy?" he asked.

"Yes, it's all so lovely," she sighed. "It must be great to have a place like this that you can get away to."

"It's good to be here with you." he whispered. "I'm usually here on my own." Olivia was sitting across from him in a white squashy armchair. He held his hand out to her. "Would you come and sit with me?" Olivia hesitated for a moment. "I promise I don't bite," he said playfully, "even if you do think I'm a wolf."

He looked so beautiful, sitting on the couch with his hand extended to her. She thought about what Lottie had said to her that morning: *be careful your principles don't get in the way of you having fun.* She was deeply attracted to this man, and she felt the warmth of arousal spreading through her body.

Rising out of the chair, she headed over to the couch to sit beside him. He laid down and pulled her up close to him, so she was sitting between his legs. She leant her back against his chest, and they snuggled together silently for a while, staring into the fire. Olivia could feel her heart racing, and she consciously tried to slow her breathing.

He stroked his hands on her arms as if he were trying to warm her up. "You're nervous, sweetheart; don't be." She didn't respond, but instead, she took his hand and traced around his knuckles with her finger, distracting herself with the pattern she was making. After a while, he spoke again. "Olivia, I really like you and I want a chance to be with you. I have a sneaky suspicion you like me too. What's holding you back?"

She turned her head to look at him. "It's obvious, isn't it? Look at your life and then look at me. Fancy events. Lots of press attention. I'm not sure where I fit into this. I can't give you any of that, I'm not even sure I would want to."

He was silent for a while and then he said, "In view of all that, can I ask why you came with me today. Why did you decide to give me a chance?"

She smiled to herself. "Well, you didn't seem to want to take no for an answer. But also it impressed me that you stared crazy in the face and didn't back down. Most men would have run for the hills long before now."

"What do you mean?"

"In the short period we've known each other, I've lost my shoes during an expensive lunch, dissected my sandwich, dressed as a dragon, made inappropriate comments about your magic dick, and danced my ass off wearing only a sequin bra. I'm very well aware I'm not normal or easy, Daniel. You've definitely got guts just inviting me here. Either that or a death wish."

He laughed into her hair and kissed the top of her head. "I think that's the point. I've been living this life on autopilot for so long that I hadn't realized how discontented I was. When I met you, it felt like everything got shaken up, like one of those snow globes. I don't think I want to be that person anymore, I want something else. Something more."

Finally, she spoke. "I'm really attracted to you, but I'm not very good at this kind of thing. I guess I'm not very... experienced. I feel you have this ideal image of me, but I think in reality I would just be a disappointment to you. There's only so much quirkiness people can take before it wears thin."

"That's funny because I feel the same way, that I'll be a big let-down to you. You have so much joie de vivre. I don't want to crush that out of you. I don't know what I can offer you. I've never been able to offer very much of myself to anyone. I'd like to change that." He rubbed his hands down her arms again. "God, this is all getting too intense. I'll take care of you, I promise. Just try to relax and enjoy being here. No pressure, okay?" She nodded and allowed herself to settle back into his chest. She had to admit that laying there in his arms felt amazing, if a little surreal.

After a while, he said, "I knew you wouldn't be prepared to stay, so I've brought something for you to change into. I hope you don't mind." She lay still, not saying a word. "I think you will be more comfortable if you change. If you head upstairs, I've put some clothes in one of the spare bedrooms for you. You can take a shower as well if you like. You'll find plenty of toiletries in the bathroom." Olivia didn't move for a moment. "It's okay, Olivia. I won't come up. You'll be quite safe."

In a dream state, she left the couch and headed up the narrow stairs of the cottage. There were four bedrooms on the second level, all painted white with lovely cast iron bed frames in each room and quilts over the beds. Each room was very similar, except the largest, which Olivia guessed was Daniel's room. In the next room along the hallway, she turned on the light, and laid out on the bed was a beautiful soft-grey cotton camisole with ivory lace edging and a pair of lounge pants. Beside it was a matching robe. Was this what he wanted her to wear? She checked the other rooms, but they were empty.

She closed the door of the bedroom and shimmied out of her tight jeans before taking off her panties. She pulled her t-shirt over the head and removed her bra and then headed into the adjoining bathroom. The bathroom was pristine and looked like it had never been used. As promised, she found beautiful bottles of shampoo and shower gel and fluffy white towels plus a new toothbrush and toothpaste. He'd clearly thought of everything. She felt like she was staying in a fancy hotel. She washed the salt from her hair and her body. Searching through the drawers, she was happy to find a hairdryer. If her hair was towel dried, it ended up looking like a haystack.

When she was dry, she slipped the cool camisole over her head. It felt so soft against her warm skin. Sitting on the edge of the bed, she took some calming breaths. *So, this is what seduction feels like,* she thought to herself. Up to that point, her sexual partners had been few and far between, and there had definitely been no seduction involved, more like awkward drunken grappling.

She and Mark had fallen into their sexual relationship by accident after consuming a bottle of red wine and several glasses of rum and coke one night. It had kind of evolved from there. *This man is an expert at this kind of thing,* Olivia pondered. Everything he had done up to this point was with one goal in mind: smooth and well orchestrated. She wasn't sure whether she should be flattered or annoyed.

Heading back downstairs, she noticed Daniel was waiting for her at the bottom, and he caught his breath when he saw her. "Be careful, sweetheart. I don't want you to fall on the stairs. They are a bit steep." His tone caused her stomach to flip. She felt like she had left the earth and was in another dimension. Only last week, she was at home in the apartment with Mark, who was flicking through the sports channels, oblivious to her, and now, here she was with a publishing god, being treated like a goddess.

As she reached the bottom of the stairs, he caught her in his arms, and it knocked the wind right out of her sails. She felt herself melt into him, burying her face in his chest and breathing him in.

"At last," he murmured, stroking her hair. "Here is the real Olivia. I knew she was in there somewhere." He led her gently over to the couch and swung her legs up, covering her with a cotton blanket. He looked at her gently. "Now, I want you to stay here and not move a muscle, okay? I'm going to take a quick shower and then I'll be right back. Enjoy the music and the fire."

She heard him run up the stairs, taking two at a time, and she smiled. Soft and lazy jazz music was coming from the speaker, making her legs feel like jelly. She watched the flames flicker in the fire and listened for the sound of his feet on the stairs. She felt wonderfully relaxed. She knew that she was being drawn into something, but she didn't know how to stop, and she wasn't sure she wanted to, even if she could.

Moments later he was in the doorway, and she could feel him walking towards her, although she didn't turn her head. He came around to the front of the couch and looked down at her peaceful body. "Hey there, beautiful. You're not falling asleep on me are you?"

She smiled up at him drowsily, shaking her head, and he pulled her gently to her feet and into his arms. "I want to dance with you again; you dance so beautifully."

He was wearing thin cotton lounge pants and she could feel his hard arousal pushed up against her. Sade was coming through the speaker, her husky voice thick with emotion. He stopped dancing and held her face between his hands, staring into her eyes. Although she was expecting it, his kiss still knocked her off her feet. He held on tightly to her, gently exploring her lips with his tongue. All the sloppy, fumbling kisses she had shared in the past had never felt like this. When she returned his urgency with her own tongue, he groaned softly; it was the most erotic sound she had ever heard. He stopped kissing her, and she released a little cry of loss.

He gazed into her eyes and the deep blue met the sparkling green, like the layers in the ocean they could hear outside the window. "Olivia, would you like me to make love to you?" he asked quietly.

Smiling up at him, she nodded before reaching up and reclaiming his mouth with renewed determination. Now that she had decided to be with him, she felt impatient. She had been holding herself back, believing that this was a bad idea, but now that she was in his arms, it felt like the best idea she'd ever had.

He took her hand and led her to the stairs, where they ascended silently. Drawing her into the master bedroom, he pulled her into his arms again and resumed the exploration of her mouth. His mouth journeyed down her neck, nibbling and kissing and making her moan with pleasure. Putting her hands under his t-shirt, she gently stroked his back, feeling the control leaving her body. The wetness between her legs was warm and sticky and there was a dull ache deep inside her that would only be helped by one thing. She pulled at his shirt with shaking hands, trying to lift it over his head, her body shuddering with desire.

Daniel helped her with his shirt and then enveloped her in his arms again. "It's okay, Olivia. There's no need to rush. Let's take it slowly, honey. Slowly, slowly," he crooned softly. "Is it okay if I take off your clothes?" She nodded, guiding his hands and helping him. Seeing her naked body made him gasp with pleasure.

"Oh my God, Olivia. You are so beautiful, so soft and beautiful." Leading her over to the bed, he sat her down on the edge and she pulled at his lounge pants. "No, not yet," he smiled. "Remember, slowly. I want to give you pleasure first. I want to look into your eyes when you come for me. And you will come for me," he said hoarsely. "Over and over again."

He lay down on the bed next to her, placing soft kisses on her breasts before taking a nipple in his mouth and sucking tenderly. The gentle rhythmic sucking was driving her crazy, and she grabbed at him with her hands, pulling him closer, guiding his mouth downwards. He ran one finger down the length of her abdomen to just above her pubic bone and rested it there, teasing her with its presence.

She knew what she wanted, and she moved her body up the bed for her clit to make contact with his hand. He was determined to make her wait, and he moved his hand away, back up to her breasts. He smiled down at her, "Waiting is half the pleasure. It will make it so much better when we finally get there."

She felt like she was going crazy. She really needed him to rub her where that ache was, and she moaned in protest. "Is there something you want to say to me, Olivia?" he teased.

"Please make me come," she said in a voice that didn't sound like her own. "I need you now!"

He looked at the urgency on her face and brushed the hair from her eyes. "So passionate, darling. I can help you with that." The way he was talking to her was so damn hot. The caring tone in his voice was mixed with an edge of control, as if he knew he had the situation completely in his hands. He knew he could hold her on the edge as long as he wanted to, and he seemed to enjoy doing just that. His hand slowly moved down towards her clit again and he felt along the length of her sex, feeling the beautiful, sticky wetness.

"Wow, Olivia. You are one hot little girl, aren't you? Did you get wet for me like this the first time we met? I know I was hard for you. I was sitting in that restaurant with my cock so hard I couldn't move away from the table. When you pulled that pencil out of your hair and shook your head, I thought I was going to come then and there."

He gently slid one finger inside her, working it around, feeling the sensitive spots. She rotated her hips, moaning in pleasure and longing. He withdrew his finger and worked on her clit, gently rubbing in circles. He knew she was already so close it wouldn't take much, so he went slowly. He saw her climax rising, so he pulled his hand away, gently sucking on her lips and pushing his tongue into her mouth.

"No, don't stop. I'm almost there." She felt herself getting frantic.

"Call me Mr. Lane," he whispered in her ear in a soft seductive tone. "It sounds so damn hot when you say that."

She looked into his eyes, pleading with him. "Please don't stop, Mr. Lane."

He moaned a little. "Oh, my hot little baby. I think I am going to have to let you come." He moved his finger back onto her clit and moved in circles, a little faster this time. She screamed in pleasure, the orgasm rushing through her body and causing her to writhe on the bed. It seemed to last forever, wave after wave, until tears streamed out of the corners of her eyes. He sat her up and pulled her tightly to his chest, caressing her back.

She was desperate to feel him inside her, so she pulled again at the edge of his pants. This time he allowed her to, and she could see the full extent of his amazing body. She drew breath at the sight of him; he was so beautiful. She took him in her hands and moved her fingers up and down in gentle strokes. He moaned softly, calling her name, and took her face in his hands again.

Reaching into a drawer, he grabbed a condom and deftly sheathed himself in one swift movement. Laying her down, he raised her hips up onto a pillow, and then he gently pushed himself inside her. It was such an amazing sensation it made her gasp. Slowly he inched his way in until she could feel all of him, filling her completely. "This is what I've wanted to do since the first time I saw you in my office," he murmured, staring down at her. "You feel amazing, sweetheart." His voice had the soft cadence of an erotic lullaby.

He started to thrust harder, adjusting the angle until he could see her pleasure rising again. He watched her face with a slow smile, noticing that the noises she was making were becoming more insistent, so he went faster. Olivia burst into orgasm again and he followed with a cry of relief and pure pleasure.

They fell together, Olivia crying and Daniel murmuring gently in her ear. "Shh, it's okay, baby. You really needed that, didn't you? We needed each other. That was fucking amazing. God, you're so beautiful."

He covered them both up with a quilt, so she wouldn't get cold, and then they lay together for a long time in silence with their arms and legs entwined, both of them too exhausted and wrapped up in their own emotions to speak.

Finally, he broke the silence. "Would you like to take a shower baby?" She nodded appreciatively and climbed out of bed to head for the bathroom. She climbed into the double shower and turned on the hot water, allowing it to run all over her and bring her back to her senses.

She rubbed the shower gel over herself, lathering it up into a soapy foam when she became aware he was stepping in beside her. When she looked down, she realized he was hard again. Hard for her. He placed his hands around her on the shower wall, enclosing her. "I couldn't resist joining you." He smiled. "I thought you might need some help." Facing her, he took the shower gel from her and soaped her back, working down to her backside. He let his hands cup her ass, gently caressing it. Then he applied soap to her front, working into her breasts and down to her soft stomach. She widened her stance as his hands reached for the delicate tissues between her legs, and he smiled with pleasure when he realized she was wet and sticky again. "You really are a hot little minx, aren't you?" he murmured.

Turning her around, he bent her over, and she felt his fingers glide across the small of her back. "Well, well, I've been desperate to find this." He'd obviously found her tattoo tucked away at the base of her spine. "*L'amore vince sempre*. Fuck, that is so hot, you bad girl." She felt his fingers trace over the script before he gently eased into her again, using his free hand to explore her clit.

It didn't take long before she could feel the pleasure rising through her body again, as she pushed herself back against him, willing him on to orgasm. He stopped thrusting long enough to let her catch up, and then when he knew she was near the edge he started to thrust again, harder and deeper. She screamed his name as she came and with one last thrust, he fell forward on to her. She could feel his powerful body shuddering with pleasure. He turned her around roughly and held her to him so tightly she felt she had no breath left in her. "God, Olivia. You're gonna kill me, baby. You're just too much."

They dried themselves off with the fluffy towels and headed back to bed. He straightened out the sheets and then returned to the bathroom to grab a robe. She wondered what he was doing. "Well, I don't know about you, but I'm starving. Would you like a snack?"

Olivia laughed with relief. "I thought you'd never ask. All that physical activity has given me an appetite." She wrapped herself in the robe he handed her, and they headed downstairs together. He riffled through the fridge and came out with some delicious soft cheese to accompany the crusty bread, plus some sweet strawberries they'd eaten earlier. Olivia chewed happily and Daniel smiled across at her.

"So. Are you still offended at me for wanting to get you into bed?" His smile was gentle and teasing.

She reached across and caressed his face with her hand, "Beautiful, bad man," she murmured. "You planned all this. You knew you would break down my defences, eventually."

"Not bad, honey. Just driven. Surely, you're not calling what we just did *bad*?"

She narrowed her eyes at him. "You are twisting my words. *That* was mind blowing sex. I'm talking about you and your nefarious plan."

He smiled sheepishly. "A man can dream. You were pretty mad when I told you we had to spend the night. I figured you would either sleep with me or punch me." He paused for a moment. "I'm glad you think it was mind blowing." He laughed. "I knew if I could win you round you'd be one hot, passionate little minx. I could see it in your eyes the first time I met you. You wanted me as much as I wanted you. You just didn't want to admit it." He reached across and grabbed her hand with a mischievous smile, placing gentle kisses on her upturned palm.

Olivia tried not to look embarrassed. He was right, of course. She had wanted him since that day they had lunch together. She'd just never imagined that he would want her in the same way. She wondered how they would navigate all this when they got back from the weekend.

They finished their snack and cleaned up. She went to the window to watch the lights out on the ocean. Some small boats were anchored offshore, and their lights bobbed around with the movement of the waves. She had always loved looking out to the ocean at night when she was a child.

Daniel came and wrapped his arms around her. "I'm glad you like this place as much as I do, Olivia. Because I was hoping you would agree to spend every weekend here with me. It could be our little secret."

She turned around and cocked her head to the side, looking at him carefully. "What about during the week? Don't you want to see me then too?"

He held her chin and looked into her eyes with a serious expression. "I can't, sweetheart. We have to keep this quiet. You're one of our authors, and you're younger than me. Just think how this would look. We have to be careful. We can't be photographed together. At least here we won't be pursued by the press, and we can have some freedom. I can't have our relationship out there in the public domain."

She looked troubled. "Do you know, I spent most of my teenage years not feeling good enough? My mother made sure of that. I felt I was always trying to be something I wasn't. The people close to me now are the ones that stuck. They're the ones who accept me despite the fact that I'm sometimes inappropriate and unspeakably weird. If you're ashamed to be with me, it won't work for me. I refuse to shred my self-esteem like that again."

He frowned. "Ashamed of you? Why the heck would I be ashamed of you? You set me on fire in a way I haven't felt in the longest time. I'm attracted to you because you're different. You have the kind of freedom of expression I could never have. I envy you, Olivia." He held her close to his chest, as if he never wanted to let her go. "You have to remember this is all new for me. I don't normally see women more than once, I told you that, but with you, I can't seem to get enough. I'm drawn to you sweetheart, like a moth to a flame."

Olivia looked up at him sadly, "As long as I'm not the one who's going to get burned."

He spun her around and held her face in his hands. "I would never hurt you."

She looked at him seriously. "There is one condition. If we are going to do this, it has to be exclusive. I won't survive you if I find out you're screwing around during the week and keeping me on ice for the weekend. I have to be able to trust you. If that won't work for you, then we have to say goodbye. It's non-negotiable as far as I'm concerned."

He stroked his finger around her face and stared into her eyes. "You have to understand that I haven't wanted anyone else since I met you. I'm not going to screw that up. Now, come back to bed. I need to hold you."

She wasn't sure how she felt about any of this, and she was well aware this arrangement went against her better judgement. He seemed keen, but something about this didn't feel right. She had just enjoyed the most amazing sex of her entire life, and she was eager for a repeat performance, but she couldn't help feeling she was selling herself short. She suddenly felt exhausted, and she didn't want to think about this right now, so she stood on her toes to kiss him gently. He pulled her into him, and she softened into his chest. It felt like the most natural thing in the world to be in his arms, and yet, something was muttering away in the back of her head. Ignoring the voice of reason that was whispering in her ear, she followed him up to bed and, snuggling into him, she soon fell into a deep sleep.

13 - Daniel

Daniel woke early the next morning, more from habit than anything else. It took him a few moments to realize where he was and recall the events of the previous day. The sight of Olivia still sleeping soundly next to him made his stomach flip. Her hair was spread out in a wild sea of tangles across the pillow and one arm was securely around his waist. He carefully propped himself up on his elbow so he could watch her. God, she was beautiful, and yet her beauty was contradictory. Even in repose, there was something untamed about her, but that was tempered by the innocence of her soft mouth. He felt himself harden as he watched her, and he was tempted to slip inside her just as he had a few hours ago when she had surprised him by waking him with a demanding kiss, but he decided to let her sleep. There would be plenty of time for that later.

He gently lifted her arm and she stirred, mumbling incoherently in her sleep. Carefully covering her with the sheets, he planted the gentlest of kisses on her forehead before padding quietly down the stairs. The watery morning sun was pouring through the glass doors of the dining room, and Daniel spent a few moments looking out at the ocean before putting on some coffee.

He could tell that his insistence on a weekend-only affair had hurt her, but he could see no other way around this, at least not at the moment. He could just imagine the photos of them together, him in his business suit and her in her ripped jeans. The press would have a field day with him and so would Eva, not to mention the board of directors. He hated that she felt less than worthy, when in reality, the opposite was true. He didn't want her to have to suffer the public scrutiny that he did. It wasn't fair; she was totally ill-equipped for it.

He also had his own selfish reasons. He could see that people might see his attraction to her as odd. Her beauty was undeniable, but others wouldn't understand her unconventional side. People could be cruel, and he didn't want her to get hurt. She seemed to have accepted the situation, but he was prepared to have to make allowances if it looked like he was going to lose her. He laughed when he thought about his feelings. Perhaps after all these years, he'd suddenly grown a heart.

He quietly set the table for breakfast and got busy cooking bacon and eggs in a pan. The aroma was divine, and he heard the stairs creak. There's no way his hungry minx could sleep through that. He glanced up and his breath hitched. Sleep tousled, with wild hair and wearing a white shirt she'd clearly stolen from his closet, she looked like every teenage boy's wet dream. "Good morning, Mr. Lane," she purred in a seductive voice. "I'm sorry I slept in. I missed my wake-up call." She threw her arms around his waist, grabbing him and feeling his hardness through his pants. "Ooh, there's my favourite magic dick."

Wow, she'd woken up in a playful mood. "Ms. Jefferson!" he said, trying to sound outraged. "You can see I'm trying to cook here and that is harassment in the workplace. I may have to lodge a complaint."

Olivia was undeterred and grabbed his ass. "I know something you can lodge and it's not a complaint," she whispered in his ear. He was happy she seemed none the worse for their discussion the previous evening.

Shutting off the gas, he turned around, grabbing her, pulling the shirt off her shoulders whilst nibbling her neck. She was giggling uncontrollably, and he thought she was absolutely adorable. He turned back to his job, putting bacon and eggs on two plates and carrying them to the table. The coffee was already made, and she poured it into two cups, bringing it over. She sat down and looked at the spread in front of her.

"Yummy! Bacon for breakfast and you. Every girl's dream." she sighed.

"The bacon, or me?"

"The bacon actually, but you come a close second." She winked at him playfully. "I totally don't deserve it." He smiled across at her with a wicked glint in his eyes.

"Maybe not. But I know what you do deserve." She got up to approach him. "Sit down and eat," he warned, waving his fork at her. "If you get started on me, we'll get no breakfast. Besides, I know from experience that I need to get some food inside you to keep that unfiltered mouth of yours in check." She pouted at him and blew him a kiss, tucking into the delicious spread. He smiled at the looks she was giving him. He'd obviously unleashed a beast.

Breakfast finished, she pushed away her plate and looked across at him. He had been painfully hard throughout breakfast, and it looked like he wasn't the only one who was feeling horny. She picked up the plates, silently keeping her eyes on him the whole time. He knew from the look on her face she was up to something, and he eyed her suspiciously with a smirk. She came back from the kitchen and straddled him, kissing his mouth hungrily.

He smiled up at her. "It looks like I didn't quite satisfy my little minx yesterday. I can see we are going to have to do something about that."

She rubbed herself against him, making him shudder with anticipation. "Oh, you satisfied me alright. I'm just ready to be satisfied again. Is that okay?"

She wasn't wearing anything under her shirt, and he gently parted it to access her beautiful, soft breasts, groaning with appreciation. Taking one of her breasts in his mouth, he gently sucked it. Olivia's head fell back, and she moaned with pleasure. Scooping her up in his arms, he carried her over to the couch, sitting her down and parting her legs. Kneeling on the floor in front of her, he smiled in a wickedly delicious way before using his tongue, gently rubbing up and down the inside of her thigh, teasing her. He wondered if she was going to be up for this so early into their relationship. He was pretty sure she was inexperienced, but she certainly made up for it with enthusiasm. He felt her hands run through his thick hair, encouraging his head up to where she wanted it to be. "You are so impatient, baby," he said mischievously. "You just don't know how to wait, do you?"

The lustful look she gave him nearly floored him. "I can't wait. You're just too damn hot." He started to gently work her clit with his tongue, sucking gently and then licking again. Watching her face, he could see the passion building in her, but he wasn't going to let her off that easily. "Don't you dare stop!" she warned him breathlessly, and with that, he pulled away and stared into her face, smiling. "No!" she screamed, but he just smiled lazily at her, running his finger up and down the inside of her thigh.

"It's called deferred gratification, darling."

"It's called torture," she complained, "and you know exactly what you're doing to me."

He laughed. "Of course I do. I love to see you squirm and hover on the edge like that. You are so hot. I could do this to you all day." He thought about what it would be like to be trapped in this cottage for an entire week with her, no phones, no interruptions, just her. God, come to think of it, a week would never be long enough.

She looked down at him fiercely. "I can see I'm going to have to find a way to torture you."

"Oh, sweetheart," he said, "you're already killing me." He returned to his previous position, but this time, he didn't stop, and he allowed her to reach her climax, moaning his name and holding on tight to his hair.

"Oh my God, that was amazing. You are amazing," she said breathlessly. For some stupid reason, he felt his heart swell at her praise. She was in his arms again as he carried her to the wide kitchen island with the butcher block top. Sitting her on top, he could easily enter her because of his height. Her recent orgasm was still sending contractions through her body, and he felt her clench him inside her. The sensation of her tightness made him come alive, and he thrust deeply into her. She clung onto him like her life depended on it, moaning softly in his ear. The myriad of delicious sensations pushed him over the edge, and he came with a husky cry.

She ran her nails gently over his back and he groaned with pleasure. "Ms. Jefferson. You are an evil temptress," he whispered.

They held each other for a while and then he pulled out, gently lifting her off the island. "Come on, honey. I want to take you for a walk up to the lighthouse today, and I know taking a shower with you will take longer than it should."

She wrinkled her nose at him cutely. "It's not my fault I can't keep my hands off you."

Daniel held her face and looked into her eyes, "You don't know how happy it makes me to hear you say that."

They headed up to the shower, and he was right, it took much longer than it needed to. It was 11 a.m. before they both emerged, wrapped in fluffy towels and giggling. He dived into the closet and came out with two bags from one of the expensive stores in town. "I bought a couple of things for you, because I knew you wouldn't be prepared" he said. "I hope they fit." He also hoped to God she wouldn't be offended at the amount of planning he'd put into keeping her there for the weekend.

Olivia grinned at him, looking into the bag. He'd bought a couple of pairs of beautiful white lacy panties, a pretty floral sundress, and a white sweater. It had certainly been interesting shopping for ladies' underwear, and he planned on doing it again soon. She slipped them on happily and he breathed a sigh of relief when it all fit perfectly.

"How did you know my size?" she gasped, astonished.

He grinned across at her, thrilled with her reaction. "I was holding you pretty close during that dance the other night. I guess I sized you up."

"When did you even buy all this stuff?" she asked. Daniel looked a bit embarrassed.

"Well, when you blew me off at The Red Room on Friday night, I knew I was going to have to try harder than that." He looked like he was recalling the moment. "Those eyes," he murmured, lost in thought. "Such a red-hot little firecracker." He shook himself back to the moment. "I went out early yesterday morning and picked up all the food and the clothes then."

"What if I had said no," she teased. "What would you have done with it all?"

"Oh, I wasn't going to let you say no," he laughed. "It was only a matter of time."

"You're very sure of yourself, aren't you?" She said, sliding on the lace panties and admiring her ass in the mirror.

He came over and grabbed her chin, looking into her eyes. "I don't know about that. I was pretty sure of you, though. We have some crazy chemistry going on. I knew that the first day I met you. It was crackling through the air like electricity. I'm only surprised Eva didn't notice." Of course, in reality, Eva had noticed, and she had warned him off. He tried not to think about that particular conversation.

They headed out for their walk to the lighthouse. She told him she hadn't been there since she was about twelve years old, and she was excited to be making the trip again. Talking animatedly as they walked, she said, she had imagined what it would be like to live in a lighthouse, sleeping in the circular rooms and watching the enormous light sending its guiding beam across the water. Her long, honey hair blew in the wind, and the sun made a few tiny freckles appear on her nose. Daniel loved her child-like excitement. She was uninhibited and quite wild, so unlike any woman he had every been with before, and it made him feel alive. It took his mind back to the memory of two small boys with dark curls climbing the path to the same lighthouse. The older boy put his hand out and took the hand of his smaller brother as they ran together, laughing into the wind.

Things were moving so fast, he felt alarmed that his emotions were carrying him along like this. It was so unlike him to become emotionally involved, but this girl had a touch of magic about her. She was so unaware of her beauty and her sexuality, and because of that, there was none of the haughty pride he'd encountered in women before.

His previous girlfriends had all been beautiful, but unlike Olivia, they were very aware of that fact and used it to its best advantage. He could see he would have to be gentle with her. There was an underlying uncertainty and fragility about her, despite her attempts at being strong and independent. He watched her turning cartwheels on the grass at the edge of the cliff.

He tried to imagine any of his previous girlfriends behaving in this way, and he laughed to himself. They would never allow their hair to get messed up like this, and their couture clothing wouldn't allow for cartwheels.

He pulled out his phone and took a series of photos, wanting to capture the look on her face. She either didn't care that everyone could see her panties, or she was completely unaware of the fact. When she landed clumsily, she looked up at him, smiling with that unknowingly seductive smile. God, if it weren't for the other people around, he'd like to throw her down on the grass and ravage her. Instead, he held out his arms to her, and she ran towards him, laughing, looking much younger than her twenty-four years. He caught her and swung her around, stopping in a tight embrace.

"Just stay where you are in front of me for a moment," she whispered, sliding her hand down the front of her sundress.

He looked at her, bewildered. "Olivia, what in God's name are you doing?"

"I guess this bra wasn't built for doing cartwheels. One of the girls has escaped and I need to stuff her back in."

"I could give you a hand with that." He laughed. She really was unintentionally funny. He wondered how many men she had scared off in the past with this kind of thing.

"Nope. I'm good. All is safely gathered in, as they say. They really are too big to be practical sometimes."

He tried to look shocked. "Are you kidding? They are truly magnificent. I can think of a hundred different uses for them."

She narrowed her eyes at him. "Yes, and I bet they all involve parts of your anatomy."

"Okay, we need to stop this conversation before I throw you down on the grass and test that theory out. Now, I don't really know why I'm going to ask this question, but are you hungry? I'm afraid if you don't eat soon, you might turn into a gremlin."

Olivia looked thoughtful for a moment. "I loved that movie when I was a kid. God, those gremlins had fun. Wouldn't you like to behave like that just for one day? Rip off that suit of yours and go bat shit crazy."

"I'm not sure I've ever gone bat shit crazy. They always expected me to be the responsible one."

"Ha! No-one has ever had any expectations of me. Good thing too, really. You need to drink Absinthe. That stuff will definitely make you lose your mind. Only problem is, it tastes like NyQuil."

He kissed her on the forehead. "The stories about Absinthe are not true. You probably just drank too much of it. Besides, *you* make me lose my mind in all the best ways, and no alcohol is required for that."

They went to a beautiful little bistro in the village. The décor reflected the seaside location, and he could tell from her face that she loved it. They had two steaming bowls of clam chowder with chunky brown bread and butter. She groaned appreciatively at the amazing taste of it all, savagely tearing large pieces off her bread. He smiled at the way she ate with gusto. "Mmm, this is so good," she said, making a rapturous expression.

"That's not the first time I've heard you say that this weekend," he observed. "I thought you were going to reserve those kinds of comments for me."

She threw her napkin at him. "That's my Italian blood coming out. We are passionate about everything we love. Food, wine, music, hot men..." There was a brief pause, and she finally whispered, "and of course sex."

Their weekend pursuits had clearly unleashed her unfiltered mouth. He smiled across at her, his blue eyes full of fire. "As I said before, Ms. Jefferson, you are an evil temptress." She laughed and squeezed his hand as the owner of the café smiled across at them knowingly.

The afternoon came around too quickly, and soon they were packing their things into Daniel's SUV. He secured the cottage and then they headed to the car. Olivia sighed sadly.

"Don't be sad, honey. We'll be back next weekend, remember?"

Driving back in the car, he held her hand all the way. They weren't very chatty, but there was a contented stillness between them. Olivia's entire body felt like it was thrumming with pleasure. She felt like she was on a rollercoaster, but she didn't feel she could stop it if she tried, and she certainly didn't want to. They pulled into a side road close to Olivia's apartment. They decided if they were going to keep the relationship to themselves, they needed to be careful. Olivia felt a little excited by the secretive nature of it all, but she was also disappointed she wouldn't see Daniel during the week. He held her in a tight embrace, kissing her gently.

"Thank you so much," she said seriously. "It's honestly been an amazing weekend. Nothing could top this."

He smiled gently across at her, pushing back her hair from her face. "I've had a wonderful time too, darling." Then he smiled as he said, "I think I need a good night's sleep before work tomorrow. Your stamina just kills me." She laughed and kissed his forehead. "Until next Saturday?"

She bit her lip and nodded, and then she climbed out of the car and made her way down the street towards her apartment. Daniel drove by and blew her a kiss as he passed.

When she got back to the apartment, Bill the night security guard, was already working, and she just nodded to him and smiled. Making her way into the apartment, it felt alien to her after her weekend at the cottage. She checked her phone and found several messages: one from Lottie, one from her dad, and one from Mark. She was going to have to find a way of keeping her friends and family off the scent, if she was going to disappear with Daniel every weekend.

Lottie's message was short and sweet, telling Olivia about a house party that was going on, asking if she wanted to go. Next, she listened to the message from Mark. "Hi, babes, it's me. I was hoping you might have calmed down by now and we could have a chat. I know I screwed up royally, but I miss you, babes. I really want to talk to you. Call me–please."

Olivia felt strangely guilty after what she had been doing all weekend. She realized that her brief chapter with Mark was over, but it hadn't taken her any time at all to jump into bed with another man. "You are a prize trollop, Olivia Jefferson," she said to herself. She phoned Mark back, but his phone just went to voicemail. "Hi Mark, it's me," she said lightly. "I'm not mad at you anymore, but I've had time to think things through, and I know this is the right decision for me. I wish you nothing but love–take care." She rang off, hoping she didn't sound too abrupt. She really wasn't mad at him.

It was around 7 p.m. and she felt a little lost for what to do. She wondered about phoning Lottie, but she was afraid that Lottie would hear something in her voice that would give the game away. She was really going to have to practice her poker face, which had always been terrible. She grabbed her iPod and linked it to her Bose speaker, and then she searched for some of the music she had listened to with Daniel that weekend. She turned out the main light and lit a candle on the coffee table, and then, turning up the speaker, she listened to Handel, allowing herself to drift off to the ethereal beauty of the music. She must have fallen asleep because the next thing she knew, she awoke suddenly. The candle had burned down, and it was around ten, so she decided to call it a night, heading off to her bedroom. She checked her phone once more and saw there was a text from Daniel. She clicked on it breathlessly. It was a link to a YouTube video of a Barry Manilow track. She laughed helplessly.

"*Barry Manilow! You've got to be kidding me.*" She opened up her iPad to find the link he had sent to her. *Weekend in New England.* It was a track she was familiar with because her dad had loved it. She remembered teasing him about it relentlessly. The video flashed in on the screen and there were lyrics to accompany it.

It was truly schmaltzy, but Olivia felt tears forming in her eyes as she read the lyrics and realized how fitting it was. It was so unlike her to get emotional about a stupid song. *Probably just overtired from all the sex,* she thought. Picking up her phone, she quickly texted back.

"*Good evening, smoldering executive hottie (SEH for short). I am very concerned about you. Did you get your playlist from the local seniors complex? I think you need to hang out with younger people who will steer you in a more appropriate musical direction. As a young person, I would like to offer my services. We can discuss my terms and conditions next time we meet.*"

He wrote back, "*And when will I hold you again?*"

She grinned at his response and wrote back, "*Put down your Barry Manilow vinyl and step away from the turntable. Start with Sara Bareilles. She has a song for every occasion.*"

Giggling, she put her phone on the table, and it surprised her when it immediately rang. "I wasn't going to call you, but here I am. I guess you're a little addictive."

"Ha! You're just a horny publishing god with deeply disturbing musical taste. I can see I'm going to have to take you in hand."

Daniel groaned. "Oh, yes please. Take me in hand, Olivia." He paused. "And then perhaps in your mouth, and lots of other naughty places."

Olivia felt herself blush and was glad he couldn't see her. "I suggest a cold shower, Mr. Lane. It's good for your circulation."

"Hmm. I can think of something that's much better for my circulation," he teased. There was a pause and then he said, "I was really just calling to say goodnight. Sleep tight, sweetheart."

"You too, Smoulder," she replied.

"Is that my name now?"

"I think it's very apt." She laughed before hanging up.

15–Daniel

It was getting late, but Daniel didn't feel ready to sleep. He should be exhausted after all the physical activity with Olivia over the weekend combined with a distinct lack of rest. Instead, both his mind and his heart were racing with excitement and uncertainty.

This all felt so unnatural to him. Normally he would say goodbye to a lover and go to bed to enjoy a healthy eight hours of sleep, but Olivia had unhinged him and left him wanting more. The weekend had played out better than he ever could have imagined, and it had been fun. He couldn't remember the last time he had laughed so much, and now he'd seen the possibilities he was greedy for more. This was the very thing that had been missing in his life for so long.

He also pondered the fact that being with Olivia had made him think of Simon. His brother's memory had been filed away in his mind. Finding it too painful to deal with, he rarely thought of him. He wondered if the reason he was thinking about him now was because he saw definite similarities between Simon and Olivia. His brother shared the same sense of fun and carefree spirit and cared very little for what other people thought of him. From an early age, he had been reckless and accident prone, scaring his poor parents and spending more time in the emergency room than should have been necessary.

In contrast, Daniel as the older brother had always felt a deep sense of responsibility, which weighed heavily on his shoulders. He'd envied his brother's blithe refusal to accept responsibility for anything in his life and watched as he scraped through school with barely passing grades, preferring to attend parties and date all the local girls. The night that Simon died, he had taken his motorcycle to a friend's house for an impromptu party. Daniel had asked him not to take the bike and offered to drive him, but he remembered his brother laughing it off as he took off for the night. Daniel had often looked back on that night with regret, and wished he'd insisted, but Simon was a free spirit who saw himself as invincible.

He thought about what Simon would have thought of Olivia. As kindred spirits, they probably would have hit it off immediately. *Fuck, he would have loved her,* he muttered to himself. In fact, Daniel probably wouldn't have stood a chance with Olivia if Simon had been around. With sandy blonde hair and ice-blue eyes, they were polar opposites in appearance, but Daniel could still remember his popularity with women of all ages. In a way, Daniel had envied his brother in the same way that he now envied Olivia. He remembered the stunning parties his mother had held at their family home every summer, and how Simon had always been surrounded by a bevy of beautiful girls who wanted to dance with him.

Daniel was also popular, but he felt he attracted women for a different reason. He was seen as an excellent marriage prospect, and the woman who wanted his attention were often encouraged by their mothers. It was an unspoken fact that loosely arranged marriages were still a thing in the higher echelons of society. As the older brother who would eventually inherit the family business, he always felt he should marry well as a duty to his family.

A couple of years after Simon had died, Serena had come into his life, and she truly was everything he should have wanted. Stunningly beautiful, her family owned a prestigious law firm, and marriage to her would have made sense. After dating for a year, he had asked her to marry him, but after only being engaged for a few short months, he knew he couldn't go through with it. He just couldn't resign himself to this life that had been set in stone for him from such an early age, and he always had the distinct feeling that there had to be more to life than this.

After the split, he had slid into his playboy ways and although he knew his parents must have been disappointed, they were always supportive of him. His transition from older brother to only son hadn't been an easy one, and he hated the fact that he felt his parents' happiness depended on him at the end of the day.

When he'd first joined the business, he saw it as a challenge. There was so much to learn. But lately, he had felt himself resent it, as if it were an enormous weight around his neck. Tonight, as he reflected on his weekend with Olivia, he pondered if the problem was not with his business life, but with his personal life. He had proven to himself that he could have fun. Now he just had to find a way to balance these two aspects of his life, and everything would be great. He felt more hope than he had for a long time. He could see this weekend arrangement was going to work out beautifully. No-one would be any the wiser, not Eva, or the board of directors, or even the press. No drama, no hassle, just lots of fun during weekends–perfect.

16

Olivia woke early the next morning, and her first thoughts were of Daniel. She imagined him dressing in his beautifully cut business suit and heading to the office in his red sports car. Her insides flipped over at the thought of how she had spent the weekend, and she was still reeling from the speed of how things had progressed. She had never imagined last week that she would be in this situation, but she couldn't help feeling her luck had changed. She was going to be signing a publishing contract, and she had a new, incredibly hot man in her life. She wandered into the bathroom and looked at herself in the mirror. She had a slight tan from the weekend and her lips looked full and swollen. "Oh, God Olivia," she said to herself, "you look like you've spent the weekend fucking." Which of course she had.

She wanted to work on the two unfinished copies of her travel guides today, so she was prepared to put a good day's work in. She was in a great mood as she brewed the coffee and poured it out and put some toast on for breakfast. Her phone buzzed, showing she had a text, so she ran over to check. It was from Daniel.

"*Good morning, Ms. Jefferson. Hope you slept well. Have a great day.*" There was a heart emoji at the end.

The sight of a text from Daniel sent warmth through her body. She replied, "*Good morning, SEH. Hope your day is spent with thoughts of me—I know mine will be filled with thoughts of you.*"

Putting her phone down, she tried not to smile to herself. *Hell, I've got to get over this*, she thought, *or I'm going to be walking around like the Cheshire Cat.*

Jumping up on a stool at the kitchen island, she munched happily on her toast, to which she had applied a thick layer of orange marmalade. She was just rinsing off her sticky hands when her phone rang. She bounded over, hoping it would be Daniel, but realized it was her parents' number.

"Olivia, it's Mammina." She heard the strong Italian accent of her mother and rolled her eyes, wondering what kind of mood her mercurial mother would be in this morning.

"Hi, Mama. How are you? I haven't spoken to you in ages." Olivia could hear *The Magic Flute* playing in the background and it stirred her childhood memories.

"Daddy told me you broke up with Mark," her mother continued. "I wanted to check you were okay." Her mother's voice sounded clipped and accusatory.

Olivia smiled knowingly. "I'm fine, Mama, honestly. It had just run its course. Time to move on–you know."

Her mother continued. "He was never good enough for you. You need to set you sights a little higher. It's high time you found someone and settled down. By the time I was your age, I was married. Start dressing the part, and you'll soon find someone. You'll never get a man if you dress like a hobo or a call girl. I still can't believe what you turned up in at Christmas. You should dress more like Lottie."

"Yes, Mama. I have to go, I've got things to do." Her mother did not hang up.

"Olivia, wait, I thought you and I could have lunch together tomorrow and do a little shopping. What do you think?" Olivia was surprised by her mom's offer. It had been a long time since she had seen her. Olivia and her mom were best in small doses. They were both stubborn and hotheaded, and Rosa had been exasperated at Olivia's rebellious period before college.

"Olivia pulled a face before responding sweetly. That would be lovely, Mama. We haven't done that for so long." They decided on a place to meet, and her mom said goodbye. "Ti amo, Olivia."

"Ti amo anch'io Mama," Olivia replied.

She headed over to her computer, ready to start work, but the phone rang again. "Jeez," she sighed in desperation. "I'm not going to get anything done today." Glancing down at the display, she saw it was Lottie and quickly tried to think of an excuse for the weekend.

"Morning, darling." Lottie's deep, refined voice sang down the phone. "Where were you all weekend? I thought you wanted to party." Olivia tried to think on her feet.

"Well, to be honest, Lottie, I think that tequila really did me in. I just turned off my phone and hunkered down for the weekend." Her friend laughed.

"Ha! I can't believe what I'm hearing. Olivia Jefferson floored by a little tequila!"

Olivia laughed weakly. "It wasn't a little tequila, Lottie. It was a lot of tequila." She could hear that Lottie was in a public place; probably shopping. She did that a lot.

"Had anymore thoughts about that sexy publishing god who wanted to make out with you?" Lottie laughed wickedly.

"Yes, I've thought about him a lot," Olivia said honestly. "Who in their right mind wouldn't be thinking about him. He's fucking god material." She could hear Lottie opening her car door–a black Audi convertible.

"I think you should just fuck him, darling. It would be good for you. You know, boost your morale after Mark the Moron."

Olivia giggled. "There are *other* ways of boosting your morale, you know, Lottie."

"I know, darling, but none of them are quite as much fun. Have to go. Love you." Olivia breathed a sigh of relief. She hadn't had to tell her friend many lies, and she felt good that she had escaped. *But that was only one weekend*, she thought to herself, slightly panicked. *How am I going to explain every weekend*?

The day proved to be quite fruitful for Olivia and once she was in her groove, she got a lot done. She was thrilled to get a sexy text from

Daniel at lunchtime and then again in the afternoon. She worked into the early evening and then called Lottie to see if she wanted to come over for Chinese food, but Lottie wanted to work out at a new gym in town. She wanted Olivia to come with her, but Olivia told her she was too tired. Honestly, after her other extra-curricular pursuits over the weekend, she didn't think it was a good idea. Her muscles ached in places where she didn't even know she had muscles. Who'd have thought sex could be so athletic?

She ordered in Chinese food for one and drew a glass of white wine from the box she always had available in the kitchen. She was just cleaning up when her phone rang. She thought it was going to be Daniel, but it was actually Evangeline.

"Sorry to call you so late, Olivia. I hope you don't mind."

Olivia assured her it was fine to call at any time. "We would really like to move forward with your guidebooks, and I wondered if you could come in on Wednesday to run through some of the paperwork and talk to some of our designers about your cover. We also must get a headshot done, but we can arrange that another time."

Olivia was excited to get started on her project and confirmed she could be there on Wednesday.

"We need to sign contracts and would like to offer you an advance of $5,000." Olivia felt a little overwhelmed, and she hugged herself happily. She was on her way to becoming a published author. Maybe her financial woes were going to be a thing of the past. That trip to Florence might not be as far away as she thought.

Daniel rang at around ten, just before Olivia turned in for the night, in a playful mood.

"Good evening, Ms. Jefferson. I'm just calling to check if you're in bed yet."

Olivia laughed. "Mr. Lane, my favourite executive hottie. Are you coming to tuck me in?"

"I'm sorry, Ms. Jefferson, I didn't quite catch that. Did you say am I coming to fuck you?"

Olivia felt the heat rising in her. God, just talking to this man made her wet.

"What are you wearing?" he demanded. "I want to know what you look like."

Olivia looked down at herself "Well, it's a little warm tonight, Mr. Lane, so I'm not actually wearing very much." She could hear his breath quicken.

"Describe it," he insisted.

"I am wearing an exceedingly small pair of cotton shorts and a lacy camisole. If you came over, you could see if you approve."

Daniel groaned. "I have no doubt I would approve, but I'm pretty sure they wouldn't be on for long."

Olivia was enjoying herself. She had never played this kind of game before, and she was finding it very erotic. "I was just going to rub some baby oil on my skin. I find it gets so dry in this weather." Daniel sounded like he was having an asthma attack.

"Where are you going to rub it?"

"Well, I thought I would start with my legs, and then rub up between my thighs."

"Go on," he said huskily.

"Then I think I should do my arms and my breasts and maybe my stomach. I don't seem to need any between my legs, as that area is already soaked for some reason," she said. "I can't reach the other places, and I could really use some help." Daniel groaned. She wondered if he was masturbating and suppressed a giggle.

"Unfortunately, I find myself in a hard situation at the moment," he said, "but if you are free this weekend, we can investigate the baby oil problem in more depth." Olivia couldn't hold it together any longer and she collapsed on the bed laughing.

"I'm glad you find my agony so amusing, Ms. Jefferson."

"You bring it all on yourself, Mr. Lane," she laughed, "but I am happy I have found a way to torture you."

"Be careful the route you are taking. I have all week to think up new ways to torture you, remember." His tone softened. "I missed you today, honey." The gentle admission made her heart jump.

"I missed you too. Can't wait until Saturday."

17

The next day, Olivia was meeting her mom for lunch. She dressed carefully, knowing she would be under the critical eye of her stylish Italian mama and that ripped jeans and Doc Martens would not go down well. They were going to be meeting in the part of town where all the smaller, individual stores were. Rosa Jefferson had expensive taste, but she also knew how to snap up a bargain. When she had been a singer, she had a wardrobe full of beautiful gowns. She had met Olivia's father when he was a sound technician working on one of her productions. He always told Olivia it was love at first sight, when he watched Rosa rehearse an aria for *The Marriage of Figaro*.

It sounded like Rosa had snubbed him at first, but he eventually won her over with his wicked sense of humour and his big heart. Olivia sensed her parents had a passionate marriage with its share of highs and lows. She remembered her mother shouting in her strident Italian tones, and everyone knew to take cover when she was in one of those moods. Olivia's brother Luca was four years older than her and had taken after her mother. He was tall and slim with the dark Italian looks and a heart built for romance. Olivia couldn't remember how many hearts he had broken when he was younger, and there always seemed to be a stream of love-struck girls hanging around their house. She had a love-hate relationship with her brother when they were growing up as he swung between protecting her and tormenting her. Now he was older and in a settled relationship, things were a lot easier between them, although she didn't speak to him much.

Olivia spotted her mom looking into a shop window at some rather beautiful dresses. "Mammina!" she called, running up to her and hugging her. She looked at her mom's face and thought she was looking tired.

"Olivia! You look different. What have you done to yourself?" Olivia looked down at her clothes. She was wearing one of Rosa's cast-off summer dresses and flat ballet pumps.

"I haven't done anything. These are your clothes."

Rosa smiled. "Not your clothes, child. Your face. You look radiant."

Olivia didn't feel she should tell her mom it was her "I got fucked" face, so she just smiled.

"Okay," Rosa said determinedly, "Daddy told me about your books and your publishing offer and we are both so proud of you." Olivia blushed under her mother's gaze. It was rare praise indeed. "I decided I wanted to treat you to some new clothes, so today we will have a girl's shopping day. We can't have you walking around like a tramp if you are going to be a professional woman." Olivia bit her tongue. "But Olivia," her mother continued, "please let me give you a little guidance. You must not rush in and fall in love with the first thing you see." Olivia smiled. *How ironic*, she thought.

They had a surprisingly good morning, and her mother seemed in good spirits. Maybe now she was older, things would be easier between them. Rosa was ruthless in her pursuit of a bargain, and they found several items that they both agreed upon. As usual, there was a fair bit of animated arguing, and Rosa drew the line at a pair of purple stilettos that Olivia wanted. "You have nothing to wear them with Olivia. They will sit in your closet unworn."

They were ready to have lunch, and they walked down the tree-lined street arm in arm, chatting away enthusiastically in Italian. Suddenly, Olivia saw an all too familiar, tall, beautiful man walking towards them, and her heart skipped a beat. He approached them, smiling.

"Ms. Jefferson, how wonderful to see you again. How are you?"

Olivia blushed to her roots, knowing what they had been doing all weekend, especially now she was standing next to her mother. She quickly composed herself.

"Mr. Lane. This is my mammina. Mama, this is Mr. Lane. He owns the publishing house that is going to produce my books."

Her mother was all of a flutter at the sight of this attractive man.

"Mammina?" he inquired.

"Yes, Mr. Lane, it is Italian for mommy," Rosa explained. "My daughter speaks Italian. Did you know?" Rosa was keen to show her daughter off in her best light. *God, if only she knew*, thought Olivia. Rosa and Daniel chatted easily for a while, and Olivia stared at her shoes. Her mother always had a way with men, and she was an easy conversationalist. Men were attracted to her beautiful trim figure, and her sexy Sophia Loren accent.

"I seem to remember Olivia told me you were a singer," Daniel continued "Am I right?"

Rosa looked flattered. "Yes, Mr. Lane. Opera. But I haven't sung professionally for many years." Daniel turned to Olivia. "And how about you, Olivia? Do you sing like your mother?"

Rosa answered for her, as she often did. "No, Mr. Lane, she did not follow me down that path. She could have done, but she lacks the rigid discipline you need to be a successful singer. I'm afraid my daughter is quite rebellious." She smiled. "However, she has her own qualities I suppose." Her mother's voice was soft and proud, and it touched Olivia to hear her speak in this way. Daniel smiled charmingly at Rosa.

"She certainly does. I have been extremely impressed by her enthusiasm." Olivia could see Daniel was trying hard not to laugh, and she bit her lip.

Olivia didn't think she could hold it together much longer, as she had the overwhelming urge to grab Daniel and kiss him. "Mama, let's go for lunch now, please." Olivia requested in Italian. Her mother looked at her kindly.

"My daughter is always hungry, Mr. Lane. She eats like a horse, but she must burn off her food somehow, because she never puts on any weight."

Daniel laughed. "Well, I will have to ask her for some tips on how to do that, Mrs. Jefferson. I won't keep you ladies any longer. Have a wonderful lunch." Then he strode off down the street. Rosa looked at her daughter slyly.

"He is one sexy beast, Olivia, and he likes you. I can always tell, you know. Now, that man is marriage material. As I was saying, if you only dressed a little more like Lottie and toned down your mouth, you could attract a man like that. You don't want to be a single woman forever. Time ticks on faster than you think."

Olivia looked embarrassed. "Oh, Mama. I think he was just being polite, and besides, I am not getting married. Not now, not next year, in fact probably never, so please put that thought out of your head. There's a lot more to enjoy in life than getting married and popping out babies. Now come on, before I starve to death."

They settled into a corner table at an Italian restaurant that was one of Rosa's favourites. The server brought two coffees and some water, and Rosa sighed. Olivia studied her mother's face carefully. She thought she looked older than last time she had seen her. Something seemed to be bothering her. "Mama, is something wrong?"

"No, I'm just tired. Don't fuss Olivia. You're just like your father," she said sharply.

Olivia knew better than to pursue this, so she stared silently at the table. The silence stretched out between them until her mother finally spoke.

Rosa swallowed hard. "A few weeks ago, I found a lump in my breast. I went to have a biopsy yesterday." Olivia felt her stomach go into knots. Her mother continued. "It's probably nothing, but the doctor said it's better to be safe than sorry. Now, I don't want you to worry and don't tell your brother, please. He doesn't need to know."

Olivia didn't know what to say. "Have you told Dad?"

Rosa looked down at the napkin she had twisted into knots. "No, not yet. I'm afraid he'll fall to pieces on me. I don't need that. You know how emotional he is."

Olivia shook her head. "He's stronger than you think. You need to tell him, Mama. It wouldn't be fair not to. Let him support you with this. For God's sake, you've supported us all these years."

Her mother smiled tightly. "I was just doing my job."

"Well, now your job is to look after yourself. Remember, Mama, it could be nothing. Lots of women get breast lumps. Don't think the worst." Olivia was trying to reassure her mother, but her heart was aching.

The food came and Olivia tried to lift her spirits, joking with her. She told her about finding Mark in a compromising situation. Her mother looked horrified. "It's a good thing that wasn't me, Olivia. I would have done something much worse than pour beer on his head."

Olivia grinned. "That's what Dad said."

Soon it was time for her mother to leave and they hugged warmly. Olivia was trying hard not to let her emotions get the better of her. Her mother needed her to be strong right now. "Now, phone me as soon as you have any news. Okay? And please don't worry." Her mother looked a little happier, like a weight had been lifted. Telling Olivia her news had obviously been weighing heavily on her mind.

When she got back to the apartment, she poured herself a glass of wine and sat down. She remembered what her mother had said about Luca. She hadn't spoken to her brother since Christmas, and she toyed with the idea of phoning him. She imagined her mother travelling home and breaking the news to her dad. That wouldn't be an easy conversation for sure. Greg Jefferson adored his wife, and he hung on every word she said. He had never believed his luck when she agreed to marry him thirty years ago, and he'd been pinching himself ever since.

Olivia picked up her phone and looked for Luca's number. The phone rang a few times and then he answered. "Luca, it's Livvy."

Her brother sounded shocked to hear from her but pleased. "Baby sister! Such a pleasant surprise. I thought you'd fallen off the face of the earth. What's up?"

Olivia told him about her meeting with their mother and what she'd said. "I don't want you to say anything, Luca, because it could be nothing. I just thought you should know."

Her brother sounded concerned. "Do you think I should drive down to see them?"

Olivia thought for a moment. "I would leave it for now. Let's wait and see what happens." She knew her parents would know she had talked to him if he turned up unannounced. He never did stuff like that.

"It's good to talk with you, Livvy. I'd really like to see you to catch up. Why don't you come over and have dinner with Molly and me?" It surprised her to hear him say that. He had never really wanted much to do with her in the past. Maybe they were both growing up. She agreed to phone him as soon as she had any news and then ended the call.

Olivia flopped down on the couch with her wine. For a long time, she didn't really feel hungry. Her phone buzzed; it was a text from Daniel.

"*Great to see you two gorgeous girls today. Your Mammina is one hot lady. I can see where you get that from.*"

Olivia smiled happily at the distraction. "*Yup. She's hot in all kinds of ways. You should see her when she's throwing kitchen utensils.*" She wondered if she should tell him about her mom, but she decided against it. They hadn't really known each other that long after all.

Instead, she called Lottie and chatted with her for a long time. Her friend was very philosophical and level-headed, and it was great to hear her voice. Afterward, she looked at the kitchen clock. It was only nine o'clock, but she was exhausted, and she made her way to bed.

18

Olivia woke up early the next morning, feeling a lot more positive. It was Wednesday, and she was going to be heading into Lane & Associates to meet with Evangeline. She had scored some amazing outfits while shopping with her mom yesterday, and she was keen to make a good impression. Also, there was a good possibility she would see Daniel, the very thought of which made her heart quicken. She thought of him sitting in his office wearing that sexy business suit.

She wondered if he knew she was coming in today and hoped that he didn't. Seeing her would be a surprise. The weather had been quite warm, so she wore one of the summer dresses they had bought in one of the small boutiques. She'd pulled out her favourite. It featured a cream background with pastel geometric shapes and a deep v-neckline. It hugged her figure nicely and then flared out at the bottom, accentuating her figure. She grabbed a cream cotton sweater to go with it and found some strappy sandals. She looked at herself in the mirror and wondered if it was too low cut. She could see her cleavage quite clearly. She rummaged through her jewellery box and found a chunky wooden necklace she had bought in Italy the last time she was there. She pulled her long hair into a French knot, pulling out some strands so it would look less formal. Happy with her overall appearance, she headed out the door.

Walking through the doors of Lane & Associates, she realized she wasn't as nervous as she had been for her last visit. Lumi looked up from her desk with a bored expression. "Ms. Jefferson. Do you have an appointment?"

Olivia nodded and Lumi gave her a tight smile before she headed up in the elevator. She was pleased to see Evangeline waiting for her. The older woman gave her a warm greeting.

"Olivia, how lovely to see you again. What a pretty dress. You remind me of my daughter, Lily. She likes to wear dresses too."

Olivia thought that it must be a stark change from the navy business attire she was wearing last time. She looked longingly over at Daniel's office, but she couldn't see him, so she followed Eva into her office. They immediately got down to business. There was a lot to talk about, and Olivia was soon lost in the details. They talked about what ideas Olivia had for the book cover, and Eva was telling her she would need to arrange for some headshots of Olivia, plus she would need a short bio to get publicity rolling.

She could sense he was standing behind her before she even turned around, and she felt like the air was charged with an electrical current.

"Oh, hi Daniel." Eva smiled up at him. "Olivia is here today to sign the contract and go through some details with me."

Olivia was afraid to turn around to face him. Her stomach was already doing backflips and she could feel the hairs standing up on the back of her neck. Eventually she swivelled her chair around and looked up to face him through her long bangs. He was staring down at her; more specifically, he was staring at her breasts. "Hello, Mr. Lane," she said weakly.

He smiled a warm smile. "Olivia, how lovely to see you again. Has Eva completed all the paperwork with you?

Eva nodded. "I'm just about finished, Daniel."

"Well, in that case, I would like to take Olivia for a tour of the office and introduce her to a few people. She's going to be working closely with some of these people, so she should at least meet them."

Eva nodded. "Well, as soon as we're finished here, I'll send her over."

They wrapped up their business and Eva gave Olivia a warm hug. Olivia really liked the older woman, and she was thrilled to be working with someone with her experience. Olivia wandered out of her office and down the hallway towards Daniel's office. Her legs were feeling weak, but she couldn't understand why. *Good grief, girl*, she thought to herself, *you just spent the weekend banging this guy senseless. Pull yourself together.* She knocked on the door, but noticing he was on the phone, she waited.

He beckoned her in, and she sidled into his office, sitting down when he indicated a chair. He put down the phone and looked across at her, his deep blue eyes amused.

Olivia took a breath. "I've finished with Eva, Mr. Lane."

He sucked in air at the sound of the formal address. "Good. Come with me, please." He quickly showed her around the entire building, introducing her to the Editorial Department, the Creative Department, and Sales & Marketing. "And I know you've already met Lumi." He smiled at the receptionist who shot him a rather alluring smile in exchange. Olivia was sure she was batting her eyelids. "Lumi, hold all my calls for a couple of hours, would you? I'm just going to walk Ms. Jefferson out, and then I have some business to attend to."

The receptionist interrupted him. "Don't forget, Ms. Longthorne has been trying to reach you for the last few days and also I've had several calls from Vanessa Lambert. She's desperate to speak with you. She won't speak with anyone else."

He spun around and looked at Lumi severely. "I will call Ms. Longthorne when I have time, and you already know my instructions regarding Ms. Lambert. I don't expect to be having this conversation with you now."

Lumi smiled sweetly. "Of course, Mr. Lane. It must have slipped my mind."

They made their way out of the building, and Olivia grimaced. "Uh-oh. Trouble with the staff?"

Daniel shook his head. "She's very efficient, but I get the distinct impression she sometimes likes to stir things up."

"I think she's jealous. She definitely doesn't like me. She always looks at me like I'm something the cat dragged in."

He smiled a little stiffly. "Well, her opinion is of no importance to me, and it you shouldn't let it worry you either."

Olivia felt distinctly uncomfortable, but she definitely didn't want to come across as the jealous girlfriend. She always swore to herself she would never be that person.

They walked around to the parking lot behind the building and Olivia noticed Daniel was once again driving the little red sports car. He looked down at her passionately. "You look beautiful today." She let out a sigh of relief, knowing they weren't under the watchful eye of the entire office.

"Thank you," she said. "It feels really weird seeing you in the office. It feels like everyone knows what we've been doing."

Daniel smiled. "I know. I wanted to throw you over my desk and fuck you into the middle of next week, but I didn't think that would go down well with Eva." He opened the passenger door to the little red sports car and bounded over to the other side.

She tried to look indignant. "How rude! You really have a dirty mouth sometimes. I'm only amazed they let you play at big boss. If only they knew."

"So says the girl who is obsessed with magic dicks," he laughed.

She shot him a playful look. "Now, where are we going, Mr. Lane?"

"You will soon find out, Ms. Jefferson. You will soon find out."

She thought maybe he was going to take her for lunch, but soon, he was pulling into the parkade of a tall downtown apartment block. He put a key card into the gate and the barrier lifted. "Where are we?" she was curious.

"You are so impatient, Ms. Jefferson. Just wait and see." He took her hand, and they walked towards the elevator. When they were inside, he swiped his card and they started to ascend. Olivia stood, looking down at her shoes, and Daniel looked across with a sly look on his face.

They got out on the twelfth floor, and Olivia realized there were only a couple of doors in the hallway. He swiped his card again and opened the door to the most stunning apartment Olivia had ever seen. It was obviously the penthouse, with stunning views of the city. It was a huge, expansive loft type apartment with beautiful soft leather couches, and enormous bookcases lined with books. The kitchen was modern and sleek, and everything was pristine. Olivia looked around with her mouth open. "Where are we?" she asked again.

"This is where I live during the week." he smiled. "Do you like it?"

Olivia gasped. "It's amazing. You could fit my apartment in here about five times. Look at the floor space. We could dance!" She spun around on the expanse of floor with her arms out and then dramatically flopped onto a couch.

He dropped his wallet and his key card on the kitchen counter and then turned to her. "Okay, is there anything I can get you? Tea? Coffee?" he paused for a moment "Perhaps a nice orgasm?" She smirked behind her hand.

He walked across the room and pulled her to her feet. "How dare you come into my office looking like that, totally distracting me from my work," he whispered into her ear.

"I don't know what you mean, Mr. Lane." She moaned as he started nibbling her neck. "I didn't come in to see you at all, actually. I came into see Eva. It's not my fault you came barging into her office."

"I saw your tits, and I got an instant erection," he muttered into her hair "I hope Eva didn't notice." He held her face in her hands and looked into her eyes. "My God, Olivia, you look ravishing today.

Your dress, your hair, your beautiful tits." He explored her mouth with his tongue. Olivia pulled back from him.

"Mr. Lane! I thought we weren't going to do this during the week. Business only, remember?"

"God help me, Olivia. I have no control where you're concerned. My best intentions flew out the window when I saw you in that dress. I was going to take you to lunch, but I think this is more in keeping with the clandestine nature of our relationship."

He went back to exploring her mouth and she could feel his hands on her back, seeking out the zipper of her dress. "It's a beautiful dress," he mumbled. "Now, how do we get you out of it?" He located the top of the zipper and expertly pulled it all the way down, exposing her back. Pushing her away from him, he slightly lifted the shoulders and allowed it to slip to the floor.

She stepped out of the dress, and he held her away from him to take a good look at her. She was wearing the white lace panties he had given her over the weekend with a matching white lace bra. "Oh, dear God! I've just died and gone to heaven," he gasped. Olivia giggled. She was feeling a lot more comfortable around him again. It was strange that she felt nervous around him after such a brief separation. She contemplated that she really hadn't known him very long, despite the deep level of intimacy they had shared.

He took her hand and let her into a small hallway with doors on either side. Pushing open the first door, she realized they were in an expansive bedroom. There was a huge, king-sized bed with beautiful soft grey bed linens. The room had a masculine vibe, but it was still exquisitely styled.

"You live here all on your own?" she gasped.

"Of course I do," he laughed. "Who do you think I have tucked away in here? A harem of beautiful maidens?"

"I wouldn't be at all surprised," she muttered. "You do have a bit of a reputation."

He turned her around gently to unclip her bra. "Well, there's only one maiden I'm interested in, and she's standing here with me right now." She shuddered when she felt his hands on her back and watched as her white lacy bra dropped to the floor. He knelt down in front of her, holding her hips and looking intently at her white lace panties. "Now, what do you propose we do with these?"

She was feeling incredibly aroused as she ran her fingers through his hair. "The way you're looking at me, I think you could melt the panties right off me. What do you want to do with them?"

"I could just tear them off, but that would leave you a little exposed on the journey home. Although come to think of it, thinking of you having to walk home with no panties is really hot." He gently put his thumbs inside her panties and pulled them down, allowing her to rest her hand on him as she stepped out of them.

"I feel you have me at a bit of a disadvantage here," she said breathlessly, "as it would appear you are still fully dressed."

"Strange, I hadn't noticed that. I guess my attention was elsewhere."

She tugged at his silver-grey tie, untying the knot and pulling it from his neck. She tried to undo his shirt buttons, but her hands were shaking and she struggled, getting frustrated in the process. He gently removed her hands and smiled down at her.

"You're getting yourself a little flummoxed there, darling," he whispered. "Let me do that for you." He expertly unbuttoned his shirt with one hand, throwing it on to the back of a chair.

She managed his belt and his fly as she carefully unzipped his pants, slipping them over his hips. He pulled his pants and his socks off in one fluid movement, and then scooped her up and carried her across to the bed, climbing up beside her.

"Now," he said. "You made me lie here the other night thinking about you, when you were turning me on with all your talk of baby oil." She bit her lip, remembering their conversation. "So, I think it's only fair that I get to inflict a little torture on you." Her face must have registered alarm because he said, "It's okay. I'm not going to hurt you. I would never hurt you, baby. I'm just going to make you wait a little for what you want. Now turn over, lay on your stomach, and don't move."

She heard him pad off to the bathroom and return with a small bottle of oil and a large soft-grey towel. "It's not baby oil," he said. "I think this is nicer." He warmed the oil in his hands and then he rubbed his hands over her back, alternating the movements with gentle stroking. The oil smelled delicious, a combination of lavender and sandalwood, and Olivia felt her body melt under his touch. He massaged down to her buttocks, stroking them gently with his fingertips, and then he moved down to her legs, parting them slightly so he could focus on the sensitive inner thigh area. Olivia moaned softly, feeling the wet, sticky sensation between her legs.

"Do the other side." she pleaded. He laughed softly.

"Not so fast, baby. You are so impatient. I haven't finished yet." She went to roll over onto the towel, but he held her down easily with one hand. "Listen to me, sweetheart. You will not turn over until I say so. Okay?" She moaned in protest, but she stayed where she was. He moved down to her feet gently, using small, circular movements on her delicate soles. Finally, he laid the big towel on the bed and let her turn over.

He placed two hands on either side of her and stared down into her face. "We're about a quarter of the way there. Okay?" Olivia's face was flushed, and she clapped her hand to her forehead.

"I can't wait that long," she complained.

"Well, I don't see what choice you have right now," he teased, oiling up his hands to start on the other side. He gently rubbed up around her shoulders and then paid very careful attention to her breasts. "These little babies were teasing me today, and now I'm going to tease them." He nibbled her nipples gently, making her cry out in pleasure and she drew her knees up, hoping he was ready to move down to where she needed his touch the most.

He massaged her stomach gently and then moved down to her legs, completely bypassing the area most in need. He hadn't even touched her there yet, but she felt she could orgasm at any moment. Finally, he said, "Okay, let's see what we have here," and he gently massaged her, sliding in a finger and exploring her sensitive areas. "Oh, you are a hot, wet, little minx, aren't you?"

Olivia clenched her hands, embedding her fingernails into her palms, losing herself in the moment as he circled her clit with his finger. She was trying not to show that she was on the edge of orgasm, because she knew what he would do, but he instinctively seemed to know, moving away at the height of her pleasure to focus on a new area. He did this to her several times, and it felt to her that he was keeping her hanging for hours.

She was beside herself, crying out for him to let her finish. Finally satisfied that he had teased her enough, he pushed through with her and allowed her to reach her peak. The sensation was so intense, she thought it would last forever. He stared into her face as she came, captivated by what he had created. Her entire body was shaking, and tears were streaming down her face, so he held her close, whispering gently into her hair.

"I need you inside me," she was sobbing into his chest. "I need you now!"

He caressed her gently. "Shh, calm now. So full of passion, baby."

She reached over to him, gently stroking his hardness up and down. He quickly turned her over again and got her up on her knees. "I'm going to take you from behind honey, because I want to be really deep inside you." He pushed into her gently at first, and then when he was sure she could take it, he started to thrust hard and fast, continuing to rub her clit with his fingers. As he felt himself about to come, he increased the speed of his fingers and she came too, with powerful contractions. It was enough to send him over the edge, and calling her name, he came inside her with intensity. Her knees gave way, and she lay flat on the bed with him on top of her. She heard him laugh gently from behind. "I am ruined, Olivia. You have ruined me for anyone else ever again."

"I sincerely hope so," she mumbled from underneath him, her face pushed hard against the bed.

He got up quickly. "Oh, holy crap, look at the time! Come on, darling, let's have a quick shower together, and you are not to touch me, okay? That means hands off! If I lose anymore work time because of you, my business empire will be in tatters, and I will end up in a trailer park."

Olivia pouted at him. "Am I not worth it?"

"Oh yes, baby. You are definitely worth it, but you are a lot of work. I am literally shagged out." They dashed into the shower, and he helped her wash the oil from her body, grabbing her wrists when she tried to touch him. "Not now, minx! We will have the entire weekend, okay?"

They dressed quickly, and she helped him straighten his tie, combing his hair into a semblance of order with her fingers. Grabbing his jacket and his wallet, they rushed out into the hallway, heading for the elevator. They entered the elevator and he grabbed her, dipping her down into a deep, lingering kiss. "Now, do I need to drop you somewhere?" he asked.

"No, it's okay. You get back to work. I think I could do with a walk to bring myself back down to earth." He kissed her again quickly, jumped in his car, and he was gone. She could hear his tires screeching as he pulled quickly out of the parkade.

Olivia stepped out into the bright sunlight, shading her eyes. She pulled a pair of oversized sunglasses from her bag and realized that she hadn't eaten lunch, and she was starving. She headed towards the park in search of the food truck that was usually there during the week. She bought herself a jumbo chicken and bacon wrap, a packet of chips and a diet coke. *Not very healthy*, she thought to herself, *but with the calories I've just burned off, who cares?* She found an empty bench in the park and sat down, heaving an enormous sigh. Today had turned into a great day. She basked in the afterglow, the early afternoon sun bathing her face in warmth.

OLIVIA SLOUCHED ON the couch that evening, feeling bone tired. *God, I never realized sex took so much out of you*, she thought wickedly. She was indulging her sweet tooth with a box of Italian truffles that her mom had given her. Letting them melt in her mouth felt like a sinful pleasure, although not quite as sinful as what she had indulged in that afternoon.

Her phone vibrated on the coffee table, and she picked it up, noticing that it was a blocked number. Normally, she wouldn't answer this type of call as they were usually either scammers or telemarketers, but strangely she picked up. She was met with silence, but she could hear someone breathing.

"Hello, is someone there?"

"You're making a mistake, Olivia. He's not who you think he is. Have you any idea how many women he's been through? You're smarter than that."

Olivia didn't immediately recognize the female voice, but there was definitely something vaguely familiar about it. "Who the hell is this?" she retorted.

"I'm trying to do you a favour," the woman continued. "Get out now before you get in too deep."

Olivia decided to play dumb. "I'm sorry. I don't understand what you're talking about. Maybe you have the wrong number."

She heard the woman laugh. "No, I definitely have the right number, and I think you know exactly what I'm talking about. You think you'll be the one who pins him down? Highly unlikely going by his track record. Besides, *she* is back in the picture. You know that don't you?"

"Look lady, I have no idea what you are talking about, but I suggest you have a lie down. I won't be answering your calls again."

Hanging up the call, she realized that her hands were shaking. Thinking about the conversation, she wondered about the "she" in question. Perhaps she should have pressed her for more information, but who knows what kind of person she was dealing with here. She knew you should never encourage a crazy person. It was obviously a spurned woman that Daniel had left in his wake.

The nagging voice at the back of her head was pushing its way to the front, and she could feel a headache coming on. Normally, she would phone Lottie to get her take on the situation, but she knew she couldn't do that without revealing her relationship with Daniel. The only person she could call about this was Daniel himself, and she wasn't sure she wanted to do that. She was an independent, kick ass woman. She could deal with this kind of crap herself, and she certainly didn't want to come across as emotionally needy.

Pouring herself a glass of wine, she took a few calming breaths and tried to think about it with a cool head. Clearly this woman had her panties in a twist about her seeing Daniel, although she wondered how the hell she knew. They had been pretty careful not to be seen together. If it was just a case of someone being spiteful, there was no point in talking to him about it. She didn't want him to think she didn't trust him, and she truly wanted to trust him. The voice in her head got louder. "*Player. Player. Player,*" it was chanting.

She screamed in frustration and put a pillow over her head. "I will not allow some crazy bitch to ruin the best sex of my life," she yelled. Resolving to put it out of her head, she stuffed the remaining three truffles into her mouth in one swift action.

19

The next two days burned slowly for Olivia. She had tried to forget about the suspicious phone call, and she had done remarkably well, deciding instead to focus on the amazing sex she was going to be having. She wondered if this was how her life was going to be from now on, spent in a permanent waiting game from one weekend to the next.

She had spoken to her mom after her doctor's appointment, and he had told her the results would be in at the end of next week. She sounded more like the old Rosa again; more positive and resilient. Olivia didn't ask how the conversation with Dad had gone, but she was sure it hadn't been easy.

On Friday, she had met Lottie for their usual Friday night girl's night. Lottie knew her mom's problems distracted Olivia, so she didn't press her about plans for the weekend. The evening was fun, but a little more subdued than normal, and they got home at a reasonable hour.

She had spoken to Daniel on Friday evening, and he had agreed to let her cook for them on Saturday. Olivia was an excellent cook, and her mom had taught her to cook some great Italian dishes. She decided she would make Spaghetti alla Puttanesca or Tart's Spaghetti, which she thought was very appropriate given what they had planned for the weekend. It was a pretty spicy dish with anchovies and olives, but she couldn't imagine a man with that kind of passion didn't like spicy food.

She had bought all the ingredients together with a couple of bottles of Chianti and she was all ready to go early on the Saturday morning. She realized it was the earliest she had been up on the weekend for a long time. Daniel arranged to pick her up at 9 a.m. in a discreet location, behind her apartment block. She packed everything carefully plus her clothes for the weekend and headed over to their arranged assignation. She decided to wear one of the pretty dresses she had bought with her mom with a white crocheted cardigan over the top. She enjoyed wearing dresses because they were so easy–one item and you were done. Also, Daniel seemed to like her in dresses and that was her primary aim.

Rounding the corner, she caught sight of his SUV, and her heart skipped a beat. She suddenly felt inexplicably nervous. Last week had been so amazing, she couldn't see how they could replicate that every weekend. She was concerned Daniel would quickly become bored with her and move on. And then there was the matter of the telephone call. What if the mysterious caller was genuine?

Shaking the idea out of her head, she took a deep breath and approached the car. He jumped out to help her load her bags into the back and she caught her breath. He was wearing faded grey jeans and a white t-shirt with a navy hoodie. The casual look did nothing to detract from his beauty, and Olivia stood there for a moment with her mouth open. As he bent over the car to put her bags away, she got an amazing view of his glorious ass and she murmured appreciatively. He looked around at her, concerned. "You okay, honey?"

Olivia grinned wickedly and looked down. "I was just admiring the view."

He laughed and caught her in his arms, kissing her. "Very naughty, Ms. Jefferson. You look pretty amazing yourself, although I think clothing may be superfluous for what I have in mind this weekend."

They climbed into the SUV, and he looked across at her. "Ready?"

Olivia smiled at him shyly. "I've been ready since last Sunday." He traced his finger gently around her chin and then pulled her in for a long, luxurious kiss.

Pulling away reluctantly, he said, "I think we better get going, or I might just jump you here in the car."

Driving to the cottage, they chatted easily. He told her all about what he had been working on in the publishing house, and she told him how the guidebooks were coming along. The drive passed quickly and before long, they were pulling up at the gates of the cottage. Olivia's face broke into a broad smile to see the beautiful house again. Last week she had been so uncertain, pulling into the driveway, but now that seemed a lifetime away.

Daniel helped her with her things, and they both carried the food and wine into the kitchen and unpacked. He had also brought some food and a couple of bottles of white wine. They were obviously not going to be hungry. He grabbed her from behind and kissed down her neck, starting at her ear.

"I've been thinking about you on this kitchen island all week," he whispered in her ear. "I've also been thinking about all the other places I can have you in this house. I'm thinking I should have bought a bigger house."

Olivia breathed heavily as his kisses took a downward turn across her bare shoulders.

"I know we've only just arrived," he purred in her ear, "but I can't wait, Olivia. I must have you now. Is that okay with you?"

The dress she was wearing had shoestring straps with buttons all the way up the front. To answer his question, she turned around and slowly unbuttoned her dress. She gently pushed him back away from her so he would appreciate the show she wanted to put on for him. She carefully deliberated over each button, licking her lips and looking up at him under her lashes. He spread his arms out behind him on the kitchen counter and watched her with fiery eyes. Finally, she reached the last button and her dress fell away onto the floor. She was braless wearing only a pair of blush pink lace panties, and her nipples were hard and erect; she had definitely upped her underwear game since meeting Daniel.

He moaned softly and put his head in his hands. "Holy Jesus, Olivia. If you lay one finger on me, I'm going to come. What are you doing to me?"

She said nothing but took a step towards him, lifting his t-shirt over his head. She cupped her hand around his very visible erection and smiled up at him, "This is what I want." She quickly unzipped his jeans and pulled them down so he could step out of them. Kneeling in front of him, she removed his boxers and looked up at him seductively. She had thought all week about how she wanted to give him pleasure and, grasping him gently, she took him in her mouth, licking him up and down in long strokes, moving up and down, slowly at first. The noises he was making were savage and uncontrolled, and it urged her on to move a little faster. He was grasping her hair and pushing her head, so she took him deeper and deeper. Suddenly he exploded into her with force, and she swallowed greedily, enjoying the sensation that at that very moment, she owned him completely. She sat back on her heels and looked up at the sight of him, utterly unravelled.

After a few minutes, he looked down at her, his eyes dark with passion. "Holy hell, Olivia, that was amazing."

Feeling kick ass and powerful, she smiled in satisfaction. "We aim to please. I'm glad you enjoyed it."

He held her away from him so he could look into her eyes. "I don't think *enjoyed it* covers it, baby, but you have needs too and I am going to see to them right now. Okay, let's see. We've already done the kitchen island and the couch and the bed and the shower. What other surface shall we try out?" He looked over at the dining room table "Perfect. First let's lose these."

Hooking his thumbs in her panties, he quickly removed them and scooped her up in his arms. "Hmm, might be a little hard on your back," he said, so he grabbed a cotton throw from the couch and spread it over the table before laying her on top. "Look how nicely you fit." He laughed. He was right. Olivia fit on the table perfectly, allowing him to take full advantage of her nakedness.

Pulling her forward so her legs dangled over the edge, he sat himself in a dining chair and buried his face in her. "Wow, Olivia. Just sucking me off has made you so wet." His tongue circled her clit, making her writhe around on the table. "Careful, sweetheart. We don't want you falling off. How would we explain that in the ER?" The movement of his tongue was slow and deliberate, moving up and down, plunging inside her and then returning to where she needed it the most. Her body went rigid and this time, he did not make her wait for her pleasure. She exploded into orgasm, grabbing his hair and roughly pulling him into her. "We're not done yet, honey" he said, and she noticed he was hard again. Opening her up, he pushed into her gently. In this position he could play with her clit whilst plunging into her and she thought she would lose her mind with pleasure. The contractions from her last orgasm gripped him tightly as she felt the sensations rising through her body again. As she came, he plunged faster, and together, they cried out each other's names, losing control.

Pulling gently out of her, he reached over to grab some tissues to clean them both up. He looked at her seriously. "Olivia, you realize we've only been here for just over an hour and we've already had two orgasms each."

She grinned up at him. "Not enough for you?"

He pulled her up and helped her off the table, drawing her into his chest. "Do you think it's possible to die from too many orgasms?"

Olivia looked thoughtful. "I think we should research this, Mr. Lane. I feel a new book project coming on. Would you like to take a shower with me?"

20

They had decided to go out for lunch, so they headed to the bistro they had visited last weekend. The owner smiled in acknowledgment as they went to the familiar table.

"Don't eat too much," Olivia warned. "Remember, I'm cooking tonight, and Italians always make too much."

Daniel pulled a face at her. "I don't think you should warn *me* about eating too much. Your mom said you eat like a horse, but that you burn it off. Do you think you burned it off this morning?"

Olivia looked up from her French Onion Soup and smiled. "I think with you around, I'll be losing weight. No wonder I'm always hungry. That sounds like another research project. How many calories do you burn during sex?"

Daniel pressed her nose with his finger. "I refuse to be a research project for a nymphomaniac author."

They spent the afternoon exploring several antiquarian bookstores in the town. Olivia was in heaven and bought a couple of leather-bound classics. Daniel laughed at her. "Do you honestly think you're going to get any reading in this weekend?"

She made a face at him. "I have to have something to keep me busy during the week, as I have a weekend arrangement with a very bad man."

They got back to the cottage at around four, and Olivia went to the kitchen to put on some coffee. They had bought some pastries at the local bakery to enjoy when they got home. They were going to eat on the deck, but the wind had changed and it had gotten cold, so he set about making a fire for them for the evening.

Olivia brought their pastries and coffees to enjoy by the fire, and they snuggled up together on the couch, enjoying the intimacy of silence.

"Do you mind if I ask you something?" Daniel broke the silence with his question.

Olivia shook her head. "I don't mind. What is it?"

He looked thoughtful. "It's a tad forward. I just wondered how many guys you've had sex with."

She looked up at him quizzically. "Well, there were a couple of one-night stands at college and then there was Mark. So, just three. I'm a novice by your standards. I guess I was a bit of a late starter. To be honest, sex has been a bit of disappointment up to this point. I lost my virginity to a rather lovely but inexperienced boy from Ohio after a 2 for 1 margarita night in the student bar. It was fast and not particularly comfortable, and I was seriously not impressed. I don't really think he knew what he was doing, poor guy. It was definitely not the earth-shattering experience I'd been led to believe." She pulled a face as if she were recalling the event. "To be honest, the second time wasn't much better."

Daniel winced regretfully. "Aww, sweetheart, that's a little sad. I wish I'd known you then. I would have been happy to help you with that transition."

"I'm sure you would've. Pervert." She giggled. "Remember, you're older than I am, so when I was eighteen you would have been twenty-five. It would have been a little indecent."

"Hmm. What did you look like then? Were you as... well endowed?"

Collapsing with laughter, she hit his arm. "Daniel, I've been well endowed since I was fifteen. They haven't really changed since then."

He closed his eyes and smiled to himself. "Indulge me a little. Let me have my dirty fantasy."

She wiggled herself into him. "I can feel your dirty fantasy pressing into my back at the moment. So, Mr. Confident, how would it have been different with you? No wham bam thank you ma'am?" He ran his fingers up and down her bare arm and she shivered a little.

"Well, you wouldn't have been drunk, that's for sure. I would have wanted you stone cold sober, so you would taste every kiss, feel every touch, experience it all. All. Damn. Night. Long."

Olivia fanned herself with her hand. "And then you probably would have left me heartbroken," she said dramatically. "Damn it! Now I feel angry. Look at all the amazing sex I've missed out on."

"But think how much fun we'll have making up for lost time."

"Well, one thing's for sure, since I've met you, I've realized what I've been missing. I always knew there had to be more; now I know I was right. I guess you've spoiled me for anyone else now."

He laughed gently. "Well, that was my intention, of course. I want to make sure you never need anyone else."

She turned over and lay in his lap, looking up at him. "I'm not even going to ask your magic number. I don't think I really want to know, it would just be too depressing. I guess I should just be grateful for your incredible skills in that department."

"You are great for my ego," he laughed.

She waited a minute before she asked her next question and tried to make it light. "Has there ever been anyone serious?"

He pulled his mouth into a tight line. "I was engaged for a while, a couple of years ago, but we both decided it wasn't right for either of us. After we broke up, I kind of fell into player mode. Not intentionally at first. It just seemed the most straightforward way to live my life."

Olivia tried not to feel hurt. A lump rose in her throat. She'd never really considered the fact he might have had a serious relationship. Somehow being a player was easier for her to accept than a serious relationship. She inwardly chided herself for being so naïve. "What happened?" She heard the words choke in her throat.

"Our families knew each other well. It seemed like the perfect match, but I always knew something was missing. My heart wasn't in it. I think after my brother died, I really wanted to make my parents happy. I did it for all the wrong reasons."

She looked up at him, trying not to let him see how upset she felt. "This really shouldn't bother me. Why do I feel sick about it?" she whispered.

He stroked her face gently. "It's because you are a very passionate girl, Olivia. And it's because of how you and I feel about each other. I know it's only been a couple of weeks, but I know for sure I have never felt like this before, and I think you feel it too. Am I right?"

She blinked, trying to stop her tears, and nodded. He gathered her up in his arms and held on tightly to her. "It's important you know these things, but I don't want you to dwell on them. What you and I have is unique. It's powerful and beautiful, and nothing can take that away from us."

She held onto his shirt and snuggled her face into it. "You don't think it's just because we have lots of hot sex?"

Daniel shook his head and smoothed her hair. "No, I don't think that at all. I think the sex is just one way we express our powerful feelings for one another. You knocked me on my ass the first day I met you, and I haven't recovered since. Why do you think I pursued you in that wine bar?" he asked.

"Because you're a horny bastard, I guess."

Daniel thought for a moment. "Did you realize I followed you there?"

She pulled away from him and looked into his eyes. "So, you're not only a horny bastard, you're also a stalker?"

He laughed. "Well, not exactly. I had popped out to get some wine that night, and I saw you arriving at The Red Room. I know I shouldn't have followed you in, but the temptation was too strong. I guess you're like forbidden fruit, Olivia." She snuggled closer into his chest, listening to his honeyed voice. "I arrived with the intention of just watching you, but then you started dancing with that guy and

I was insanely jealous. It's not a feeling I've ever experienced before, and it's not something I ever want to feel again."

"He's gay," Olivia whispered.

Daniel digested that information for a moment and then continued. "When I danced with you, I lost control. That rarely happens to me, but with you, it seems to happen on a regular basis. I hadn't intended to seduce you that night. It was clumsy, and you were angry, and rightly so. Christ, I thought you were going to deck me," he chuckled.

Olivia was feeling a little better. She wasn't quite sure where this conversation was leading, but he seemed to be saying all the right things. "What are you trying to tell me, Daniel?"

He took a deep breath. "Our relationship took off so fast and I pursued you like crazy. You need to know that's not normal behaviour for me. I don't chase women, at least I didn't until I met you. I was so desperate to be with you, I missed out on all the first steps people normally go through. I don't want you to think I'm only interested in the physical side of our relationship—although I have to say that is amazing."

She crawled into his lap and kissed him gently. "This is new for me too, Daniel. The intensity of my feelings for you scares me."

He breathed out heavily, as if he felt relieved. "I'm glad I'm not the only one," he whispered.

He wrapped his arms around her, pulling her closer. A warmth spread through her body; not the warmth of desire, which she normally felt, but something different. She felt safe and loved in his arms, and it felt so right. She was meant to be there. She felt the familiar insecurities drain out of her, and in their place was a feeling of pure joy.

After a while, she remembered she was making dinner, so she placed a gentle kiss on his forehead and got up. "I'm going to make you dinner. I'll pour you some wine, and I want you to stay there and relax. Okay?"

He held onto her hand to stop her from leaving. "That's not fair, baby. Let me help you."

She shook her head decisively. "No, Daniel. I want to do this for you. You don't want to get in the way of a crazy Italian girl in the kitchen. There are too many sharp objects around."

He grinned up at her. "Well, as long as you promise to be a crazy Italian girl in the bedroom later."

Olivia was in her element in the kitchen, and she danced around as she cooked. She put Taylor Swift's "*I Knew You Were Trouble*" on her iPod and ran it through Daniel's speaker.

"I didn't realize I was going to get a floor show as well," he called from the couch. She danced into the living room and shimmied in his face as he laughed. "Careful, sweetheart, or you might not make it back into the kitchen."

She laughed and danced back to her spaghetti. She made a green salad and shouted, "I hope you like it spicy."

"Are you talking about the dancing or the food?" he grinned.

She lay everything out on the table: Spaghetti alla Puttanesca, green salad, crusty bread, and the fruity, rich Italian wine. "Come and get it," she called.

Daniel barrelled into the kitchen and grabbed her, throwing her over his shoulder. "If you insist, my lady."

"Not me; the food, you fiend."

He ran appreciative eyes over the table as Olivia lit the candles. "This looks wonderful. What is it called?"

She grinned across at him. "Spaghetti alla Puttanesca which translates to prostitute's spaghetti."

He looked at her incredulously. "Do prostitutes even eat spaghetti? I would have thought it was very fattening." Olivia threw a napkin at him and sat down to eat.

She loved how the dining area overlooked the ocean, and as the light was dying from the day, she sat where she could look out to see the twinkling lights.

"Oh my God, this is amazing," Daniel gulped, taking his first few bites.

Olivia smiled proudly, twirling her spaghetti. "When I think about it, I realize my mom taught me so much," she said a little sadly. "She taught me all about opera and food and cooking and how to live with passion. I spent so much of my life fighting her, I never saw what was in front of my face."

Daniel squeezed her hand gently. "Love can be like that sometimes, sweetheart."

She was staggered that he ate three helpings of the spaghetti. "That's more than my dad can eat." She laughed. She had cleaned up most of the dishes beforehand, but he helped her with the rest before they crashed on the couch with the remainder of the wine, which was potent, and Olivia was feeling tipsy and more than a little aroused. She straddled Daniel with a wicked look on her face. "What do you want to do now?"

He smiled a slow and lazy smile and cocked his head to one side. "Sex on the Beach?" he offered.

"Oh, I don't think I should have a cocktail. I've had enough wine already."

He stood up and went to collect his jacket and a sweater for her, along with a blanket. She looked at him, confused as he crossed the room to the doors of the deck. He turned to her with his hand out for her to take. "Come on, let's go." She took his hand and followed him out the door. The cool evening air lapped around her bare legs, and she shivered. He pulled her closer to him, enclosing her in his jacket, and they made their way down the path to the small beach in front of the house.

She had never been on the beach at night. There was a full moon and there was something magical about the way it reflected on the gentle waves that were breaking on the shore. The beach was deserted, and Daniel led Olivia to a small area between an outcrop of rocks where they were protected. He spread the blanket on the sand and lay down, putting his hand out for her to join him.

"So Olivia, when I said sex on the beach, I wasn't talking about a cocktail."

Olivia giggled, enjoying the warmth of the red wine coursing through her body combined with the cool of the night air.

"Do you mind if I relieve you of your panties?" he whispered huskily in her ear. She lifted her hips high in the air as he pulled her panties clear and put them on the blanket.

"I don't want sand in them," she laughed. "Most uncomfortable."

Laying beside her, he trailed his fingers up the inside of her thighs, and she moaned gently. She could hear the waves crashing onto the beach, echoing her rising excitement as Daniel's fingers moved towards her hot, wet sex. When he reached his target, he groaned softly sliding one finger inside her and moving it around to ignite her passion. He watched her writhing on the blanket in the moonlight, with her dress hitched up around her waist and her golden hair spread out around her like the sun's rays. It was the most erotic thing he had ever seen, and he felt like just the sight of her laying there in the heat of her passion was enough to drive him crazy. He focused on Olivia's rising excitement, rubbing gently on her clit as she moaned his name. As she exploded into her climax, she clutched at her own hair and he watched her, fascinated, as she fell apart in front of him.

She sat up suddenly, clutching at his jeans, trying to free him from his clothing so he could take her. "I need you inside me now. I'm aching for you. Please hurry." Daniel loved the restlessness of her passion. It felt like she could never get enough of him; like he was the only man for her. He tugged his jeans and his boxers down, freeing his impressive erection.

"Hands and knees, baby," he told her huskily. She flipped over, exposing her beautiful, peachy ass, and he pushed himself into her, thrusting hard against her. Fingering her already swollen clit with one hand and supporting himself with the other, he brought her excitement back up to match his. Her contractions clamped around him, pulling him deeper inside her. The intensity built for both of them until she cried out and he followed her, running his hands roughly through her hair. They collapsed together on the blanket, gasping for air. The warmth of his body on top of hers chased away the chilliness of the night air, whilst on the inside she felt like her body was on fire.

Pulling out of her gently, he caressed her soft ass, making her moan with renewed pleasure. "I think we should go back darling; you feel cold." Rolling onto her back, she knelt up and threw her arms around his neck, burying her face into his chest and inhaling deeply. He took his jacket and wrapped it around her, so she felt snug and secure. They stayed there for several minutes, wrapped up in each other's arms, listening to their accompanying heartbeats.

Eventually she pulled away from him. "Let's go back and sit by the fire," she said, her voice thick with emotion. She retrieved her panties from the blanket and pulled them back on, giggling. Huddled together, as if their lives depended on it, they made their way back up the beach.

As they reached the path to the house, a large yellow Labrador came bounding down the path towards them. Olivia laughed, putting her hand out to pet the over-enthusiastic dog. His breathless owner followed a couple of minutes later, apologizing for his dog's bad manners. "That's okay," Olivia laughed. "He's beautiful!" They carried on up the path. "Phew, that was close," she giggled. "We could have been caught having sex by that guy and his dog."

Daniel pinched her ass playfully. "You see what you get me into, Ms. Jefferson? I used to be a respectable business owner."

Olivia snorted at him. "I seem to remember you suggesting this, Mr. Lane."

He turned her to face her, running his hands through her hair, his eyes full of wonder. "Seeing you there on the blanket in the moonlight, going crazy for me..." He shook his head. "I think that will stay with me forever."

21

The morning sunlight piercing through the drapes woke Olivia the next morning. Daniel was still crashed out beside her, laying on his front with his head turned to the side. She looked down at his beautiful face, thinking about how much younger and more vulnerable he looked when he was sleeping.

Resolved to make breakfast, she resisted the urge to kiss him and instead grabbed her robe and quietly padded out of the bedroom, trying not to disturb him. When she got downstairs, she went to the window and looked out over the ocean. The early morning sun was sparkling on the water, and she could see it was going to be a beautiful day. Putting on some coffee, she went to the fridge and retrieved some eggs and veggies. She decided to make a big Spanish omelette and quickly got to work chopping peppers and onions. She found a big pan and tossed in some butter and olive oil, adding the vegetables so they sizzled.

Daniel appeared in the doorway, rubbing his eyes, his hair ruffled from sleep, his chest bare and his pants low on his hips. Olivia caught her breath as she often did when she saw him, and she felt his blue eyes penetrating her. She looked away and blushed foolishly, remembering what they had been doing the night before.

He laughed playfully. "Looks like someone is feeling shy this morning." Catching her in his arms, he kissed her gently, exploring her mouth with his tongue, and Olivia felt herself relax.

"I don't know why you still have this effect on me after all we've done," she sighed.

He smiled down at her, tracing her face with his finger "I don't know either, but I kind of like it. I never know who I'm going to wake up to. Will it be shy and coy Olivia, or will it be raunchy, hot-as-hell Ms. Jefferson?"

She pulled away from him and returned her focus to the pan, afraid that the veggies were burning. "Well, right now, it's hungry Olivia. Get some plates out, would you? I'm just going to put the eggs in."

The air temperature was warm enough for them to eat breakfast on the deck, although Daniel insisted on Olivia having a blanket for her legs. Olivia thought how amazing it must be to wake up to this kind of view every day. She breathed in the sea air and sighed peacefully, listening to the rhythm of the waves as they broke on the sandy shore.

"Wow, you sure know how to rock an omelette, sweetheart," he mumbled through a mouthful of food.

She smiled at his compliment. "I'm glad I can please you in other ways."

He looked over at her thoughtfully. "Olivia, you please me in more ways than I care to count."

They ate quietly, both of them watching a small fishing boat as it made its way slowly out to deeper waters. "I want to take you somewhere special for lunch today," he said, breaking the silence. "It's a bit of a drive so we should take a shower, and besides, I need to fuck you desperately."

Standing up, she looked at him with feigned shock on her face. "Mr. Lane! I don't think that's in the terms of my contract. Not only that—you'll have to catch me first." She took off laughing and ran into the living room, putting some distance between them.

"Oh, a game! I like games, Ms. Jefferson. I'm extremely competitive, you know." They chased around the furniture for a while and then Daniel grabbed her as she was heading for the stairs, pinning her to the wall with his arms. "That was a silly move, Ms. Jefferson. You cut off your only means of escape," he said breathlessly.

He effortlessly threw her over his shoulder and started to climb the stairs.

"Don't you dare drop me," she yelled, banging on his back with her hands. He slapped her ass playfully, making her yelp louder. Taking her into the bedroom, he threw her down on the bed, pinning her arms above her with one hand. She kicked her legs like a wild thing and writhed around.

"Wow, you're like a Tasmanian Devil, baby. Anyone would think you didn't want me to make love to you."

She grinned up at him so he could see she was playing. "A girl's gotta put up a fight sometimes, you know."

Pulling her robe apart, he placed his free hand between her legs and started massaging gently. Her body stilled and calmed. "Judging by how wet you are, Ms. Jefferson, I don't think you're in any position to put up much of a fight."

Her eyes closed, and she moaned softly. "My body always gives me away doesn't it?"

"Every time, sweetheart," he murmured. "Every time."

Two hours later, Daniel was zipping up the cream dress she had worn to his office the day they had ended up in his apartment. She turned around to look at him, smiling, and he groaned. "Olivia, do you torture me on purpose? Now I'm going to be staring at your breasts throughout lunch and trying to hide my erection from everyone."

Olivia laughed and looked at herself in the mirror, smoothing her hands over her curves. "Do you think my breasts are getting bigger? Maybe I'm eating too much."

He put his head in his hands. "Your breasts are perfect. Now can we please stop the breast conversation, or we will never get out the door."

They headed out to Daniel's SUV, and soon, they were on their way. He took the coast road that climbed away from the small seaside town. The drive followed the coastline, and the view was spectacular. Eventually, he pulled up at a beautiful country inn. The green painted sign outside read "*The Laurels*." It was a magnificent colonial property with white painted siding and black shutters. Shiny, black double doors were propped open, and they could hear the noise of happy diners spilling out from the dining room.

"I've wanted to come here for ages." Daniel grinned. "Apparently the food is excellent."

They headed into the restaurant, and the server led them out to some tables outside on the patio. Olivia noticed there was a long stretch of lawn that suddenly dropped off, giving way to a stunning high-bank view of the ocean. "This place is incredible," she said, breathlessly.

Daniel hugged her close to him as they headed over to their table. "Only the best for you, sweetheart," he whispered in her ear, making her legs feel weak and tingly.

The brunch menu was spectacular, and Olivia spent forever deciding what to eat. "I want to try it all!" She laughed. Eventually, she settled on Eggs Benedict with smoked salmon, and Daniel ordered a skillet for himself.

They were sitting under the shade of an umbrella, but Daniel took out a pair of Ray-Bans and relaxed back into his chair. Olivia looked across at him. He was wearing a casual, white linen shirt with dark jeans. With his dark hair and sunglasses, he reminded Olivia a little of some of the Italian men she had met over the years, only not as vain. *What the hell does he see in me?* she thought darkly to herself. Daniel smiled a slow, seductive smile at her.

"Are you looking at my tits?" she whispered. "Because I can't tell when you're wearing sunglasses."

He smirked. "Of course I am, darling. I think every man in the restaurant is. You need to be careful you don't take someone's eye out with those."

"Daniel!" she hissed. "Don't be so rude!"

He cocked his head apologetically. "I can't help it if my girl-friend's a sex kitten, can I?" She'd not heard him refer to her as his girlfriend before and it surprised her. Is that what she was? She wasn't really sure with this weekend arrangement that they had but hearing him say it brought a warm glow to her face. "I can tell you're blush-ing even though I'm wearing sunglasses," he said teasingly. "You can't wear a dress like that and then come over all prim and proper on me."

She looked up at him under her lashes. "My mom picked out this dress, so it must be okay."

He ran a finger up her bare arm, making her shiver with pleasure. "The dress is definitely okay, but the contents are out of this world." Olivia fanned herself with her folded linen napkin. Listening to Daniel talking to her like this was causing her to become aroused, and the food hadn't even arrived yet. "Something wrong, sweet-heart?" he asked huskily.

She narrowed her eyes and shot him a look. "You know exactly what you're doing to me, so please stop. I want to enjoy my food without thinking about... *you know what.*"

He pulled her chair closer to him and took her face in his hands, kissing her gently. "I can't help it, kitten. I'm constantly aroused by you, so I think it's only fair you feel the same way."

The server arrived with their food, clearing her throat and look-ing a little embarrassed by their public display of affection. Brunch was amazing, and they shared each other's food, feeding each other, and raving about the wonderful flavours.

Once brunch was over, Daniel took her hand. "Let's look around the grounds." She was glad that she hadn't worn heels as they made their way across the long expanse of manicured lawn towards the edge of the cliff. She felt goosebumps on her arms from the stiff sea breeze, so he hugged her closer to him. As they reached the bound-ary of the grass, she realized there was a fence about three feet away from the steep drop off.

"Probably to stop drunken idiots from heading down the bank," Daniel said.

"Or clumsy ones" Olivia added, realizing she could fall into either of those categories. The view really was quite spectacular. Olivia felt like she was suspended above the ocean, looking down on it. There were several sailboats out in the bay and the wind was making them keel over towards the water. She realized there was a set of steps cut into the bank at the side of the property. She looked at Daniel hopefully, "Can we go down to the beach?"

He smiled at her expectant face. It was like the face of a child who had just asked for an ice cream. "Of course we can go down." He laughed. "Are you okay in those shoes or shall I carry you?"

She looked at him incredulously. "Daniel, I wouldn't let you carry me all the way down there. Put your testosterone away for a moment." And with that, she took off down the steps in front of him. She was glad of the handrail which she gripped all the way down to the bottom.

She gasped when she saw the small, white sandy beach at the bottom of the steps. It was the most beautiful little horseshoe-shaped bay. The wind didn't feel so chilly down on the beach and Olivia kicked off her shoes and stretched out on the sand, enjoying the warmth of the sun on her face. "I feel we're a little overdressed," he laughed.

"I don't care." Olivia grinned "I just want to feel the warm sand on my skin."

Daniel lay alongside her, staring down at her serene expression. "You really like the beach, don't you?" he said.

"I love it." She grinned. "I love the smell and the sounds of the waves and the feeling of the wind and the sun on my face. I can't think of anywhere more perfect." He stroked his finger around the outline of her face gently and bent over to kiss her softly on her lips.

"Don't get any ideas, Daniel." She giggled. "I think we are in full view of others."

He looked up to the top of the cliff where he could see other people relishing the view. "I'm just enjoying you," he whispered. He lay his head on her chest and listened to her heartbeat, slowing his own to match hers.

"I could fall asleep like this," she murmured, wrapping her arms around him.

They lay in silence for a while, feeling totally calm and rested. Eventually Daniel sat up slowly and sighed. "We have to get back, honey. I have to drive back to the city, and I don't want to leave it too late."

Olivia pulled a face. "Do we really have to? I want to stay here forever."

He stood up and put his hand out to help pull her up. She felt dizzy from laying in the sun, and she stumbled against his chest. He was ready to catch her and enveloped her in a warm hug. "I'm not that keen about heading home either, but I know I have a busy week ahead of me. It will still be here next weekend."

Once they reached the car, he ran a finger down her bare arm, making her shiver. She looked across at him, her green eyes turning dark with arousal. "I want you to make love to me one more time before we leave. I'm very keen to make up for lost time as you put it."

Grinning, he pulled out of the parking lot. "You are an insatiable minx. Tell me what vitamins you take because I think I need some if I'm going to keep up with you."

Pulling back into the cottage, they both raced inside, giggling, not making it any further than the hallway before he fell upon her. "I think this will do just fine," he said, then laughed.

An hour later, they were pulling onto the highway to head back to the city and their separate lives. It had been another blissful weekend and Olivia hummed softly to herself as they drove, holding

Daniel's free hand and gently tracing his knuckles. The unpleasant phone call she had received the previous week was now just a distant memory. Daniel was so sweet and attentive. She felt there was no way on earth he could be faking it.

She felt tired to the bone, but it was a blissful kind of tired. The kind you only felt after a day at the ocean. She remembered back to when she and Luca were kids and how she felt heading back to their rented cottage after spending all day on the beach.

She groaned as he pulled in behind her apartment block and helped her unload her things from the car. "Make sure you unpack right away." He smiled, stroking her face. "You look exhausted, baby." She nodded, allowing herself to be swept into a deep and lingering kiss. She felt as if a halo of joy surrounded her, and it resounded through her body with a magnetic energy.

22

Heading into her apartment, she flicked on the lights and dumped her bags on the floor. Daniel was right. She should unpack straight away, especially the food she'd brought home. She put things away in the kitchen, taking a moment to pour herself a glass of wine from the ever-present box on the countertop.

She took the duffel containing her clothes into the bedroom and scattered her clothes out on the bed. *Definitely laundry day tomorrow*, she thought grimly. She noticed a piece of parchment-coloured paper in her bag and, pulling it out, she realized something was written on it. It looked like a poetry card purchased from a gift store and she scrutinized it:

> I will wait for you in a place where
> the sea meets the sky.
> Where ocean waves swell against
> gentle white shores.
> Where the familiar path ends and
> the unknown begins.
> I will wait for you...

Olivia gasped at the beauty of the words. Daniel must have slipped it in her bag before they left; that was why he wanted her to unpack. She felt tears welling up in her eyes as she held the piece of parchment close to her chest. Rushing over to her purse, she grabbed her phone and sent a text.

Thank you for my poem. It's so beautiful, and I am unravelled by you once again. You never fail to amaze me.

Putting down her phone, she placed the poem on her nightstand, next to the bed. Within seconds, her phone buzzed in response.

It says it better than I ever could. My sweet Olivia. You have me completely under your spell. What's a man to do?

Just keep doing whatever it is you're doing. I'm overwhelmed–truly. Do I really have to wait a whole week before I see you again?

There was a pause for a while and Daniel did not respond immediately. Olivia was concerned she sounded too needy, but to be fair, he was also coming on pretty strong. She sat staring at her phone for several minutes before trundling off into the kitchen to pour herself another glass of wine. He was obviously considering his answer, and she certainly would not rush him. She sat down heavily on the couch and took a large gulp of pinot grigio. The warmth of the alcohol flooded through her body, and she rested her head back, breathing steadily. Suddenly her phone buzzed, and she grabbed it:

Olivia, you know we can't do that. I lose focus when I'm around you and I can't think straight. I love it, but I think it's best that we keep it like this for now. If you were around all week, I'd get nothing done and I really want to keep my finger on the pulse with the company. We're at an important stage in our development. Do you understand?

Olivia instantly felt guilty. He had just given her another amazing weekend and here she was, whining. Lots of couples managed long-distance relationships and didn't see each other for weeks. She only had to go for five days. It was just that she knew he was so close and her longing to be with him overwhelmed her. She typed out a quick response:

I'm sorry. I didn't mean to come on so strong. Thanks for the wonderful weekend. Sleep tight.

She put the phone down on the coffee table and went to sort out her laundry for the morning, but she hadn't crossed the living room before her phone rang; it was Daniel.

"I hope I didn't upset you, baby. Please understand it's not because I don't want to see you. I want that more than anything."

Olivia listened to his beautiful voice pleading with her and took a breath, trying to sound light. "Daniel, please don't worry. I'm fine–really. I know your business is important to you and I know I'm a big distraction."

He breathed a sigh of relief. "Thank you for being so understanding, honey. I know it must seem weird to you."

Olivia laughed. "Well, we've already established you're a horny bastard and a stalker, so I think I can deal with weird."

She could tell it relieved him to hear the humour in her voice and she vowed to not be so intense. They had a great thing going, and she didn't want to blow it by becoming too dependent on him. She knew guys hated that.

"As long as you're okay. You will tell me if you're not, won't you? Don't be afraid to talk to me, Olivia."

"I'm fine, Daniel. Now I have to go as I seem to have a lot of laundry to deal with. Mostly panties for some strange reason. Thanks for an amazing weekend." She hoped he felt reassured that she wasn't upset with him.

"Okay, I'll let you go and deal with those panties. Only problem is, now I'll be thinking about your panties all evening. I can see I won't sleep tonight."

Olivia laughed. "Good night. I'll speak to you soon."

She felt relieved that she had left things on a more even keel, and after she put a load of laundry on, she picked up the phone to catch up on her calls. She wanted to get the worst one out of the way first–Lottie. She knew Lottie was going to be suspicious, so she tried to think of a good excuse for why she had been unreachable all weekend. Not being able to think of anything, she dialled her number and hoped for the best. Luckily for Olivia, Lottie's family had booked a one-month break to the Caribbean, and she had decided to go with them, so she was full of her holiday plans and what she was going to wear. Olivia was relieved just to listen to her friend babbling on excitedly.

Lottie suddenly stopped short. "God, Olivia, I'm so sorry. I haven't even asked how your weekend was."

Olivia smiled. "Well, I've been pretty busy. I have to get those two guides finished so I really need to buckle down." She was happy with her answer. It was evasive enough without being too untruthful. She really was going to have to get her finger out and complete them.

"Well, you know what they say about all work and no play. Make sure you have some balance, darling." Olivia blushed, remembering just how much play she had got in that weekend. Lottie was going to be flying on Wednesday and busy shopping until then, so they wouldn't be seeing each other. When she hung up, Olivia breathed a sigh of relief. She loved Lottie, but she could be a little intrusive. Especially when she was trying to maintain a clandestine relationship.

Next, she called her parents and spoke to her mom. Rosa was feeling upbeat about her test results, which were due on Thursday. "I'm sure it's going to be nothing, darling. I feel great," she enthused. Olivia wasn't sure if it was for her benefit or if Rosa was just trying to boost her own confidence. She also got to speak to her dad, who seemed slightly more subdued than usual. She could hear the situation was stressing him out, but he clearly didn't want to let Rosa know. She felt so bad for them both. Waiting for the results must be the hardest thing. Rosa promised she would call on Thursday evening with the results, and they both called out, "I love you" before ending the call.

It was still only 8 p.m. and Olivia thought she would veg out in front of the TV for a while. She looked in the fridge and found some Swiss cheese to go with some crackers she had found. Taking her wine to the coffee table, she made herself comfy on the couch with a blanket. She had only been settled for 5 minutes when her phone rang. Cursing, she dashed to the kitchen to see who it was. Mark's name flashed on her call display. She thought for a moment and then answered the call. "Hi Mark, how are you?" she asked brightly.

"Olly! Babes, you're home. I'm so glad I caught you. How are you?"

It was surprisingly good to hear Mark's voice, and the softness and familiarity in his tone made her smile.

"I was wondering if I could come around to see you this week, maybe Wednesday evening?" he continued. "I could bring some Chinese food and a bottle of wine if you like?"

Olivia hesitated before responding. It would be nice to see him, but she wasn't sure about his motives. She knew for sure she didn't want him back, and she didn't want him to make a scene. She responded thoughtfully, "I'm happy for you to come around Mark, but I want you to know that we are not getting back together. That ship has sailed, I'm afraid."

He was silent for a moment and then he said, "Well, I'd still like to see you. I just feel we have unfinished business." She agreed, and they arranged he would arrive at six on Wednesday. *Perhaps we can just be friends*, she thought to herself as she slid back down onto the couch.

After she had spoken to Mark, she felt restless and thought about Daniel's revelation about his previous relationships. The idea that he had once been engaged made her insanely jealous, and she was desperate to know whom he had been engaged to. She fired up her laptop and did a few Google searches on Daniel. She felt guilty, but her curiosity was piqued, and she would not let this go.

Her first searches turned up some recent photos of Daniel at some charity functions, always with a different, beautiful woman. He looked amazing in a tux and her heart skipped a beat at the sight of him. At first, she thought she wouldn't uncover the mysterious fiancée, but going back to earlier entries, she suddenly found a photo of Daniel with a tall, stunning woman.

Olivia took a breath when she saw her. This was the kind of woman she would expect to see on Daniel Lane's arm. Her long, glossy black hair fell around her shoulders and her lips were parted to show off her perfect teeth and smiling scarlet mouth. She wore a fire engine red evening dress, and it reminded Olivia of Lottie's sense of impeccable style. The woman was holding Daniel's arm and leaning into him with an air of possession, and she was obviously comfortable in front of the cameras. Olivia read the caption underneath the photo: *Publisher Daniel Lane and his fiancé Serena Longthorne attend the annual Publisher's Gala Dinner.* The date of the article was three years ago, and she wondered how long ago they had split up.

Now that she had a name to work with, Olivia googled *Serena Longthorne*. She was obviously a barrister, and she found some articles relating to cases she had represented. *So, she's beautiful and smart and successful*, Olivia thought. She felt sick at the thought of this beautiful creature being part of Daniel's life. Her mind went back to the mysterious phone call. Was this the "she" the woman was referring to, and if so, what did she mean about her being back in the picture? "Why do you do this to yourself, Olivia Jefferson?" she yelled at no-one in particular. Having opened Pandora's Box, the contents could not be unseen. She slammed her laptop shut with a bang and headed to bed.

23

Olivia spent the next couple of days buried in her work. She was in a good mindset and stayed out of the fridge as much as possible. She set herself goals for her days and was thrilled when she achieved what she wanted to with her writing. Daniel called her in the evenings, although she was careful not to get too hot and heavy with him, despite his constant innuendos. Seeing the photos of Serena had given her the feeling that she needed to protect her heart a little.

When he called on Tuesday, she told him about Mark coming over on Wednesday evening. Daniel was quiet for a moment. "That's your ex, isn't it? Is there something I should know?"

Olivia laughed. "Keep your boxers on, Daniel. He's just coming over for a chat. I think he feels we have things we need to discuss."

She heard Daniel inhale. "He's going to try to win you back, baby. You better be prepared for that."

She snorted. "He can try all he likes. Unless hell freezes over, that's not happening."

"I'm concerned about your safety. Do you want me to come over and be with you while he's there?"

Olivia giggled. "And how am I going to introduce you two? *Mark, this is my secret boyfriend who no-one else knows about. Secret boyfriend, this is my ex-boyfriend.*"

Daniel laughed, but he didn't sound convinced. "Olivia, a lot of assaults on woman are carried out by people they know."

He was obviously concerned, so she tried to reassure him. "I honestly don't think Mark would do something like that, Daniel. He's the most innocuous person I know. He doesn't seem like the weirdo type. Don't worry about me; I'll be fine. I'll call you when he's gone and let you know how it went."

On Wednesday afternoon, when she returned from the library, Olivia cleaned up the apartment. She wanted to show Mark how great she was doing without him, and she didn't want to give him the satisfaction of walking into a pigsty. At 6 p.m. sharp, the house phone rang, and she spoke to Mark in the lobby before buzzing him in.

She had to admit he looked good. He'd obviously just gotten out of the shower and his blond, wavy hair hung over his chocolate brown eyes, giving him a hot surfer-boy vibe. He looked like he had made an effort with his appearance with clean jeans and a white short-sleeved shirt. His arms looked large and muscular, and she wondered if he had been working out more than usual. Olivia remembered how her heart had jumped the first time he had asked her out.

"Come on in," she said breezily, desperate to keep things light. He padded into the kitchen with familiarity and put the wine in the fridge and the food on the table. He'd clearly remembered how much she ate because he had brought a ton of food with him.

Turning around from the fridge, he looked at her appreciatively. "You look amazing, Olly. What have you done to yourself?" His pet name for her got her hackles up immediately.

"Mark. I think you should know that I have always hated you calling me Olly. You can call me Olivia, or Livvy, or even Liv, but please don't call me Olly anymore."

He looked astonished, like she had slapped him. "You never told me you hated it."

She smiled sympathetically at him. "I think I did. Maybe you just didn't hear it."

She grabbed plates from the kitchen and a couple of wine glasses she had bought recently. They spread out the food on the table and tucked in. "Would you like to watch TV?" she asked, "I'm sure I can find some sports match for you."

He shook his head. "I'm here to see you Oll—I mean Livvy." She shrugged and tucked into the Chow Mein.

"So, what have you been up to, babes? I've called you a few times, but you never seem to answer. Have you been avoiding me?"

Olivia felt her face redden when she thought about what she had been *up to*, so she did a fake cough to make it look like she was choking. Mark sat closer to her, rubbing her gently on the back and she instantly moved away from him.

"I've been busy," she said truthfully. "Lane & Associates have agreed to promote my travel guides and I'm working hard trying to finish the last two."

He looked genuinely impressed. "That's great, babes. You must be really stoked. I know how much you wanted them to be a success." She couldn't help grinning at him. He had known how frustrated she had been dealing with publishing houses and trying to just get her foot in the door.

"How about you? How is work going?"

He nodded, finishing a mouthful of fried rice. "It's going good. They're sending me out on different assignments, so I think it's going well." Olivia was genuinely pleased for him. Perhaps they could be friends. They certainly shared a lot of history.

He put down his chopsticks, and the elephant entered the room. "And how's your love life, Livvy? Anyone new on the horizon?" He asked the question casually, as if he was discussing the weather.

Olivia thought for a moment while she sucked up a noodle. "Actually, there is someone, but I don't want to talk about him. It's all a bit new and I haven't told anyone about him yet."

He looked at her suspiciously. "Not even Lottie?"

She shook her head. "Especially not Lottie. She's the biggest gossip in town."

He laughed. "So, a mystery man who no one knows about. Is he married by any chance?"

Olivia spluttered indignantly. "No Mark, he is *not* married. What kind of question is that? By the way, how's Kimberley? Are her tits a bit warmer now?"

He winced. "Well, I guess I deserved that. Kimberley and I aren't dating. We never were. I just got carried away that evening and I ended up losing the best thing that ever happened to me." He looked at Olivia with brown puppy dog eyes. She remembered he had a habit of doing that when he was in deep shit. She had forgiven him frequently when he used that trick, but it wouldn't work tonight. "I know I never told you before, but I love you babes. You know that don't you?"

Olivia stood up to put some distance between them. "You don't love me, Mark. You just think you do. I've found a different life now, and I don't want to go back to the old one. We've both grown up and we need to move on."

His eyes narrowed, and he looked at her sullenly. "So, what's this new guy got that I haven't?"

She was about to reply *"everything,"* but she thought that would be cruel, so she simply said, "He makes me feel special, like I'm the only person in the room. I don't have to compete with soccer or baseball or anything else. There's only me."

Once she had put it into words, she realized why Daniel was so special to her. No-one had ever treated her the way he did. Suddenly, she didn't want to be in the same room with Mark any longer.

"Thanks for bringing dinner, but I think you should go now. I've got a headache and I want to go to bed. Probably too much monosodium glutamate."

He smiled a slow, seductive smile. "I could come in and give you a massage. You always used to like that. That will get rid of your headache." He took a step towards her. She glanced around to see what she could grab to fend him off and her hands wrapped around the empty wine bottle.

"If you take one step closer, Mark Hazelton, I will hit you so hard you won't see straight for a week."

Instead of putting him off, her words only seemed to fire him up. "You always were fiery, babes. That always turned me on about you."

He stepped closer with a determined look on his face, and Olivia knew she had to think fast. In one quick movement, she vaulted over the couch and grabbed the house phone, calling for night security. Mark was almost on her when Bill answered. "Bill!" she screamed. "It's Olivia Jefferson. I need you up here now."

He snatched the phone away from her, throwing it onto the floor and grabbed her in his arms, pushing her into the wall and trying to press his lips against hers. She twisted herself around like a snake, trying to avoid his alcohol-laced breath. Mark was strong and she could feel his hands tightening his grip on her arms. He had a cruel expression on his face she had never seen before. She didn't recognize this Mark.

The loud knock on the door told her Bill had arrived, and she screamed, "Bill, help me!"

Suddenly the door flew open, and Daniel barrelled through the door with Bill close behind. Daniel grabbed a handful of Mark's hair and hauled him off Olivia, throwing him out the door and into the hallway with force. Olivia collapsed onto the floor, sobbing until she was pulled up into Daniel's arms, weeping hysterically.

Mark took one look at the fury in Daniel's eyes and realized it was time to give up. Bill had taken over and already had him in a tight arm lock. "You want me to call the cops, Ms. Jefferson?" he said, looking at her with concern.

She shook her head, unable to speak. "Then I will just dispose of this garbage outside," he said, preparing to frog march Mark out of the building.

Olivia managed to choke out a hurried thanks to Bill, and he proudly pulled himself up to his full height and smiled. "Glad to help, Ms. Jefferson. And I'm glad Mr. Lane was here to lend a hand." And with that, he bid her goodnight before escorting Mark to the elevator.

24

D aniel sat on the floor with Olivia, rocking her and speaking to her softly. "It's okay, baby, I'm here. No-one can hurt you now." Her arms were burning with pain where Mark had grabbed her, and she looked down to see new bruises emerging.

"Come on. Let's get you on the couch," Daniel whispered. He helped her to her feet and got her to lie down while he went to get some ice for her bruises. When he saw she was shaking, he grabbed the blanket from the back of the couch and wrapped it around her, snuggling up to get her warm. Holding her limp body to his chest, he stroked her back in a circular motion and after a while, she felt calm return to her body.

She looked up at him through tear-stained eyes. "I feel so stupid. You told me to be careful. I thought we could be friends." Her eyes flared with anger. "I thought I knew him, and he attacked me."

Daniel shook his head. "I blame myself. If I'd been here, it never would have happened."

She looked at him sadly. "You can't blame yourself, Daniel. If you and Bill hadn't come in when you did, I dread to think what would have happened. I would have just become another statistic like poor Georgie." Thinking about her friend brought tears to her eyes again, and she buried her face in her hands, sobbing. "I'm so stupid. So fucking stupid. The whole reason I wrote my guides was to help women to feel safe and not end up like Georgie and look what I did." She rambled on about Georgie's rape in Rome and how it had ruined her life.

Daniel straightened up, grabbing her hand. "I won't let you beat yourself up about this," he scolded. "I'm going to help you take a bath and then I'm going to put you to bed."

She heard him pad into the bathroom and turn on the taps. He returned shortly and took her gently by the hand, leading her into the bedroom. Sitting her on the edge of the bed, he helped her undress, tenderly stroking the emerging bruises on the tops of her arms with a sad expression. He helped her to the bathroom, and she realized he had found some of the expensive bubble bath she kept for special occasions. He had also lit the candle she kept on the side of the tub, and a soft glow flickered around the room.

"Okay, in you get, honey." He held her hand as she carefully lowered herself into the hot water. She laid her head back and closed her eyes, allowing her body to relax in the warm water.

He looked down at her and smiled. "Still hot as hell, Ms. Jefferson, even after a rough night."

She allowed herself a small laugh, which choked in her throat, and he bent down and kissed her forehead. "Will you be okay here for a moment?"

She looked panicked. "You're not leaving, are you?"

He shook his head. "No, darling, I'm not going anywhere. I just wanted to clean up the food on your table, so you don't have to face it tomorrow." His thoughtfulness brought a lump to her throat, and she let out a small sob. Stroking her face, he teased her, "Are you crying because you were hoping to finish the food later?"

She smiled and shook her head. "You're a good man, Daniel Lane. I don't know what I've done to deserve you, but I thank my lucky stars every day for you."

Daniel disappeared into the kitchen, and she could hear him shuffling food containers into a garbage bag he found. She was glad she had cleaned up the apartment that day and it hadn't been the unholy mess it normally was. He came in carrying a cup with a small amount of amber fluid and handed it to her to drink. "What's this?" she asked, looking at it suspiciously.

"Brandy. It will help with the shock." She knew she didn't have any brandy, and she wondered where he had magicked it up from. Drinking the hard liquor, she pulled a face and shuddered as it went down, but it soon filled her with a warmth which slowly flowed through her bloodstream.

He grabbed a towel from the rack and held it out for her. "Come on. I don't want you getting cold in there. Let's get you out." He wrapped her in the towel, rubbing her gently, taking care to avoid her sore arms. Leading her into the bedroom, he sat her on the bed.

"Now, Ms. Jefferson. What are you wearing to bed tonight?" Olivia pointed to her pillow, and underneath Daniel found the soft grey lounge set he had bought her a few weeks ago. "I recognize these," he said, his tone warm.

He helped her step into the pants and then pulled the camisole over her head. Pulling back the covers, he swung her legs around before covering her up with her duvet. He sat on the edge of the bed, stroking her hair and staring into her face. "How are you feeling, sweetheart?"

"A little better. I'm so glad you're here. Would you get into bed with me?"

He looked a little uncertain. "I'm not sure that would be a good idea."

She looked at him with pleading eyes. "Please, Daniel. I just want you to hold me."

He laughed softly. "The problem is, darling, I don't know if I *can* just hold you. You know what it's like with us and you've had a nasty scare." Looking at her sad eyes made him relent, and he silently stripped off his clothes down to his boxers. Climbing in beside her, he got her to face away from him and then spooned into her, holding her close. "How does that feel?" he asked huskily.

"It feels good. It feels really good," she mumbled sleepily.

Before long, he heard her breathing change and realized she'd fallen into a deep sleep. He snuggled closer to her, trying to adjust his erection so it wouldn't push into her. "For God's sakes, man, get a grip," he muttered to himself. Stroking her hair, he whispered in her ear, knowing she couldn't hear him. "Sleep tight, angel."

25

Olivia woke with a start in the middle of the night. The events of the previous evening came flooding back to her, and she sat up, rubbing her arms. Daniel was still beside her, sleeping soundly. She felt fully awake, so she grabbed her robe and padded into the kitchen to grab a glass of water. Sitting on the couch, she digested what had happened. A man who she had known and trusted had turned into a predator. She knew that had Daniel and Bill not arrived, he would have raped her. She knew that if she had reported the incident to the police, it would ruin him, but she didn't feel comfortable with the possibility that he might do it to someone else. She also knew she couldn't face the process involved if she reported it, and that made her feel like a coward. She tried to think back to the evening to see if anything she had done provoked him, but she just kept coming back to the fact that she never should have allowed him to come over.

She heard Daniel's soft footfalls approaching. "There you are sweetheart. You okay?"

She blinked up at him. "I'm fine. I was awake, and I didn't want to disturb you."

He came and sat beside her on the couch, wrapping his arms around her. "I don't mind being disturbed. That's why I'm here." He was silent for a moment and then he asked, "What's going on in that beautiful head of yours?"

She sighed. "Probably just the usual stuff. Did I provoke him? Should I report it? Why am I so stupid? That kind of thing."

He took her face in his hands. "Why are you so hard on yourself, Olivia? None of this was your fault."

"You knew this would happen, didn't you? Is that why you were here? How come you turned up at exactly the right time?"

Stroking her face, he smiled. "I'm afraid the little green monster came to visit me. I knew he was coming over tonight, and I didn't feel comfortable about it. Short answer is I was going crazy with jealousy. I came over and saw him arrive, and then I hung out with Bill for a while. I guess I just lucked out with the timing."

She smiled ruefully. "I'm very flattered I have that effect on you. But what I can't understand about Mark is that he spent six months acting like I hardly existed. I think he just didn't want someone else to have me. He went a little crazy when he found out I was seeing someone."

"Why do you find it so hard to believe that you're every man's dream? You're definitely my dream, although I have to say, my dreams have taken a bit of a filthy turn since I met you." He sat back, laughing quietly to himself.

She snuggled into his chest for a while and then she said, "Daniel, would you make love to me? Please?" The last word came out as a plea, and he looked into her eyes.

"I'm not sure it's a good idea, honey. You're still upset."

"I need that closeness, Daniel. I need you."

He took her hand and led her back to bed. Removing her camisole and pants, he gently lowered her onto her back. "If you need me to stop, you have to tell me, okay?"

She nodded and then added, "I never want you to stop, Daniel. Never."

He treated her so tenderly it felt like veneration. His soothing voice and caressing fingers chased away the horror of what might have been. Only when he was inside her and they were soaring together did things feel right again. As she exploded into orgasm, she felt like a phoenix rising out of the ashes. He had put it all right and set the world back on its axis again. She went back to sleep, murmuring his name, over and over like a prayer.

26

Olivia was aware that Daniel was getting dressed. She stirred and saw the sun streaming through the bedroom drapes. "What time is it?" she murmured sleepily.

"It's only 6 a.m., kitten. I have to go back to my place to get dressed for work. I'll fix you some coffee before I go. Will you be okay? Can I call someone to come and sit with you?"

Olivia shook her head and stretched. "I'm feeling much better." She smiled. "I'm going to be fine."

Daniel looked down at her, unconvinced. "When I get to the office, I'm going to contact the head of security for your building. I don't want anyone getting in who's not supposed to be here. You need to be safe in your home, Olivia."

She pulled herself out of bed and hugged him. "You don't need to do that, honestly. After what happened last night, there's no way they'll let Mark anywhere near the place."

Olivia pulled on her robe and padded into the kitchen to put on some coffee. When Daniel appeared behind her, kissing her neck, he was already dressed.

"I was going to do that for you," he complained.

"I often wondered what it was like getting up at this time of the day," Olivia joked. "Are you staying for coffee?"

Daniel looked pained. "I would love to, but I really need to get my ass into gear if I'm going to make my first meeting."

Olivia held up her index finger. "One minute. I'll make you one to go." She quickly grabbed a travel mug from the cabinet and made his coffee the way she knew he liked it. She grabbed him and kissed him passionately. "Thank you so much for what you did for me yesterday. You saved me when I needed you most. I still can't believe you came charging in my door the way you did."

Daniel laughed. "I have to admit, the look on his face was priceless." His expression grew serious. "I will always be there when you need me. You're stuck with me; you know that don't you?"

Olivia stroked her finger around the outline of his face. "I am very glad to hear that. Now, go to work; I don't want you to be late because of me." He dipped her down, kissing and tickling her, and then headed out the door.

She heard the elevator arrive, and then there was silence. It was a silence that thrummed through her body and was almost deafening, making her eardrums pound. She was too awake to go back to bed, so she headed off to find her iPod and her laptop.

In the bedroom, she saw the poem that Daniel had given her. Picking it up, she traced the words with her finger, smiling to herself. She knew in that moment that she had fallen in love with him, and she felt a shiver run through her body. It was a scary thought. She had only known him for a few weeks, and yet, it sometimes felt they had been together for a lifetime. She thought about the beautiful woman in the photograph on Daniel's arm and looked at herself in her mirror. There were dark circles under her eyes, and her thick hair was sticking up like an unwieldy haystack. "I hope he's not just dicking you around, girl," she said to her reflection.

....

Olivia felt like she was on a roll with her writing and the morning went by quickly. It was only when her stomach rumbled that she realized it was lunchtime, so she closed her laptop and headed to the kitchen to make a sandwich. Hearing her phone ringing from the bedroom, she dashed across the floor to answer it. She was surprised that it was her mom, as she wasn't expecting to hear from her until tomorrow.

"Olivia, it's Mama. How are you precious girl?" Her mom's voice sounded weak and distant.

"Mama, what's wrong?"

Her mother sounded like she was choking back tears. "The results came back today, Olivia. I have cancer." Olivia could hear her mother sobbing quietly. Feeling all the blood drain out of her face, she sank to the floor. She knew it wasn't the time to fall apart, so she took a deep breath, trying to suppress her own feelings.

"Mama, tell me what the doctor said."

Rosa tried to compose herself. "There are a couple of options. I can have something called a lumpectomy or I can have a mastectomy. Dr. Johnson thinks it will be safer all round if I go for the mastectomy, so that's what I'm going to do."

Olivia drew in a breath, thinking of her beautiful, proud mama. *This must be killing her*, she thought. She knew immediately what she had to do.

"Mama, can you get my room ready? I'm coming home for a while."

Her mother protested wildly. "Absolutely not, Olivia. You have your own life to lead. I am going to be fine."

Olivia was resolute. It was her turn to be strong. "I don't care what you say, Mama. I'm getting the first train out of here. I should be home by this evening."

After she put the phone down, she allowed the tears to fall. She wrapped her arms around her knees, sobbing until her ribcage hurt. The unfairness of it all made her angry and sad. Her mother had always taken such good care of herself. How the hell had this happened? She knew she had to phone her brother, so she pulled herself together and dialled his number.

"Hey sis, what's happening?" Luca's familiar voice felt like a warm hug. She couldn't say much, so she kept it brief.

"Mama has cancer, Luca. I'm heading home. I'm going to the station now."

She heard her brother's voice crack. "Oh, no, no, no. Not Mama. No." Luca rarely showed emotion, and his words drilled into her heart. She wished he were there with her so they could hold on to each other and rage together at the injustice.

Throwing some clothes into her small carry-on case, she quickly texted Daniel so he would know where she was:

Just had some bad news. Have to go home to be with Mama for a while. This is my address...

Once she was safely on the train, she checked her phone, seeing there were two messages. There was a text from Luca saying he was also heading home at the weekend, and a text from Daniel:

Sweetheart, I am so sorry. I'm not sure what's happening, but I wish I could be with you to hold you. You must be going through hell. Please let me know when you get there safely.

The train journey was only a couple of hours, but it seemed to last a lifetime. Olivia had packed a couple of chocolate bars, which she ate as she watched the time tick slowly away. She texted her dad to let him know what time the train would be in, and he promised to pick her up from the station. She thought about the cancer that had been growing away silently in her mother's beautiful body, like a sinister and uninvited stranger who refused to leave. Her thoughts turned to her father and how he must be feeling. The thought made her shiver a little, and she pulled her coat closer around herself to chase away the chills.

As the train pulled into the station, she quickly texted Daniel:

Train just pulling in. I can see Daddy on the platform. I'll speak to you later.

She climbed off the train awkwardly, pulling her bag behind her. Looking at her father's face at a distance told her everything she needed to know. His normally tanned face was ashen white, and his sparkling green eyes were dark with stress. Catching sight of her, he rushed across the platform and threw his arms around her. He didn't speak, but she could feel him sobbing into her shoulder like a child. Eventually he found his voice.

"What am I going to do, Olivia? She's my life."

Olivia summoned the strength that she knew her dad needed. "Dad, you cannot fall apart. She needs you right now and you're going to have to be strong for her; we all will. You need to be positive and not think the worst. This is not a death sentence."

He calmed and looked into his daughter's eyes. "I always thought you were like me, Olivia," he whispered, "but you are much stronger. You are just like your mother. I never realized." He shook his head as if this new insight confounded him.

Hand in hand, they walked to the car and her dad loaded her case in the trunk. On the way back to the house, she pressed him for as much information as possible. Things were obviously moving rapidly, thanks to Rosa's determined specialist, who was pulling strings to get her procedure as soon as possible. It seemed likely that the surgery would take place some time the following week, and that Rosa would just be in the hospital overnight before being discharged. There would then be tests to see if the cancer had been completely removed and possibly follow-up treatments after that. Olivia had done lots of research since her last meeting with Rosa, and she knew they were all facing a long road ahead, but she also knew how important it was to be positive and optimistic. Negativity would help no one, particularly Rosa.

Pretty soon, they were pulling up at Olivia's childhood home. Her heart skipped a beat as she saw her family home again. The house was painted a sunny yellow with bright blue shutters. A colourful sea of flowers bloomed in the front garden behind the white picket fence. Her mom saw the car pulling up outside and came to the doorway to greet her. She covered her with kisses, telling her in Italian that she shouldn't have come and that she was okay.

"Well, I'm here now," Olivia said grimly, "and I'm starving. So, what's for dinner?" It was just the thing Rosa needed to hear, and she clapped her hands and headed to the kitchen. Her daughter was home for her to feed and care for, and her problems were about to take second place.

After dinner, Olivia headed to her room to unpack and to hopefully give Daniel a quiet call. She didn't want her parents to know about her relationship, especially not while there was so much else to worry about, so she wanted to keep it to herself. Walking into her old bedroom, she hugged herself. Her room had a view of the leafy street outside, including a streetlamp that she could use to read by, long after she was supposed to be sleeping. Her room had changed very little, although her dad had given it a fresh coat of blue paint a couple of years ago. This was the room where she had discovered great works of literature, spending hours tucked away, reading. It was also where she came to escape from Rosa when they had another of their epic fights. Her dad was right; she and Rosa were similar in a lot of ways. She called Daniel's number and was relieved when he answered.

"Sweetheart, how are you? I've been so worried about you."

Olivia told him the circumstances of the day and he listened carefully. Just having him on the phone made her feel calmer and more focused. "I'm going to be here a while" she told him. "I don't want to come back until after Mama's surgery. It will be a couple of weeks; they need me right now."

She heard Daniel inhale deeply. "I understand, honey. I'm just going to miss you so much. What am I going to do without you?"

She giggled. "Well, I guess you could think about all the ways we are going to make up for lost time when I come back."

"I don't think that's a good idea." he teased. "I'll be in that cold shower permanently." His voice became serious. "You know, if you need me, I'll take a few days off and come and stay in a hotel close by. Just if you need my support." Olivia was touched by his thoughtfulness.

"I'm okay right now and my brother Luca will be here over the weekend. Family life is about to get interesting again." She laughed. "My parents will be glad to see the back of us when we go."

27

The next couple of days plodded by in a strange new reality. There were lots of phone calls from the doctor and the hospital, arranging appointments for Rosa. They had her scheduled to come in for her surgery on the following Wednesday, and Olivia took her in for all her pre-op checks on Friday. That evening, Luca arrived home to much excitement from Rosa.

"Ah, Mama's beautiful boy is home," Olivia teased. It surprised her when Luca took her in his arms for a big bear hug. He seemed reluctant to let her go and buried his face in her neck. She held him away from her and looked at his face. He was looking tired and was clearly taking Rosa's diagnosis badly.

They all sat down for dinner for the first time since last Christmas and the noise level rose, as it always did when they were all in the house together.

"Why didn't you bring Molly?" Olivia asked Luca.

"She has a shoot this weekend," he replied. "Swimwear." Luca had the good fortune of being engaged to a rather beautiful underwear model. Olivia loved Molly because she was so uncomplicated. She reminded Olivia of a bouncy Golden Retriever, always seeing the best in people and ready for fun. She had blonde beach waves and a figure to die for, and she had captured Luca's heart the first time he laid eyes on her.

Looking at Luca, Olivia could see the attraction. When they were growing up, the few friends she had always came around to her house to swoon over Luca. He looked like Rosa, tall with dark eyes and dark curls. He dressed in skin-tight jeans and t-shirts and would have fitted in well drinking coffee in any piazza in Rome.

After dinner, Rosa put on *The Marriage of Figaro* to listen to, and she insisted they all play cards. It thrilled her to have her entire family around the table, and Olivia thought it was probably the best

199

medicine she could have. Even her dad had relaxed, and he was looking more like his old self again. Olivia remembered how tense it had been in their house in the past, when Rosa was angry with her or Luca, or both of them at once. When she had left for college, she couldn't wait to get away, but now she felt she needed to spend more time at home again.

On Saturday morning, there was a knock on the door and Olivia shouted for Luca to open it. He came back clutching an enormous bouquet of white roses with a huge, smug grin on his face. "Well, Liv. It's hard to believe, but I think someone has the hots for you." He tried to make a grab for the card, but Olivia was too fast for him, and she grabbed it first, plunging it into the back pocket of her jeans. Luca called to their mom in a sing-song voice.

"Mama, Livvy has a secret admirer."

Olivia stuck out her tongue at him and took the roses to the kitchen to find a vase. Her mother looked at her with a knowing smile. "Are we going to find out who sent you these beautiful flowers?" she asked. Olivia said nothing, smiling secretly to herself. "I wonder if they are from Mr. Lane?" Rosa added.

Olivia looked at her, shocked. "Mama, how did you know?" Her mother looked like the cat who got the cream.

"I know men, Olivia. When that man looked at you–I knew!" Olivia blushed, trying to hide behind the roses as she put them in water.

"It's nothing, Mama. Really."

Her mother snorted. "A hundred bucks worth of roses plus delivery is not *nothing* child. He has it bad for you. Mark my words."

Olivia disappeared up to her room to read the card that came with them. It was cryptic; a YouTube link, then signed "SEH" with a bunch of kisses. He was trying to be discreet but had failed miserably because of her nosy Italian family. She grabbed her laptop and put the link into the search:

Richard Marks–Right Here Waiting for You.

Olivia listened to the song and read the lyrics and immediately saw the meaning behind the cryptic note. It was Saturday of course, and they would normally be at the beach cottage. She wondered if he had gone down to the cottage on his own as she dialled his number.

He immediately picked up and said hurriedly, "Hang on a minute, baby."

She heard his footsteps go, and then music starting, and then, she heard him *singing*. Richard Marx and Daniel made it all the way through the first verse and refrain before he headed back to the phone. He had a great singing voice, which didn't surprise her as he seemed to be good at everything.

Olivia was laughing through her tears. "You are a romantic fool. What is it with you and these ancient songs? It is seriously disturbing."

"The old ones say it the best." he laughed.

"Thank you for the beautiful roses. Mama knew immediately you had sent them. How do you think she knew?"

Daniel thought for a moment. "Your mom is a wise woman, Olivia. I guess I must have given it away that day we bumped into each other. How are things going?" Olivia updated him on all the news and told him about Rosa's surgery the following Wednesday. She told him that Luca had taken some time off work and was going to be staying as well. "That's great, honey. Your mom must be thrilled to have you all together at a time like this."

"Are you at the cottage?" she asked quietly. She wasn't sure how she felt about him being there on his own. At least she hoped to God he *was* on his own. She shook her head and told herself to stop being so ridiculous. It was his place, and it was only right he should spend the weekend there.

"I'm here, but I'm not sure if I'm going to stay over. It just doesn't feel right without you here, angel. I miss you so much."

Olivia felt reassured. "Well, hopefully it won't be too long before I can come back. Probably not next weekend. We must see how Mama does with the surgery."

Daniel sighed. "Take all the time you need, darling. I can't be selfish at a time like this."

Olivia hung up and headed back downstairs. Luca was leaning against the wall with a stupid smirk on his face.

"Did you thank lover boy for the roses?" He made kissy noises with his mouth, so Olivia smacked him across the back of the head as she went by. He chased her, screaming into the kitchen, where her mother swore in Italian.

"Mamma Mia! When are you two going to grow up?" she exclaimed.

Luca put his arm around Olivia's shoulder and kissed her affectionately on the top of the head. "We're fine, Mama. We're just having fun." Rosa smiled at the unfamiliar warmth between the two siblings. All those years of discord and fighting and finally things seemed to be settling down between them.

28

The days dragged by in the Jefferson household. As they got closer to Rosa's surgery date, things became more tense. Olivia's dad took to going out for long walks. *Typical male avoidance*, she thought. She knew it was eating away at him, and sometimes it seemed he couldn't bear to look at her mom without getting emotional. In contrast, Rosa seemed resigned to her fate and had accepted everything with her typical stoicism. On Wednesday morning, Olivia would not allow her father to drive Rosa to the hospital.

"You'll fuss too much, Dad. She doesn't need that," she had told him the night before.

Rosa and Olivia set out early as Rosa had to check in at 7:15 a.m. After they had taken all her details, she wanted Olivia to leave.

"You can't do anything now, child. Please go and come back later."

Reluctantly, Olivia walked out of the hospital into the bright sunshine. Birds were singing and the early morning traffic trundled along the highway as people headed to work. It amazed her how everything seemed to continue as normal whilst her world felt like someone had turned it upside down. She was determined to be there later when her mom woke up, but the nurse had told her to not come back until at least 1 p.m.

It felt so strange to be back in her hometown again and walking down to the corner Starbucks brought back lots of memories. She ordered a latte and a chocolate croissant and sat down at a corner table. Looking at her watch, she realized it was 8:30, and she wondered if Daniel was in the office yet. Sipping her coffee, she shot him a quick text.

Good morning, beautiful. Sitting in Starbucks, thinking of you. Mama is under the knife. All I can do is wait. I miss you so much.

Her phone rang and when she answered it, the sound of Daniel's husky voice made her want to cry.

"Hey, sweetheart. How are you holding up?"

Olivia had been trying to hold it together for her mom, but now she was alone, she just wanted to break down. She was aware she was in a public place, so she turned her back to the other people in the coffee shop. "I'm okay." She sniffed. "I just wish you were here to hold me. It's so hard being strong for everyone, Daniel."

"You've been amazing, darling. You're such a brave girl. I could be with you in a couple of hours if you need me."

Olivia shook her head and blew her nose. "No, you need to work. I have to go back to the hospital at one and see if she's back. Luca and Dad are coming in later." Olivia watched a young mother walk along the sidewalk outside the coffee shop, holding her young daughter's hand. They were looking at each other and smiling in mutual adoration. Her heart broke. Daniel could not see this scene being played out in front of her eyes, and he kept speaking gently to her.

"I've been putting in a lot of hours in while you've been gone, darling. I thought maybe we could take off for few days when you get back. What do you think?"

The thought of spending time with Daniel alone lifted her spirits. "That sounds lovely. I'd really like that."

He sounded happy. "Great! When you're back, we will plan to do that. I can't wait."

She finished her coffee and headed back out towards the town centre and one of her favourite places from her childhood—the town library. Walking through the heavy double doors, the familiar smell took her back to the hours she had spent there, curled up with a book. While other girls her age were swimming or riding horses, Olivia was discovering the wonders of Jane Austen and Emily Bronte.

The library was a beautiful heritage building which had once been the town post office. Inside, it was painted a muted green, and comfortable brown leather chairs were arranged in seating groups throughout the main floor. When Olivia was a teenager, the librarian had befriended her. Hettie Clark had been a stylish woman, small and slight with a silver-grey bun and black cat's eye spectacles. She always wore pencils skirts with cashmere sweaters with pearls, giving her the appearance of a chic Parisienne.

Hettie and Olivia would camp out in her office, drinking copious amounts of tea and munching away on chocolate digestive cookies. Olivia had been going through a troubled period in her life, and her fights with Rosa were legendary. The library was a place of refuge for her, and Hettie always seemed to know what to say. She also guided Olivia's reading choices, introducing her to the classics, but also to contemporary material that spoke to her differently. Hettie was one reason Olivia had pursued a journalism degree. Olivia didn't think she could still be working there, but she wanted to check, just in case.

Approaching the librarian's office, she couldn't believe her luck. Sitting behind the desk squinting at the computer screen was Hettie Clark, looking slightly older, but very much the same as Olivia had remembered her. Olivia knocked on the door with a big smile on her face.

"Hettie! Do you remember me?"

The older woman looked up and gasped with pleasure. "Olivia Jefferson as I live and breathe! I don't believe it!" Olivia embraced her warmly and Hettie led her over to a group of leather chairs so they could sit and chat. "I'm going to brew up some tea. This calls for a celebration. I'm sure I have a new pack of chocolate digestives somewhere." Handing Olivia a mug of steaming hot tea, Hettie settled into a chair. She looked a little comical as her feet didn't quite touch the floor.

"You know, I often think about you, Olivia, and wonder what you're up to. You were such a confused little thing, but my, have you ever grown into a beautiful young woman? You have become the swan, my dear." Hettie giggled in delight.

Olivia told her all about university and her desire to be an author, and her guidebooks, and about her part-time job at the library. Hettie clapped her hands in delight. "I knew it! I knew you were destined for great things! As soon as your books are ready, I want several for the library and we can do an author's feature on you. Maybe you could come down and give a talk. People always love to hear about local talent." Olivia grinned at her enthusiasm. She really hadn't changed in all those years. Talking to Hettie really lifted Olivia's spirits.

Olivia told Hettie about her mom, and Hettie grimaced sympathetically with her hand on her heart. "Don't worry, Olivia. There are lots of survivors out there. I'm one of them."

Olivia was shocked. "Really?"

Hettie nodded. "Five years ago. I thought my world was falling apart at the time, but I came out the other side and I'm still here, kicking the mister's ass." Hettie was referring to her husband, Frank. "Your mother has a journey ahead of her. She's lucky she has you. If she needs someone to talk to, tell her I'd be happy to have a cup of tea with her anytime." Olivia was grateful for her kindness and grasped her hand.

The hours flew by as she was catching up with Hettie and Olivia was shocked when she looked at the clock and realized it was 12:30. She hugged Hettie and said goodbye, promising to let her know as soon as her books were launched. Heading down the library steps, she turned onto the main street and headed back to the hospital. She thought about picking up some lunch on the way, but she really didn't feel hungry. *Must be the first time ever*, she thought grimly.

29

Walking into her mom's hospital room, Olivia was shocked. Her mom, who was normally a force to be reckoned with, looked so small in the hospital bed. She was hooked up to lots of monitoring equipment and she hadn't fully woken up yet. Olivia pulled up a chair next to her bed and reached for her hand. She had been raised as a Catholic, but never really had a lot of time for the church. However, praying seemed like the right thing to do at this moment, so she closed her eyes and silently pleaded for God to restore her mom to health. When she looked up, blinking away tears, her mother was looking at her drowsily.

"Olivia," she whispered hoarsely. "I'm so thirsty." Olivia called for the nurse, who brought some ice chips for her mom to suck on.

Throughout the afternoon, her mom drifted in and out of sleep with the nurse coming in regularly to check on her and top up her pain meds. At four o'clock, Luca and her dad arrived, carrying brightly coloured helium-filled balloons and flowers. Her dad blanched when he saw Rosa, but Olivia shot him a warning look to pull himself together. Having everyone in the room seemed to bring Rosa back to full consciousness, and the nurse carefully sat her up, so she could talk to everyone.

"Now, you are not to stay too long," she reproached. "She needs plenty of rest if she is going to go home tomorrow."

After an hour, it was clear that Rosa had had enough, and she was looking tired, so the nurse asked everyone to leave. Olivia spoke to her mom before she went. "Are you okay for me to go, Mama? I could stay, you know."

Her mother smiled weakly. "Yes, darling. Go on home and feed your father and your brother. I've left plenty of food in the fridge for everyone. I will be ready and waiting for you tomorrow." Olivia kissed her gently on the forehead and headed out with Luca and her dad.

When they got home, the house felt empty without Rosa's presence. It was so obvious that her fiery passion gave their home its flavour; for better or worse. Olivia busied herself in the kitchen and Luca came in to lend a hand, chopping up the salad. When she looked over at him, she saw his shoulders were heaving with big, silent sobs. She walked across to him and took him in her arms, running her fingers through his thick dark curls.

"Luca Jefferson, you are one big softie," she whispered. "Mama is going to be fine. We are all going to be fine. Have faith, Luca."

He grabbed a piece of paper towel and wiped his eyes. He looked down at her with a look of amazement. "I never realized it before, Liv. You're really just a blonde, pint-sized version of Mama. That's probably why you two found it so hard to get along."

Olivia smiled ruefully. "Well, I'm hoping that's all behind us now, Luca. Now come on, finish that salad, or we'll never eat," she chided.

Sitting around the table, it was clear that Olivia's dad was struggling with his emotions. She insisted on putting on some of her mom's music and suggested that they all play cards. She knew she was putting on a brave face and trying to keep everyone afloat, and she also knew that's what her mom would want. She kept her dad busy, giving him a job while clearing the table and making him dry the dishes while Luca washed. *We just need to keep jumping over the hurdles*, she thought to herself.

At ten the next morning, she headed back to the hospital to collect Rosa. When she entered the room, it thrilled her to see her mom sitting in a chair and looking much better. Rosa had even applied some makeup, and she was looking much more like her regular self. Olivia walked over and kissed her mom on the cheek, afraid to hug her in case she hurt her. The nurse went through all the at-home instructions for the drain and wound care and went through the meds with Rosa and Olivia. Rosa's doctor stopped by before she left and told her how well she had done and that things looked great. He would see her later in the week to follow up.

Rosa took Olivia's arm, and they slowly made their way out of the hospital into the bright sunshine. Rosa smiled as the sunlight hit her face. "Well, I'm so happy to be seeing the back of that place!" She laughed with relief. Olivia carefully helped her into the car, and they set out for home.

When they walked in, Luca and Greg had put up a 'welcome home' sign and they'd filled the house with flowers and Rosa's favourite music. Luca and Greg both looked very pleased with themselves, and Rosa looked a little taken aback. "Oh, you shouldn't fuss," she grumbled, but she was obviously pleased and happy to be home.

Olivia took over the cooking for the next several days whilst her dad fussed over her mom, driving her to distraction. Olivia smiled as she heard her cursing at him in Italian. She was obviously on the mend.

On Saturday, Luca decided it was time to go home to Molly, happy that his mom was in safe hands. He hugged everyone and said to Olivia, "I expect to see more of you from now on. Promise me. We're only half an hour away from you."

Olivia agreed and hugged him tight. She felt for the first time in her life that she had a brother she could genuinely love, and she was looking forward to building a new relationship with him.

On Wednesday morning, Olivia was up making breakfast, and her mother wandered into the kitchen. She was looking so much better. The colour had returned to her cheeks, and she was moving about without that pained expression on her face.

Olivia put her breakfast down at the table, but Rosa didn't sit right away. Walking over to Olivia, she held her face in her hands and kissed her on the forehead. "It's time for you to go back to your life, my darling. You have been amazing, and I will always love you for what you have done, but it's time for Daddy and me to start living our new normal. I will be fine now."

Olivia looked at her doubtfully. "I'm happy to stay, Mama. Really."

Rosa shook her head. "I'm kicking you out, child. Go back to your Mr. Lane and live it up." Looking into her mother's face, Olivia realized she was right. Her mom and dad were going to be fine, and it was time to give them some space to work it all out. They had weathered the storm as a family, and Olivia was so glad she had made the time to do it.

By mid-morning Olivia was heading to the station with her dad. He was almost back to his old self, and they spent a much happier journey than when she arrived a couple weeks ago. Greg Jefferson wheeled his daughter's case onto the platform and waited with her for the train to arrive. He hugged her close to his chest. "I can't tell you how proud I am of you, Olivia. For the past two weeks, you've held us all together. You're an amazing girl; your mom and I love you so much, sweetheart."

Olivia waved to her dad from the train and settled into her seat for the journey. She picked up her phone to let Daniel know she was on her way, but she changed her mind. Smiling to herself, she thought about keeping it as a surprise. She would wait until she got back to the city and then come up with a plan to spring it on him.

She watched the elderly man on the seat opposite her put his newspaper down on the table between them. "Do you mind if I read it?" she asked.

The man shook his head. "You go ahead, my dear. I'm finished with it. Not much news today."

She flicked through the paper and had to agree that he was right. There didn't seem to be much going on. As she turned over to page six, she froze at the headline: *Double Dating Daniel*. Under the banner were two photographs. One was undoubtedly a picture of Daniel kissing her before they got into his car the previous weekend. All you could see of Olivia was her back, but anyone who knew her would instantly know it was her. It was a great shot of Daniel as he bent down to kiss her. The caption read: *Daniel Lane getting hot and heavy with a mystery blonde.*

It was, however, the second photo that made her blood run cold. A picture of Daniel looking devastating in a tux beside a beautiful and instantly recognizable woman. The caption read, *And for his second conquest this week, Daniel Lane was seen leaving the Annual Spring Fling with barrister Serena Longthorne.* The event had obviously been held the day prior, but he hadn't mentioned it to her. Daniel was walking with his head down and Serena was walking beside him, looking directly at the camera with an alluring smile.

Olivia felt the colour drain from her face and she was afraid she might throw up. She tried to remain calm and told herself there had to be a logical explanation for all this. Picking up her phone, she tried to call him, but his phone was going straight to voicemail. There seemed little point in leaving a message. This was something she needed to talk to him about in person, and she needed to see his face when she did. Tearing the page out of the paper, she shoved it into her bag, out of sight, and rubbed the pain in her chest, trying to think about something positive. He had been so sweet and supportive while she had been away. It seemed impossible that he had been carrying on behind her back.

No matter how she reasoned the situation, the voice in the back of her head that she had been trying to ignore since she met Daniel was now yelling in her ear. He was an accomplished player. By his own admittance, it was a lifestyle he had perfected for a long time. It made no sense that he should suddenly change his ways and become someone else, particularly for her. It was obvious that she was no match for the likes of Serena Longthorne. Perhaps she had been right all along. She was just an amusing distraction. What was the saying—a change is as good as a rest? Well, she had certainly been a change for him.

Outside the station, Olivia grabbed a cab and headed back to her apartment. It felt strange walking into the place. It smelled different; not like home at all. She felt flat and lonely, so she put on some music and brewed a pot of coffee. She decided she would try to see Daniel at his apartment that evening. She would leave it until around six, and then hopefully he would be back from the office.

She looked through her closet for something to wear, realising she needed some power dressing, and noticed a dress that she had bought on her shopping trip with her mom. She hadn't had a chance to wear it and it seemed a little formal for her, but tonight would be the perfect opportunity. It was not something she would have picked out herself, but her mother was adamant she should have it. The green V-neck sheath dress hugged her curves perfectly, ending at her knees. The green picked up the colour of her eyes and suited her colouring impeccably.

Later in the evening, as she dressed, she felt like she had a lead weight in her stomach. This should have been a joyous homecoming, a celebration, but instead she was going to see him with a feeling of dread, afraid of what she might discover. She hadn't seen Daniel in over two weeks, and although there had been regular texts and calls, it felt like there was distance between them. With everything that had been going on, it was as if there had somehow been a shift in the universe. Things felt different, but she wasn't sure why. Maybe now she knew the answer to that question. Added to that, she wasn't sure how she would get into his apartment building, but she figured if she couldn't, she would just call him from outside.

She took a cab across town and sighed at the familiar sight of his building. Remembering that glorious lunch hour they had spent together the last time she was at the publishing house, she almost cried.

As she was approaching the building, a young man was entering at the same time. She figured honesty was the best policy, so she approached him. He smiled at Olivia, his eyes running over her appreciatively.

"I'm sorry to bother you," she began, "but my boyfriend lives in this building, and I want to surprise him. I wonder if you would help me get into the elevator."

He cocked his head to one side and looked at her. "Well, I guess it wouldn't hurt. You look too cute to be a master criminal."

Olivia blushed at his compliment and thanked him profusely. They got in the elevator together and Olivia pushed the button for the twelfth floor. The young man got off at the sixth and turned back to her as he was leaving with a smile.

"You know if things don't work out with your boyfriend, I live in 612. Just come down and knock." She smiled sheepishly at him and thanked him for his kindness.

Getting off at the twelfth floor, Olivia recognized the layout immediately. She headed down to Daniel's apartment and nervously knocked on the door, smoothing down her dress. After a couple of minutes, a beautiful woman in a white bathrobe opened the door. Her skin looked damp from the shower and her long black hair hung down in beautiful waves onto her shoulders. Olivia could hear soft jazz playing in the background. She recognized her instantly; it was Serena Longthorne.

Serena looked quizzically at Olivia, but when she failed to speak, she spoke for her. "I guess you're here to see Daniel?" Olivia nodded dumbly. "He's just gone out to buy some more wine. I expect he'll be back soon."

Olivia felt the elegant woman look her up and down and then she smiled seductively and said, "I'm sure Daniel would want you to join us. Please come in and wait."

Looking down at Serena's beautifully manicured hands, Olivia noticed a large diamond ring sparkling in the light. Shaking her head, she backed away from the door, feeling the colour drain from her face. Everything suddenly became very clear to her. "No. It's okay. Thank you." She turned on her heel and rushed back towards the elevator, tears pricking in her eyes. She held onto the handrail in the elevator, feeling like her knees would give way beneath her. Hurrying out onto the street, she gulped in large breaths of air, trying to steady herself. Hailing a cab, she collapsed onto the back seat and sobbed her heart out. "I'm so sorry," she said to the driver between her sobs.

"Don't worry, love. I've had them all in here. Some laugh, some cry. I just drive."

She asked the driver to drop her at the back of her building as she couldn't face running into any of her neighbours in the lobby, so she got in the elevator in the parkade. Entering her apartment, she dropped to her knees and wept. That was what the weekend arrangement had been all about. The nagging doubt that had been in the back of her head all along had materialized. He had been maintaining both of them very cleverly. She wondered if Serena was aware of the arrangement, or if she was also being fooled. Maybe this was a regular occurrence, and it was just something she tolerated. She had just been the next brief fling he needed to get out of his system.

Suddenly she was overwhelmed by the need to get as far away as possible. She dragged herself to her feet and flipped open her laptop. Luckily, she hadn't touched the advance she'd received from the publishing house. Looking at a website, she took out her phone and dialled the number. "Hello. I want to book a flight to Florence. I want to leave tomorrow morning if possible. No, I just need a one-way ticket, please. I'm going to need a hotel as well."

Once everything had been arranged, she picked up her phone again and called her brother. She noticed that she had a text from Daniel, but she deleted it without reading it and blocked his number.

She knew if she spoke to him, she would fall apart, and she didn't want that. "Luca, it's Livvy. I need your help."

Luca was surprised to hear from her so soon. "My baby sis! What's up, Livvy?"

"You're not going to like it, Luca. I need to ask a big favour." Through sobs, Olivia asked if she could stay with him and Molly for the night and if he would drive her to the airport in the morning.

"What is going on, Olivia?" he asked sharply, but she just assured him she would tell him in the car. He hesitated for a moment, and then said, "I'm on my way. I'll be at the back of your building in half an hour." Somehow Olivia knew he would come through for her when things got rough.

Grabbing her passport, she hurriedly packed some things in her carry-on case that she had only unpacked that afternoon. She was determined to travel light. This would be the ideal opportunity for her to do some research for her next guide, and it would put some safe distance between her and Daniel Lane. Maybe if she got far enough away, she could think more clearly. It was her fault, of course. If she had seen it for what it was and hadn't fallen in love with him, she wouldn't be in this mess now. Her own stupidity was coming back to bite her on the ass yet again.

Luca was true to his word and pulled into the parkade within half an hour. Olivia noticed that Molly had come too, and she bounded out of the car towards Olivia, her beautiful blonde waves blowing behind her, running effortlessly in six-inch heels. "Holy shit, Liv. You've given Luca such a scare," she said, embracing Olivia in a tight hug. "What's going on?"

The girls both bundled into the back of the car and Molly put her arm around Olivia, holding her close. Luca started the engine and then looked back sternly at Olivia. "Okay, sis. Spill the beans. What the hell is going on?"

"Just drive, Luca. Please," she sobbed. "I'll tell you when we get back to your place."

Olivia spent the journey curled up on the back seat of the car with Molly. Even Molly's normally unsinkable spirit was in submission, so she just clung to her, stroking her hair. By the time they arrived at their townhouse, Olivia had calmed down somewhat, and Luca took her arm and helped her into the house, depositing her into one of his squishy leather armchairs. Molly went to the kitchen to grab a bottle of wine. "Don't say anything until I'm back" she gasped. "I don't want to miss anything."

Olivia took a large slug of her wine and inhaled deeply before she spoke. "As you know, Luca, I've been seeing Daniel Lane, but it's been a bit of a strange arrangement."

Molly interrupted. "Not *the* Daniel Lane, Olivia. That sexy publishing guy?"

Luca shot her a jealous look and Olivia nodded weakly. "That would be the one." Molly looked like she was going to burst with excitement.

"Anyway, we were pretty hot and heavy, and I thought things were going well. While I was on the train this afternoon, I read a copy of today's Tribune, and this is what I saw." She pulled the folded page out of her bag and handed it to Luca, who read it with a frown. Olivia continued, "I decided the best thing was to confront him about it and see what he had to say, so I went to his place tonight when I got home."

Molly was on the edge of her seat with her fingernails digging in the arms of her chair. She loved any kind of drama.

"When I got there, I was greeted by his supposed ex-fiancée in a bathrobe, only she was wearing a very large and sparkly engagement ring. She'd just gotten out of his shower."

Molly clapped her hand over her mouth dramatically. Olivia thought she was going to spontaneously combust, and she shot her a wry smile. "Did you see him? What did he say?" Molly asked.

Olivia shook her head. "No, I got out of there as soon as I could and went home and booked my flight. It's obvious what's been going on. He's been feeding me this shit about only wanting to see me on weekends, and now I understand why. I really thought we had something special going on. I guess I've been ridiculously naïve. He's just a player. Well, he certainly played me, that's for sure."

Luca looked furious. "I've got half a mind to go round there and beat the shit out of him."

Olivia held up her hand. "No, Luca. That wouldn't solve anything. I just need to get away and put some space between us. I need time to think. At the end of the day, I want to walk away from this with my head held high, and I can't do that now. I feel like a train wreck."

Molly poured everyone another glass of wine. "I can't believe you're just heading off to Florence, Liv. You're such a badass! God, I wish I could come with you."

Olivia didn't feel like a badass. Her chest ached from crying, and there was an empty space inside her where all her emotions had been. She couldn't believe how badly he had deceived her. She knew his seduction techniques were polished when she met him, but this was so hurtful. *Of course*, she told herself, *he never meant for me to find out*. She wondered how long he had intended to string her along before he dropped her for the next cute new author. Maybe this was serial behaviour. She clapped her hand to her head to try to still the swirl of thoughts that were swimming around up there.

"What time is your flight tomorrow?" Luca asked.

"8 a.m.," Olivia said, wincing apologetically. "I'm sorry it's so early, Luca. I can get a cab if you don't want to drive me. We must be there by 6:30 at the latest."

Luca shook his head. "I'm taking you, it's the least I can do. You're my baby sister and it's about time I started looking out for you more. I've been such an ass in the past. I'm really sorry Liv."

Molly grinned and jumped on top of Luca, hugging him hard. Her overblown happiness had returned, and she was proud of him.

Luca looked concerned. "When do you plan on coming back, Olivia? You can't hide forever you know."

Olivia swallowed hard. "I'm not sure. I might make this a longer trip; I only bought a one-way ticket. I thought back in the summer about finding work in Italy for a while, and this might be the ideal opportunity. I'll start in Florence and see what work is around. I thought I could visit Uncle Pietro as well. He only lives an hour outside of Florence."

Luca looked slightly horrified. "I don't like this, Liv. I don't like it one bit. You're in no fit state to suddenly make such big life changes. Besides, you'd lose your job at the library and everything; you love that job. Why don't you just go for a couple of weeks, and we can talk about you making it more permanent when you come back? I don't want to have to fly to Florence to haul your ass back here if you get in trouble."

Olivia shot him a determined look. "It's time I grew up a bit. If I'd been a little savvier, I wouldn't be in this mess now. Who knows? This could be a new start for me."

Luca sighed in defeat. "Well, if we're going to be up at the crack of dawn, we should turn in."

Molly wandered off to fetch Olivia some fresh towels, and Luca stared at his sister's beautiful face. Her normally sparkling eyes were red and empty of expression, and her face was blotchy from crying. "Can I give you a hug or will it set you off again?" he asked.

Olivia walked towards him, wrapping her arms around him, and burying her face in his chest. Luca was the same height and build as Daniel and if she closed her eyes she could almost imagine she was in the arms of her errant lover. Her brother smelled good, but nothing like Daniel. His arms were strong, but he didn't hold her like Daniel did. She would have to get used to the fact there would be no replacing Daniel Lane.

30

L uca took Olivia to the airport early the next morning to catch the first flight to Florence. She was travelling light with just a carry-on bag.

"Are you sure you have enough stuff?" he asked her. Olivia nodded. "Jeez, if I was taking Molly, we'd probably have three enormous suitcases."

When it was time for her to pass through security, he held her in his arms and gave her a tight squeeze. It felt so good to have that connection with her brother. *At least something good has come out of this*, she thought. He held her chin the same way that Daniel so often did and looked at her face.

"Are you sure you know what you're doing, Liv? It's a heck of a long way to go to escape a guy, even Daniel Lane, *that sexy publishing guy*," he said sarcastically, echoing Molly's words. "Mom's going to go batshit and I'll have to deal with it."

Olivia smiled ruefully at him. "I'm sure you'll be able to turn on the charm with her, just like you always do." She tried to ruffle his hair, but he jumped out of the way, laughing. He gave her one last kiss on the top of her head and sent her on her way.

Sitting in the departure lounge waiting for her flight, Olivia made the mistake of looking at her phone. Of course, Daniel had tried to contact her from his office and had left several texts and voice mails. She didn't want to torture herself, but she couldn't resist the temptation to look at a few of his texts. Looking at his increasingly desperate pleas almost made her lose her resolve and her finger twitched to call him, but she stopped herself by sitting on her hands for several minutes. Eventually she scrolled to the last text he had sent and replied with a simple link to a song–*Gravity* by Sara Bareilles. *Says it better than I ever could*, she thought to herself, before switching off her phone.

The flight seemed endless, and Olivia was restless. She normally enjoyed flying and got immersed in the complete experience of it, but this time she just tried to shut out the empty feeling that she couldn't shake. She had to change flights in Rome after a short layover and she sat in the airport watching all the elegant Italian women with their expensive bags and designer clothes. She thought about the beautiful woman she had seen in Daniel's apartment and found it hard to hold back the tears that were stinging in her eyes. She realized she should have trusted her instincts in the first place. She had just been a bit of fun for Daniel; his little piece of weekend rough. This beautiful socialite had obviously always been waiting in the wings.

Eventually, she arrived at her hotel in Florence, absolutely exhausted. She felt drained, physically and emotionally, but she hoped she was going to enjoy her experience there. She had last visited Florence several years ago with her parents, but she had always wanted to return. It was such a magical city. She had booked into the only hotel in her price range. It was comfortable enough, but Olivia was concerned about the area it was located in. There was a noisy bar downstairs and a couple of nightclubs down the street. She hadn't had enough time to do the research she normally would.

"Single, but not very safe," she said to herself as she lay down on the bed. Exhausted, she drifted off into a restless sleep, dreaming of horseshoe-shaped bays and ocean waves.

She woke up late the next morning, disorientated for a while, with a pounding headache. She wasn't sure where she was or what she was doing there. Then, reality started to sink in, and she remembered why she was there; the huge empty void returned to her chest.

She had a shower, and then she unpacked her small suitcase. She had packed light, learning from past experience, and she had brought just enough clothing to take her through the next two weeks, washing underwear in the sink as necessary. It would give her a chance to work out what she was going to do long term. If she were to stay, there was so much she would have to do to sort out things at home, but she couldn't get her head around that just then.

She'd packed some nice things, but nothing too dressy, as she knew she would be eating on a budget. She had hoped to get out to the opera one night as a treat to herself, so she had packed a beautiful turquoise blue dress that she'd bought with her mom on their shopping expedition. The dress had a halter neck, and the turquoise changed to a lovely sea blue at the bottom. When Olivia saw it in the shop, it had reminded her of the colour of beach glass. She hung it up in the closet with a sigh of regret and then headed out to find a late breakfast and do some sightseeing.

She spoke in Italian to the front desk staff, and they helped her with a route for where she wanted to go. She explained to the girl behind the desk that she was a single woman travelling alone, and that she would appreciate any tips for safety at night. The young woman was very helpful, and Olivia was grateful for the conversation. She had tucked her money belt inside her clothing to prevent pickpockets and headed off to Caffe Gilli, a popular tourist destination with a lovely outside area to sit and watch the world go by.

When she arrived, she was pleased to see there was a free table outside for her, and a friendly waiter led her over to her seat. The patio was shaded, so she took off her sunglasses and wrote in her journal that she always carried when she was travelling. She liked to make brief sketches of some of the places she visited, and her notes would help her with her next guide. Today she lacked inspiration, and she tried to bite back the tears that were threatening again.

Soon, the waiter brought over a beautiful latte with a leaf pattern in the froth, and a delicious pastry. Sitting there was heaven, but she couldn't dispel the heavy feeling in her heart. She decided travelling alone was not for her anymore. Perhaps this would be her last trip.

She would have to think about something else to write about; maybe a self-help book on how to mend a broken heart.

An attractive, young, Italian man passed her table, did a double take, and then came back towards her. He looked very much like many of the young men in Florence; very stylish, with tight denim jeans, a striped t-shirt, and a mop of black curls. *Italian Stallions*, Rosa called them. He was tall and slender, and he smiled at her in a friendly way.

"Mi scusi signora," he said. "Can I ask you, do you speak English?"

Olivia looked up at him. "Yes, I speak English. Why?"

The young man parked himself on a chair at the table and carefully formed his sentences. "Please, miss, may I join you? My name is Alessandro, and I am learning English. I would like to practice with you. Is this okay?"

Olivia shook her head and spoke to him in Italian. "I'm really not in the mood today. I don't think I would be a very good conversationalist. I'm sorry."

He looked at her eyes and tried again. "You have cried. You are sad. Are you on holiday?"

She sighed and nodded. "You should say, *'you have been crying'*. Yes, I am sad, and I am on holiday."

"But all alone? That is sad. Is that why you cry?"

She wrinkled her nose at him. "You need to say, *'is that what made you cry?'*" she corrected. "And no, I don't mind being alone. I am escaping from a bad man who broke my heart." She pulled her sunglasses down over her eyes as just the thought of her broken heart was making tears well up in her eyes.

"I will not allow you to be in Florence alone," he continued dramatically. "It is too sad. You can come with me tonight?" She was just about to tell him she would rather be on her own when she heard a familiar voice.

"Excuse me. I'm sorry to bother you, but do you mind if I sit with my girlfriend?"

Alessandro spun around to find himself face to face with Daniel Lane. He looked back at Olivia. "Is this the bad man?"

Olivia nodded in disbelief, "That would be him, but I have no idea why he's here."

Alessandro looked confused and Daniel reassured him. "I don't know what my girlfriend has been telling you, but don't believe a word of it. She is a minx."

Alessandro creased his eyebrows "Minx? What is minx?"

Daniel grinned. "It means she is an extremely difficult woman." Alessandro nodded knowingly at Daniel and then looked regretfully back at Olivia and decided he should be on his way.

"Thank you for talking to me, Olivia. Have a good holiday." She smiled sadly at him and gave a brief wave.

Olivia turned to Daniel, furious. "What the hell are you doing here?" she hissed.

"I could ask the same thing myself," he retorted.

"How did you even know I was here?"

Daniel gave a strained laugh. "Your big brother paid me a visit yesterday morning after he dropped you at the airport. He was pretty pissed. He asked me what I had done to you, along with a few other things. In fact, he said this could be a permanent move for you."

Olivia clapped her hand to her head. "Oh, Luca!" she said in frustration. "I should have known he couldn't keep his mouth shut." Staring down at her coffee, she stirred it furiously, refusing to make eye contact.

"So, the question is, Olivia, what exactly did I do to you that meant I had to come half-way round the world to find you?"

She looked at him with narrowed eyes. "Well, if you don't know, I'm certainly not going to tell you. Let's face it, Daniel, I was always just a bit of fun to you; a nice fuck on the weekends when your fiancée wasn't around. I should have known better. I was so naïve! My fault as usual." Her voice was coming out in a fast and rising crescendo and her hands were gesticulating wildly; people were starting to stare. She opened her mouth to start again, but Daniel raised his hand.

"So help me Olivia if you don't shut up, I will put you over my knee in front of the whole damn piazza, and I don't care who sees. Now I have no idea what you're talking about, so let's not play games. Just tell me why you are so angry with me?"

Olivia put on her sunglasses to hide her eyes, which were now filling with tears. After a moment, she choked out her response. "I'm not angry with you, Daniel," she whispered. "I'm heartbroken. How could you deceive me like that? I knew you were experienced, but I never thought you were cruel. I trusted you." Large tears that she could not contain leaked out the bottom of her sunglasses and ran down her cheeks. "You've broken me."

The waiter, who could see what was going on, shot Daniel a murderous look. Daniel looked devastated. "Darling, don't cry. You're killing me. Come here." He tried to take her hand and pull her into his lap, but she pulled her hand away sharply and turned her back on him, unable to control the deluge of tears. It was as if the floodgates had opened and all the pain from the past few weeks was suddenly unleashed. She sobbed into her hands, and he pulled her chair around, so she was facing him. "It's okay, darling, I'm here. Everything will be okay now. Don't cry, please."

After a few minutes of gut-wrenching sobs, she calmed herself and lay with her head against the back of the chair, defeated. She felt like a balloon that had been deflated, lying empty and useless.

After a while, Daniel spoke. "Is it okay if I ask you a few questions?"

She nodded, unable to fight anymore.

"When you left your parents' house that day, you came to look for me, didn't you?"

She nodded as she tried to dry her tears with a tissue she found in her purse. "Yes, after I'd seen this!" she spat, grabbing the balled-up paper from her purse and throwing it at him. She watched as he carefully smoothed it out and looked at it silently.

"Hmm. I thought you might have seen this. I tried to speak to you before you did something stupid, but you've been blocking my calls, haven't you?"

She refused to answer him, and instead, shot him an angry look.

"Okay, so you saw this, and you came to my apartment; Serena answered the door, didn't she?"

"Yes," Olivia spat. "Wearing a bathrobe straight out of the shower. She told me you had gone out to buy some wine."

"Okay," Daniel said. "What happened next?"

Olivia looked incredulous. "I left, of course. Did you expect I would stay for a little ménage à trois?"

Daniel looked at her gently. "I think you missed one very important detail during these events. Think, Olivia. What did Serena say to you?"

Olivia looked at him, confused. She couldn't understand why he didn't just let it go. It was very obvious what had been going on. "She said you had gone out to buy wine."

"And what else?" he pressed.

Olivia thought "And that I should come in and wait for you, but I certainly wasn't going to do that. I could see what had been going on. Me on weekends and her during the week. I knew there had to be a reason you didn't want me as your full-time girlfriend and there it was, staring me in the face. Because you were still engaged, you bastard!" Her voice was starting to rise again, so he gently put his finger over her lips.

"And during any of this, did it not occur to you to phone me and call me out on this shit?" he asked.

Olivia shook her head. "I couldn't speak to you because I knew I'd get pulled into your gravitational force of bullshit and charm. I was heartbroken. I had to get away, so I could think more clearly."

"Most women, when confronted with this kind of crap, would come over and slap me and call me something unspeakable, but not you. No, you took off half-way around the world without giving me a chance to explain, you little hothead." He raked his hair with frustration. "Okay, Olivia. I need you to listen to me very carefully." He took off her sunglasses and looked into her reddened eyes, wiping the tracks of her tears with his thumbs. "It's a real shame you didn't take up Serena's offer to come in and wait, because if you had, you would have met her *husband*, Mike, who was my best friend at Harvard. They were just staying with me for a couple of nights. When Serena and I broke up, she started going out with Mike. It all worked out well and there are no hard feelings between us. In fact, I was best man at their wedding."

"But the photograph," she spluttered.

"Yes, the press are brilliant, aren't they? Look more closely, Olivia. Look at Serena's right hand."

She stared down at the paper, confused. "Her right hand isn't in the photograph."

"Yes, they've cut it out. Probably because it wouldn't have made much of a story to show her holding her husband's hand. We just all happened to be attending the same function and walked out together."

Olivia looked stunned.

"Now, did you even bother to read the name of the reporter?"

"Name of the reporter? What do you mean?" she choked.

"Look at the article again and read the name of the reporter. It's right there in black and white, as they say."

She looked at the article again, but she was finding it hard to make her eyes focus. She was tired, and she'd cried so much over the past two days nothing seemed to be connecting. Eventually she scanned down the page until she read: *Report by Mark Hazleton*. She looked up at him, completely confused, "But he's a sport's writer. Why would he be writing for the society pages?"

He raised his eyebrows at her. "Why indeed? I guess revenge is a dish best served cold. They took the shot of us outside your apartment building before he attacked you. I think he's been planning this since he found out you were seeing me. I will have a chat with his editor when we get back." He contemplated the paper thoughtfully. "It's a great shot of your ass though, isn't it?"

Olivia's mouth opened and closed, but she wasn't able to say anything. Daniel smiled.

"Well, well. It looks like I have finally silenced the minx!" Daniel fixed his steely gaze on her. "Now, listen to me, Ms. Jefferson, and no interrupting. We are going to go to your hotel to collect your things. Then we will take your things to my hotel where you will stay with me. I am not going to let you out of my sight."

Olivia didn't argue. They walked to her hotel in silence and collected her single carry-on bag. Daniel was clearly mad at her, and she didn't blame him. She talked to the friendly front desk assistant, who took a shine to Daniel as soon as she saw him, and they climbed into a cab to take them to Daniel's hotel. In the back of the cab, she kept her eyes down on her clasped hands, unable to look him in the face, while he stared out the window.

His hotel was gloriously opulent, in stark contrast to the tourist class place she had been staying in. The room was beautiful with two queen-sized beds, she noted. She knew where she was going to be sleeping tonight, and it wasn't with him. Although she felt remorseful about her mistake, she still felt uncomfortable about what had been going on. She realized in all of this that she didn't want the role of part-time girlfriend. As amazing as the weekends with Daniel were, she wanted a more permanent arrangement, and she wasn't sure he was prepared to do that.

She wheeled her suitcase into the expansive closet and turned to face him, but he had his back to her. He was staring out of the enormous balcony windows that overlooked the main piazza. "Daniel," she began, but he held up his hand as if he didn't want her to speak. They stood there for a few minutes in silence, and Olivia felt like she wanted the ground to open up and swallow her. Needing to say what was on her mind, she tried again. "Look, I know I made a mistake, but all of this made me realize something. I can't do this, Daniel. I can't be your part-time secret. You never told me you were going to that function or that you had your friends coming over to stay. It's as if I only exist to keep you happy on weekends. You can't blame me for jumping to conclusions if you're not prepared to share your life with me. I can't just be shoved away in a convenient little bubble."

When he turned to face her, she saw a look on his face she had never seen before. Tears sparkled in his blue eyes, and she realized he was in agony. "Christ Olivia, I've really messed this up. I thought I was protecting you, but all I did was drive you away. I listened to that song, and it almost broke me. Is that how you really feel? You want me to set you free?"

She winced regretfully. It really was a painful song. "Daniel, when I sent you that link, I thought you'd been cheating on me all along. Part of it is still true, though. I'm so consumed by you, I'm afraid I might lose myself. I'm scared I love you too much." It was out there now, and she hung her head, afraid of the implications of her confession.

He crossed the room in one, long stride, gathering her up into his arms and kissing her. He kissed her with such a forceful urgency that she felt like she couldn't breathe. "Don't you realize it's the same for me? My love for you is so intense it sometimes feels like it's going to implode inside me. I know this weekend arrangement has caused you pain, but you have to understand I was trying to protect you from all the crap I have to face on a daily basis. When we're at the cottage, it's just you and me. It's like another world that hasn't been contaminated by all the rumours and gossip that seem to follow me wherever I go."

He held her face in his hands and stared into her now tear-stained face. "Olivia, I have never been so afraid in my entire life. I sat on that plane, thinking about all the things that could happen to you here on your own, and I almost had a full-blown panic attack. Knowing I'd caused you to run away killed me."

He pulled her down on the bed with him and she crawled into his lap, wrapping herself around him. She felt like she couldn't get close enough and she wanted to climb inside him. All her grief from the past couple of days was dissipating, and in its place was a feeling of peace. He loved her, and that was the only thing that mattered for the moment. He interrupted her thoughts. "Say something, sweetheart. Please."

"I'm sorry I scared you and that I made you come all this way. I told you I was a disaster that first day we met. I'm never wrong about these things."

His face relaxed a little, and he smiled. "Well, Ms. Disaster. A ten-hour flight certainly gives a man some serious thinking time, and I have come to some decisions." She looked up at him curiously. The warmth of their connection was returning, and she could feel it flowing through her body like molten lava. "From now on, I am not going to let you out of my sight. Where you go, I go. It's as simple as that. It will drive me crazy, but someone's got to look after you and I want that someone to be me."

Olivia looked incredulous. "You can't do that! You need to go to work, and I can't go with you. I'd be too much of a distraction."

Daniel smiled at her wickedly. "You can say that again. You're one big distraction, you naughty minx." He gently nibbled down the side of her neck and she moaned with pleasure. "Then I will lock you in my apartment all day. I'll leave you plenty of food–you'll be fine. I'll have to lock all the alcohol away, of course."

Olivia tried to look shocked. "You're just trying to turn me into your own personal sex-slave."

He unbuttoned the front of her shirt. "Now that sounds like an excellent idea. Why didn't I think of that? We need to talk about this some more, but first, I need to hold you for a while and then I need to make love to you. Is that okay with you?"

She clung to him, trying not to cry. "I love you so much. It killed me when I thought you were with someone else. I have no idea why you love me, but I am so happy that you do."

Holding her away from him, he contemplated her thoughtfully. "That's exactly it, Olivia. That's why I love you. You are totally un-aware of how beautiful and funny you are. Every time I see you, it's like meeting you for the first time all over again. I never know exactly which Olivia I'm going to get, but I love each and every one of them." She giggled as he reached behind her to unclip her bra. "Now, let's get you out of these clothes. We've got some catching up to do."

They spent a bliss-filled afternoon, and Olivia watched the sun sink down over the horizon, wrapped in Daniel's warm embrace. *It doesn't get any better than this*, she thought to herself.

31

He told her they would be going out for dinner, so they showered together. He had vowed not to let her out of his sight, and it seemed like he was going to keep his promise. He was shaving in the bathroom, so she slipped into the beautiful turquoise dress she had brought for the opera, and carefully applied her make up. She tied her hair back into a French knot and looked at herself in the mirror. The pinkness had returned to her cheeks and her lips were swollen from an afternoon of pleasure. "*Who needs lip fillers?*" she thought to herself, satisfied with her appearance.

When he walked out of the bathroom, he looked stunning in a white tuxedo shirt undone at the neck and black dress pants. Olivia stared at him, mesmerized for a moment. "You take my breath away every time I look at you," she murmured.

He stood perfectly still, staring at her with deep blue eyes that she was finding hard to read. Silently, he held his arms open, and she ran into them. He held her in an embrace so tight she thought she would be crushed. She wanted to hold on to the moment forever, but Daniel assured her he had booked a table at a great restaurant, and he didn't want to lose the reservation.

He ordered a cab, and soon, they were on the way to the restaurant. In the back of the cab, she clung to him like a child. She never wanted to let him go again. He stroked her bare back under her wrap, and she purred with pleasure. "Don't get carried away darling," he whispered in her ear, "or we'll never eat."

They soon arrived, and he helped her out of the cab. The restaurant was a beautiful Tuscan-style with traditional furniture and low lighting. The waiter led them through the restaurant to an outside patio. It felt like a secret garden with high walls surrounding the terrace. White fairy lights were strung around, and slow, dreamy music was playing. There was a small rectangular dance floor, with tables arranged around the outside.

Some couples were on the floor, dancing, and the waiter led them to a table in a corner nook. Daniel ordered some wine, and he pulled Olivia's chair closer to him so he could hold her. After a while, Daniel excused himself and wandered off to chat with the head waiter. They had an animated conversation, and the waiter looked thrilled when Daniel handed him something. He came back to the table with a smile on his face.

"What was that all about?" asked Olivia.

"Oh, I just requested that he keep the wine coming," he said with a smile. "Now I said we needed to talk and now is as good a time as any while we're waiting for our food. Hopefully, it won't take too long, or God knows what you'll do."

She rolled her eyes at him, but she found it impossible to be annoyed when he was being so playful. He handed her a white envelope, and she looked down at it, perplexed.

"Well, open it," he urged.

When she opened the envelope, she found two regular keys and a swipe card, all on a smart key chain. "What's this?" she said with a puzzled look on her face.

"Keys. One set for the apartment and one for the cottage. I want you to move in with me. Sorry, I'll rephrase that—I *need* you to move in with me."

She looked down at the keys and then back up at him. "Daniel, I'll drive you crazy. I drive everyone crazy eventually. Do you really think this is a good idea?"

He laughed. "Sweetheart, you've been driving me crazy from the first day we met. You have made it impossible for me to live without you. I'm miserable as sin when you're not around, and I don't want to live like this anymore. I want you in my life 24/7."

"But I'm really loud."

"I don't care."

"And messy."

"I have someone who cleans for me. She'll just have to come more frequently."

She blinked up at him, finding it all too much to take in. He wanted her in his life as a permanent fixture. It seemed too much to comprehend.

"You're not saying anything, kitten, which is unusual for you. Do I take that as a yes?"

She nodded with a huge grin on her face. "Yes, but don't say I didn't warn you."

He took a deep breath and put his head back. "Great! That was part one. You might take a little more convincing for part two. I need you to come and sit on my lap for this one."

She narrowed her eyes at him. "Are you just trying to do something dirty to me?"

He tapped his lap. "No, I promise. Come on over." She got out of her chair suspiciously and he wrapped his arms around her as she sat down. "Now, I think I have you restrained. I'm just a little concerned you might run off to Timbuktu when I do this." Releasing one arm, he rummaged in his jacket pocket. Olivia was growing more and more intrigued.

He continued, "Now most men do this on one knee, but I don't trust you enough for that, so we have to do it like this. You might just kick me over and run off." He put a small turquoise box on the table and put his hand back around her, keeping her in a firm hold. "Go ahead, you can open it."

Puzzled, she picked up the small box, noticing there was a small button that you had to press to open it. As the lid flipped open, she gasped at the sight of the most beautiful diamond ring nestled in black velvet. She looked up at him, almost afraid to believe what she was seeing.

"I know we haven't known each other for very long, but I knew the first day I met you I wanted to spend the rest of my life with you. If I searched forever, I would never find anyone like you. Beautiful, funny Olivia. Marry me, sweetheart?"

"You want to marry me? Are you sure?"

He smiled and tucked her hair behind her ear. "Do you know the moment I knew I wanted to marry you?" She shook her head. "It was in the restaurant that first day when you pulled that pencil out of your hair. You were so provocative and so innocent all at the same time. I have been captivated by you ever since. Now, are you going to give me an answer, minx? Just tell me you're not going to run away so I can release you and slip this ring on your finger."

"Yes," she squeaked. "This is crazily fast and unexpected, but I can't think of anything I want to do more than spend the rest of my life with you."

"Well, thank God for that." He laughed, slipping the ring on her finger. Taking her face in his hands, he kissed her like he never wanted to let her go.

The waiters all cheered loudly and rushed over to shake Daniel's hand and kiss Olivia on both cheeks. Then they insisted on taking photos of the two of them, and then of them all together, and the whole restaurant soon got involved. Champagne corks popped and the other guests came over to congratulate them profusely in Italian, whilst Olivia tried to hurriedly translate for Daniel. The entire scene turned into one big party and the wine flowed freely, whilst everyone danced.

Suddenly, she heard a familiar song over the speaker system as Barry Manilow's soothing voice came through loud and clear. Daniel looked at her and grinned as he gently took her hand. "I knew you couldn't resist dancing to Barry." He laughed.

Olivia rolled her eyes. "Oh, Lord. I really don't want to encourage this. It's just too disturbing for words." Nevertheless, she allowed him to pull her to her feet and onto the small dancefloor.

Olivia didn't remember eating much that night, and it was late before they managed to tear themselves away from their new best friends, with promises to return later in the week. They got back to the hotel at around midnight, clinging to each other and giggling as they stumbled into the room. Olivia looked at the clock and counted on her fingers to see what time it was at home. She turned and looked at Daniel.

"Please, give me one moment." He looked puzzled but amused. She dug around for her phone and started to dial. "Mammina!" she cried. "I'm getting married!" Daniel grinned as he heard Rosa Jefferson shriek on the other end of the phone as Olivia babbled away in Italian.

Eventually the call was over, and she turned to face Daniel, smiling widely. He smiled back at her with a wicked glint in his eye. "Now, Ms. Jefferson. As we seem to have had a rather unconventional relationship, I wonder how you feel about having the honeymoon before the wedding."

She knew where he was going with this. "So, I guess that would make tonight our wedding night?" She laughed.

"That's absolutely correct. I suppose I should have carried you over the threshold. Shall we go back out and do that again?" They walked out in the hallway, trying not to wake the other hotel guests and he scooped her up in his arms, carrying her back into the room and depositing her on the closest bed.

"Now, Ms. Jefferson, I have no idea what people get up to on their wedding night. Do you know?"

Olivia's green eyes sparkled, and she giggled. "I think we'll work it out, Mr. Lane."

32

The sun was peeking through the gap in the heavy drapes, alerting Olivia to the fact that it was time to get up. She threw them open and looked out at the expansive ocean view. Squinting at the cloudless sky, she realized it was going to be a beautiful day.

There was a gentle knock on the door. Grabbing her robe, she rushed over to open it, only to be greeted by the excited faces of Molly and Lottie.

"Happy Wedding Day!" they squealed in unison. She noticed that Lottie was carrying a breakfast tray full of delicious goodies, bagels, cream cheese, and smoked salmon.

"You need to keep your strength up today, Livvy," she grinned.

The girls came in and they all sat around the small corner table to enjoy a private breakfast together. Lottie had even summoned up some mimosas.

"I can't believe you beat me to the altar," Molly complained through a mouthful of bagel. "Luca and I have been engaged for over a year. You and Daniel pulled this off in six months!"

Olivia squeezed her hand sympathetically. "Well, we were going to have a long engagement, but you know how Daniel is when he gets an idea in his mind. I guess he didn't want to wait, but don't worry, I have a feeling this might spur my brother into action. I know how much he loves you."

Olivia was thrilled that Molly and Lottie were going to be her bridesmaids. She couldn't think of anyone she would rather have to support her on this special day. They had, of course, been shocked when she announced her engagement, especially Lottie.

"Honestly, Olivia," she had complained. "I go away on holiday, and I come back to find my best friend has bagged herself the most eligible bachelor in the state."

After breakfast, the girls presented Olivia with a gift bag of naughty goodies. There was a black, barely-there baby doll lingerie set, a bottle of champagne and a very saucy looking vibrator. "That's for when Daniel gets tired." Molly laughed.

Olivia grinned. "I don't think Daniel ever gets tired actually, but I'm sure we will have some fun with this."

Lottie pulled a face. "Oh go on, rub it in. He's not only gorgeous, he's also gifted in the sack!"

The girls sat around laughing and enjoying each other's company. "So, tell me, Livvy. Does this mean you're a reformed character now? Are you dispensing with the wild outfits and the inappropriate behaviour?" Lottie laughed.

Olivia shook her head. "Oh, no. Daniel rather likes my wild clothes, and he particularly loves my inappropriate behaviour. I do think I'll need to dial it back when we attend his fancy events. I can do it when I need to, you know. I'll just have to stay off the tequila." She looked down at her manicured nails. "I want to make him proud, Lottie."

Lottie snorted. "Good grief, how could he not be proud. You've got the finest pair of boobs in the state, and they're real. Just slide that into the conversation at these charity dos. They'll all be green with envy."

The rest of the morning was taken up with hair styling and make-up and by eleven o'clock, Rosa arrived. She had wanted to come and help Olivia dress, and she looked amazing. Wearing a beautiful coral dress and jacket, she could have easily passed for someone ten years younger. Her dark hair was styled in a chic up-do, and she was carrying a coordinating fascinator for later. She hugged all the girls and settled down for a glass of champagne, enjoying all the excited girl talk in the room.

Lottie unzipped the huge, white dress bag that was hanging on the back of the door, and she carefully took out Olivia's dress. She had known it had been "the one" when she tried it on the day Rosa took her dress shopping. It cost a lot more than she had wanted her mom to spend, but Rosa had insisted. "This is the only dress for you," she had said through her tears.

The white, fitted bodice had a portrait neckline, sweeping into a full skirt of Italian lace. Olivia was going to be wearing a veil tucked into the back of her hair and she would carry a simple bouquet of white roses, which reminded her of Daniel. Zipping up her dress, Rosa gently fingered the beautiful lace. "This dress was made for you, darling," she whispered.

The hair stylist came into the room, clutching a white pencil. "Are you sure you want this, Olivia?"

Olivia grinned at him. "Absolutely, the pencil is essential." Her hair had already been secured into a French knot, so he carefully inserted the pencil into her updo, before securing her veil behind it, so it couldn't be seen. "Daniel's going to flip when he sees it," she laughed.

Molly and Lottie dressed in their beautiful blush-pink dresses they had chosen together. Olivia looked at them proudly. "There's no doubt about it. I have the two most beautiful bridesmaids ever." The photographer came and took photos of Olivia seated in the expansive window seat, and then some of her with Rosa, and finally, the whole group.

Olivia looked at the clock nervously. Looking out the window, she could see the beautiful white chairs set out in rows, and the marquee for later. Daniel and Olivia had known immediately that *The Laurels* was the only place they wanted for their ceremony, and they were thrilled that an early September date was available.

People had started to arrive, and she could see Luca, looking stunningly handsome in his tux and talking to guests as they arrived. She wondered where Daniel was, and she figured he was probably inside with his best man, Mike, getting some Dutch courage.

Rosa clucked at her nervously. "Come away from the window, Olivia. You mustn't let Daniel see you yet. It's bad luck."

There was a knock at the door and Greg Jefferson walked in, looking every inch the movie star with his honey blonde hair and smart suit. Rosa clutched her hand to her chest. "You are one sexy man, Greg Jefferson."

He smiled at her with so much love in his eyes and kissed her sweetly. Then he turned to Olivia and clasped his hand over his mouth. "My little girl," he choked.

"Dad, please don't, or I will bawl and ruin my make-up." He kissed her gently on the cheek and squeezed her hand. Rosa headed out with Lottie and Molly to join the guests, and Greg and Olivia were left alone.

"How are you feeling, love?" he asked her gently.

"Nervous," she said. "I could do with a stiff drink. Have you got anything stashed away?"

"There's still time to change your mind," he joked. "We could be out of here like Thelma and Louise." He looked at her seriously. "You are sure about this, sweetheart, aren't you? We really like Daniel, but it was just all so sudden. You flew off to Florence, heartbroken, and came back with a ring on your finger."

Olivia smiled gently at him. "Dad, I have never been this certain about anything in my entire life. You remember how you felt when you met Mom? Well, it's the same for me. I love him desperately and he loves me. I have no idea why, but he does. Best bag him now before he realizes what he's doing and changes his mind."

Greg looked indignant. "Daniel Lane should think himself lucky. My daughter is the catch of the century."

Greg took Olivia's arm, and they headed down the wide sweeping staircase. "If I just get through the day without falling on my ass, I'll be happy." She giggled.

They exited through the black double doors where the smiling staff stood at either side in quiet reverence. The first strains of *Pachelbel's Canon in D* played, and they turned the corner to make their way up the aisle.

Daniel stepped forward from his seat to receive them and seeing him made her heart soar. He was wearing a black tux with no tie and his top button undone, as she had requested. When he watched Olivia progressing down the aisle on Greg's arm, his face was full of emotion. She felt like she was floating, and she wondered what spirit had possessed her body and robbed her of her usual clumsiness. Everyone's eyes were on her, and she noticed many familiar faces, including Evangeline from the publishing house, wearing a serene and knowing smile on her face. In the row behind sat Hettie and her husband, Frank. She had shed her usual library attire and was wearing a chic sheath dress and a jaunty hat. Harry from the library, resplendent in a brightly embroidered waistcoat, and his elderly mother, beamed at her from the end of the row.

Reaching the archway, Greg gently kissed her on the cheek and passed her hand to Daniel. "She's all yours, Daniel," he said, his voice thick with emotion. "Take care of her, son."

Daniel leaned forward to whisper in her ear. "You look like an angel, darling. You're breathtaking."

She whispered back, "Hey, beautiful. I'm so nervous."

He squeezed her hand and smiled reassuringly at her. "We've got this, sweetheart."

They had written their vows together and as they delivered them, they stared into each other's eyes, oblivious to anyone else. As Daniel spoke to her, Olivia knew it was useless to try to stop her tears, and he produced a white handkerchief from his pocket and dabbed gently at her eyes.

It was a beautiful ceremony, and Rosa surprised everyone by singing *O Mio Babbino Caro*. It was the first time she had sung in front of an audience in many years, but her voice was still incredible. Greg looked proudly at his wife with tears in his eyes, and the Italian relatives who had come over for the wedding jumped up out of their seats cheering, "Bravo!"

After they exchanged their rings, the officiant beamed and announced, "By the power vested in me, I now pronounce you husband and wife. I think you both know what to do next." Taking her in his arms, Daniel pulled her in for a deep and poignant kiss, accompanied by loud clapping and cheering.

The afternoon was a complete blur to Olivia. As much as she wanted to enjoy the day, everything seemed to move too fast with photographs, and the beautiful meal, and speeches. They had erected a large marquee on the lawn for dancing. It had been strung with white fairy lights and was exquisitely decorated with candles on all the tables. Olivia gasped with joy when she saw it.

She intended to dance the first few dances in her formal gown, but first, she needed to remove her veil, so she grabbed Daniel and pulled him privately to one side. "I need you to do something for me."

He smiled seductively at her. "I think you should wait until later, darling."

She crazily felt herself blush, and he laughed. "Not that, you fiend! I need you to help me take off my veil. I'll turn around; it's just fixed with a comb in the back." She felt his fingers on her carefully, trying to take it off, and then she heard him laughing. He was clearly delighted.

"Mrs. Lane, have you had that pencil in there all day?" She turned around and smiled at him.

"It's for you. I thought it would bring back memories."

He took her face in his hands and kissed her passionately. "And do I get to take it out and watch your hair fall around your shoulders?"

"Later," she promised.

At that moment, Luca walked past, grinning. "Jeez, get a room you two. It's disgusting."

Olivia poked her tongue out at him and laughed.

Daniel led Olivia onto the floor for their first dance as husband and wife. They weren't sure which track to use, but in the end, they decided on *All of Me* by John Legend. They didn't want to choreograph their dance because they wanted it to be natural, and they danced really well together, anyway. Olivia rested her head on Daniel's chest, but he lifted her face up as they started to dance. "I need you to look at me, baby." She stared into his eyes, and he sang softly along to the song.

Olivia felt the rest of the people in the room melt away as she focused on the depth of his blue eyes. She remembered thinking when she met him, they were eyes you could lose yourself in, and she knew at that moment she was utterly lost. As the dance ended, he wrapped his arms around her, kissing her passionately until she felt she couldn't breathe. "I love you so much," she whispered breathlessly.

After, Olivia danced with her dad, and Daniel danced with his mom, to *Weekend in New England*. Olivia had met Daniel's parents when she returned from Florence wearing an engagement ring, and she had been nervous about what they would think of her. Luckily, they seemed to love her almost as much as Daniel did. Daniel's mom, Trish, had been a teacher for many years and she reminded Olivia a little of Hettie. Both women had bonded over literature and before the end of the evening, it felt like she had known her forever. After dinner, Trish had taken Olivia for a stroll in their garden.

"I'm so glad he's found you, Olivia. He seems so happy. He took Simon's death badly, and I thought for a while he would never be happy again. He's a good man, Olivia. He will look after you."

Olivia smiled back gently. "Don't worry, Trish. I fully intend to look after him too. Always."

Daniel's dad, Robert, was really a grey-haired version of Daniel; tall and distinguished with twinkling blue eyes. They both seemed relieved that Daniel had found someone he was deeply in love with, and they shot each other little knowing looks at Daniel's affection towards Olivia.

Once the formal dances were over, the dancefloor heated up and Olivia wanted to slip away to change into her evening dress. She was also glad it would give her a few minutes alone with Daniel, so she asked him to help her.

Lottie playfully scowled at her. "Hey, that's my job, Olivia. What's he got that I don't have?"

Olivia rolled her eyes. "Do I really need to answer that, Lottie?"

He took her arm, and she swept up the curved staircase, feeling like an extra from *Gone with the Wind*. Once they were in Olivia's room, they stood facing one another, both with expressions of wonder. She bit her lip to stem the tears. "My heart is so full I don't know what to say to you."

He gently took her in his arms. "You don't need to say anything, baby. You've made me the happiest man alive." Releasing her, he smiled seductively at her. "Now, I seem to remember something about getting you out of this beautiful dress."

"And *into* another one," she reminded him.

"Yes, but there has to be a period of transition between those two activities, and I am just wondering how we could fill that."

He turned her away from him, unzipping the beautiful lace gown. It had bra cups sewn in, so she was just wearing white lace panties, a garter, and stockings underneath. He carefully hung her dress and then he turned her back around to face him, his eyes dark with passion. Kneeling down in front of her, he planted butterfly kisses on her stomach making her shiver with pleasure.

"Do you think we should, Daniel?" she asked huskily. "Everyone will wonder where we are."

He looked up at her in amusement. "Firstly, Olivia, there is no way I can't, and secondly I think everyone knows where we are and what we're doing. We don't have to be gone long. It can be a warm-up for later." Olivia put her hands on her pink cheeks as he removed her panties. "I think the stockings can stay on, Ms. Jefferson. Very sexy."

"I'm Mrs. Lane now, remember?"

He laughed softly. "At times like this, my darling, you will always be Ms. Jefferson."

With those words, prim and proper Olivia left the room, and her raunchy alter-ego entered. He knew that just his voice alone could push her over the edge. Her green eyes misted over with passion, and she licked her lips. He registered the change in her immediately.

"There she is. She's back. I knew once we got that dress off, she would make an appearance."

After spending as long together as they thought was decently possible, she headed off to the bathroom to fix her hair and makeup. She removed most of the pins from her hair, just leaving the pencil in place. Meanwhile, Daniel got back into his tux and tried to make himself look presentable again.

She unzipped a second dress bag to reveal her evening dress. It was a beautiful white backless midi dress, embellished with sequins and a full skirt. When she bought it, she thought it would be great for dancing, and it was the kind of thing she could wear again.

Daniel zipped her up and looked at her. "Good grief, Olivia. We need to get out of this room or I'm going to jump you again. You look amazing."

She put up her index finger. "One last finishing touch." She laughed and turned around. "You can take the pencil out now."

He looked at her passionately. "No, go sit on the edge of the bed. I want *you* to take it out, like you did that day in the restaurant. Do you remember what you said?"

She closed her eyes and thought for an instant, trying to recall the moment, and then she looked up at him seductively. "Yes, Mr. Lane. The pencil is, in fact, mine. I got the idea from YouTube. Look!" She pulled out the pencil slowly and shook her head and miraculously her hair fell in perfect tendrils around her shoulders.

Daniel sank to his knees. "That's it. I'm dead. You have officially killed me."

They reluctantly headed out of the room and back down to where they could hear the thrumming of the music. Lottie looked up at them with a disgusted look on her face. "And why exactly did that take so long?"

Olivia shot her a sweet smile. "My make up was a mess. I had to start all over again."

Daniel at least had the good grace to look a little sheepish. Olivia turned and grabbed his hand. "Okay, Mr. Lane, I want to dance. As it's my wedding day, I may just dance on the table, but you need to promise to catch me if I fall off." He bowed chivalrously.

"I will always be there to catch you, my lady." She wrinkled her nose and grinned.

"Oh, and one more thing. If you do try to get me into bed, I think it might just be your lucky night."

33

Much later that evening, Daniel and Olivia climbed into his red M.G., which had been decked out with all manner of decorations for the journey. As they drove down the hill, he stopped and removed the tin cans that Luca had tied to the tailpipe. He grinned across at her. "Well, Mrs. Lane, how are you feeling?"

She sighed contentedly. "I feel like I'm floating, and I never want to come back down."

He grabbed her hand, drawing it up to his mouth to kiss her knuckles. "Well, it's not over yet. In fact, in the words of Karen Carpenter, we've only just begun."

Olivia threw her head back and laughed. "I am going to bring your musical tastes into the twenty-first century if it kills me."

They had planned to stay at the cottage for a few days to unwind before heading out for a three-week trip to the Amalfi Coast in Italy for their honeymoon. Olivia would have been happy to just stay at the cottage, especially after they had already been to Florence, but Daniel insisted she should have a proper honeymoon. He had also promised to build extended travel periods into his work schedule. He wanted to make sure Olivia fulfilled all her travel dreams, and besides, he was determined to stand by her side in that lavender field in Provence.

As they approached the cottage, Olivia gasped. Daniel had it decked out in white fairy lights, and it shone like a little jewel.

"Okay, stay in the car," he insisted, as they pulled into the driveway. "There are a couple of things I need to attend to." Olivia wondered what he was up to as he dashed into the house. After a few minutes, he reappeared, breathless. "Okay, I'm ready for you, Mrs. Lane," he said, helping her out of the low sports car.

He scooped her up in his arms, carrying her through the door and she clasped her hand over her mouth in wonder as she saw what

247

he had done to the cottage. Vases of white roses covered every surface and in between there was, what had to be, hundreds of candles flickering gently. In the dining room, he had moved the table, a mattress from one of the beds upstairs had been brought down, covered in beautiful white linens, and the doors to the deck were open.

"Do you like it?" he asked her nervously.

"Daniel, it is the most beautiful thing I have ever seen," she said with tears sparkling in her eyes. "You did all this for me?"

He nodded solemnly. "Olivia, I would go to the ends of the earth for you. I thought we could sleep on the deck tonight, so we could hear the ocean, but I have plans for you and it may not be private enough."

She grinned. "I can't think what *plans* you have for me."

"Oh, you're going to find out, baby. Anyway, we can sleep here, and we will still hear the waves with the doors open. I don't think you're going to be cold."

He caught her in his arms and kissed her gently. "Do you remember the first time I brought you here? I was so worried I'd blown it at The Red Room. I was really nervous."

She smiled. "Well, if it's any consolation, you didn't seem nervous at all. In fact, I was thinking you were an expert in the art of seduction, and I was just another conquest."

He looked concerned. "But you know now that's not true."

She nodded. "Do you know you almost persuaded me that night on the dance floor? I was pulled to you by a force so strong, it took every ounce of my fortitude to say no."

He lowered the straps of her dress, and it slipped to the floor with a slinky, rustling sound as the sequins brushed against the wood. "But you did, you little firecracker. You said *no* in no uncertain terms, but you won't say no to me tonight, Ms. Jefferson, will you?" he said huskily.

"No, Mr. Lane. I don't think I will say no to you ever again."

He smiled at her in total adoration. "Now, wedding nights. Remind me how it goes. I'm so glad we had a dry run in Florence, because I think I know what I'm doing now."

....

A week later, Olivia was lying on a lounger in front of their hotel in Sorrento, enjoying the spectacular view of the ocean. She had her journal propped up on her knees and she was sketching the coastline in pencil. Daniel returned, holding cocktails for them both. Lying down next to her and putting the drinks between them, he smiled across at her. "What are you doing, darling?"

She looked at him and sighed. "I never tire of looking at that beautiful face. Or that beautiful ass, come to think of it. Bring it over here, please. I want to do some fondling."

He looked indignant. "Mrs. Lane, will you please behave yourself? You are supposed to be a respectable married woman now, you know."

She pulled a face at him. "You know very well I will *never* be that." Standing up and draping her arms around his shoulders, she showed him her sketch pad. "I have an idea for a new book."

He looked interested. "Single and Safe on The Amalfi Coast?" he asked.

She shook her head. "The Lover's Guide to Italy: featuring the most romantic places to stay, and to eat, and to make love, of course."

He smiled seductively. "I feel a lot of research might be needed for this particular project. Would you like to come back to our room and pitch it to me?" She nodded, her eyes full of passion. "I can never say no to you, Mr. Lane."

Don't miss out!

Visit the website below and you can sign up to receive emails whenever Sophie Penhaligon publishes a new book. There's no charge and no obligation.

https://books2read.com/r/B-A-UPZN-PNBWB

BOOKS 2 READ

Connecting independent readers to independent writers.

About the Author

Sophie Penhaligon was born and raised in the South West of England before moving to the Canadian Rockies, armed only with a snow shovel and bottle of Southern Comfort. She currently lives in the Pacific Northwest with her family and her rather naughty black Labrador.

Sophie enjoys writing novels about heroines she can relate to and heroes she can fall in love with, and she is a voracious reader of fun and sexy romances. She has a master's degree in education and has enjoyed a variety of interesting careers, drawing inspiration from her colourful life experiences.

Read more at https://www.sophiepenhaligon.com.

Printed in Great Britain
by Amazon

40749900R00145